"Campbell is a horror writer's horror writer. A MASTER. [OBSESSION is] a superior novel of horror."

—*Publishers Weekly*

"I don't want granny to be harmed," he said over and over each night before he fell asleep, "please just let her go away," and felt so relieved each morning when he heard her and knew she hadn't been harmed that he thought he might be sick, until he realized that neither had she gone away. Nothing else would happen, the accident outside the museum had been a lucky coincidence. But on the first day of the autumn term he learned that Steve's bugbear Gillespie had had a stroke and would no longer be teaching, and on the fourth day Jimmy's father won the pools.

Obsession

Also by Ramsey Campbell
published by Tor Books

Obsession

Ramsey Campbell

TOR

A TOM DOHERTY ASSOCIATES BOOK

OBSESSION

Copyright © 1985 by Ramsey Campbell

Published by arrangement with Macmillan Publishing Company

A TOR Book
Published by Tom Doherty Associates, Inc.
49 West 24 Street
New York, NY 10010

ISBN: 0-812-51656-7   Can. ISBN: 0-812-51657-5

Library of Congress Catalog Card Number: 84-21831

First TOR edition: February 1986

Printed in the United States of America

0 9 8 7 6

for RICHARD *and* JEAN, *with love*
(it's all a bit like life, really)

Acknowledgments

I have to thank Peter Caradine and synchronism for help with the first section of this book. While I was writing the early chapters, his program "Turn Back the Clock" on BBC Radio Merseyside was devoted to the events of 1958, and he was unfailingly helpful when I asked him for information I needed.

Old friends were helpful as ever, John Thompson, especially, and Jack Sullivan and Robin Bromley gave me a room in New York in which to write several chapters. Dr. Anne Biezanek advised me on medical matters, and my Norfolk friend Jay Ramsay helped me with the setting.

But it is Sylvester Stallone, the writer, director and actor, whom I must thank for the idea. Had he not made his boxer character accept a favor without knowing what the price might be, in *Rocky III*, you would not be holding this book now. I hope he will forgive me for having paid less attention to the remainder of his film than to the flood of ideas I experienced.

Then

Chapter I

TWENTY-FIVE YEARS LATER, when Peter realized at last what they had signed away, he had still not forgotten that afternoon: still remembered the waves flocking down from the horizon to sweep up the fishing boats; the glass of the classroom windows shivering with the wind; chalk dust drowsing in the September sunlight; his throat going dry as he realized that everyone was looking at him. "Well, Priest?" Mr. Meldrum said.

Peter stood up quickly, the folding seat bruising his thighs. "Sir?"

The teacher tugged his black gown over his thin shoulders. "I said," he said with a hint of impatience, "you ought to be able to tell us about that."

Chalk dust clogged Peter's throat as he tried to think what that might be. The teacher's voice had jarred him out of reliving the day on the common, reliving it as though that could make him have failed to persuade the others, Steve grinning skeptically and scratching his dimpled chin

3

where he was growing a beard for the summer, Robin
biting her pale lips and looking doubtful, Jimmy's heavy-
lidded eyes almost closing as he questioned him. . . .
"Courage," someone whispered behind him in the classroom, and Peter realized that the whisper wasn't meant to
hearten him, only to remind him what Mr. Meldrum wanted
to hear.

*The boy stood on the burning deck whence all but he
had fled.* . . . Of course, they were discussing that today,
having read it aloud around the classroom, Steve stum-
bling over the last line of his verse, and Mr. Meldrum had
said that Peter should be able to tell them about courage.
Just now courage felt like one of Peter's headaches; it
wasn't knowing you had to protect your grandmother because you were fifteen years old now, it was doing it
though you wished you were somewhere else, anywhere at
all. Mr. Meldrum wouldn't want to hear that, or anything
else; his stare made it clear that he hadn't been asking,
only commenting. Peter held onto his chipped inky desk
and felt trapped, betrayed by himself, and then he heard
someone whistling in the corridor.

Peter reached behind him to make sure the seat didn't
squeak as he sat down unobtrusively, but all at once he
couldn't move. The whistler had begun singing "Luck Be
a Lady," off-key. It was Jimmy.

Just because he was happy, that needn't mean— Peter
felt Steve's stare, but he wouldn't have responded even if
he had been able to move his pounding head on his
throbbing neck. Jimmy stopped singing in mid-phrase as
he opened the door, as if he'd just remembered where he
was. Mr. Meldrum turned, chalk dust whirling as his gown
flapped. "Good of you to drop in, Waters. I hope you've
some reason to be cheerful other than having taken half my
period for lunch."

Someone sniggered in case he'd meant to make a pun
about falling in water. Jimmy looked as if he was trying to
seem abashed, but his round good-humored face with its

small mouth wasn't made for it. "My dad's won first prize on the football pools," he said.

Both he and Peter heard Steve gasp. Jimmy glanced at Steve, then quickly at Peter, and the expression he'd been trying to suppress in front of Mr. Meldrum—an incredulous grin at his good news—froze before it could quite take over his face. "God," Steve muttered, and Peter's headache spread down his neck into his shoulders. It was true, then. There was no more room for pretending. Peter had only one thought, so intense that it felt less like thinking than like part of the ache his head had become: he wondered how he would ever dare go home.

Chapter II

THAT SPRING OF 1958 it seemed hardly to stop raining, even in East Anglia. Peter spent the weekends in the shop, his mother shooing him from place to place as she dusted the buckets and spades and toy windmills, the postcards of Seaward and the comics and sixpenny remainders, the tins and packets of food on the shelves, until sometimes he wished he were still small enough to huddle under the counter, out of the way, and she would dust his face for grimacing. He liked helping in the shop, liked the smells of paraffin and soap powder, liked serving customers and carrying the morning papers, fattest on Sundays, down to the hotels on the East Promenade. Most of all he liked unpacking deliveries, especially of books or magazines.

That Saturday toward the end of March the carton was of remaindered American magazines. "*Weird Tales* for weirder people," his father said, twitching his nose to send his thick glasses back up to the bridge. "Here's one for you, Bernie: *Curse of the Eyeless Heads*," he called to

Peter's mother, and pretended to read the rest of the contents page: " 'Eyes of the Headless Curse,' 'Heads of the Curseless Eyes,' 'Less of the Curse-Eyed Heads' . . .''

"Less of the lot of them if I had my way." She looked up from arranging sweets in tiers on the counter and wiped her hands on the Queen's face on her apron. "I wouldn't give you sixpence for a hundredweight of them.''

"Better than getting a fat bum and a fat head sitting in front of the telly, my dear."

"The day one of those machines comes into my house I go out the door. Go on, Peter," she growled, seeing him watching, "find something to read if you must, but don't show it to me."

He found a couple that were new to him and read out the advertisements to make her laugh: "Man! Be Big," "Throw Away That Truss," "I Need 500 Men" . . . His father found "Learn to Mount Birds," which had her holding her sides and trying to be solemn when a lady came in to buy rubbers. "Children's erasers, for school," the lady said, staring as if she thought Peter's mother wasn't quite all there.

When the lady had left with her packet Peter's father switched off the lights in the window. The rain had stopped, the sky was clearing. "I'll go and see granny, shall I?" Peter said. "She might want some shopping."

"That's a good boy. She'll be glad to see you." As Peter went out, toggling his duffel coat, he heard his mother saying, "We ought to keep an eye on her just now."

Rain streamed down the gutters as he climbed the gentle slope, past shops on first-name terms—Tommy's Pets, Frank's Fish and Chips—and white pot-bellied terraced houses faced with stones from the beach. In the unexpected sunlight the red mailboxes with their spiky crowns and the street-corner benches with their memorial plaques looked freshly painted by the downpour. The slope grew steeper once he'd crossed a few streets. He climbed above the houses, scrambled up the clay steps to the common and stood panting.

Seen from here, the cape on which Seaward was built looked like a ship forever surging forward into the North Sea. The disused lighthouse on the tip was the figurehead to which the common rose. Grass lay flat as cat's fur on the common, a few trees leaned backward with their branches outstretched, away from the almost constant wind.

Peter walked across the half-mile of common to the northern edge. Below him streets sloped to the lesser hotels. The cliff curved round to Seaward Forest, which stretched inland to the museum and the village that had grown up around the mansion the museum had once been. The road from the village forked at the far end of the common from the lighthouse and led down to opposite ends of the promenade. He held onto the handrail as he climbed down the stone steps to the first of the streets.

Most of the white Georgian houses were divided into apartments. More and more people were retiring to Seaward. At the foot of the slope, beyond several hairdressers and a poodles' beauty parlor, a band played a Viennese waltz under the iron and glass roof of one of the Victorian shopping arcades on the North Fork.

A stray dog was cocking its leg against a bubble car parked on the corner of the street where his mother's mother lived. A van that looked vaguely official except for cardboard license plates stood outside the house whose ground floor she rented. Peter was looking forward to hearing stories of her Victorian childhood, eating her scones with a cup of hot sweet tea, listening to her old 78s, ballads that sounded like growing old: "Just a song at twilight . . ." The front door was ajar, and he walked in.

He took his comb out of the breast pocket of his blazer and stopped in front of the hall mirror to rake his hair back from his high forehead. His gray eyes stared back at him from his oval face. Apart from his protruding ears and his long chin that was almost the same shape as his forehead, he supposed he didn't look too bad. He knocked a phrase of an old song on his grandmother's door next to the mirror and went in.

The first thing he saw was his grandmother standing against the far wall, beyond the mahogany table with its folding leaves and matching straight-backed chairs whose seats made the room smell of leather, a hand over her mouth. The man whose hand it was glared back over his shoulder at Peter and brandished a knife in her face, a knife with a curved black blade that tapered to a sharp point. It was a fragment of one of her records, all of which lay broken beside the overturned gramophone. Her father's paintings had been pulled off the walls, leaving patches like plaques. So much Peter saw before someone flung him the length of the room.

He crashed into the rocking chair and fell against the dresser. A willow-patterned plate fell from the top shelf, barely missing his temple, and smashed at his feet. He crouched off balance, his left elbow a blaze of pain where it had struck the chair, and wondered if his arm was broken. The man who'd stepped from behind the door had already followed Peter down the room in one quick lithe movement. His face was pinched and mottled, his clothes were grubby; Peter could smell his sweat and shabbiness. There seemed to be no expression on his face.

"Do yourself a favor, son," said the other man, who was thin and shabby too, but older. "Pretend you never saw us and tell your old mum here to, for the good of her health."

Without warning she lashed out at him, buried her nails in the hand over her mouth, scratched his face with her other hand, just missing one eye. Peter was as shocked by her violence as by anything else that was happening, and terrified for her. He tried to regain his balance before the younger man could notice, though his heart was pumping so hard he was afraid he might faint instead.

The other man grabbed the old lady's mouth in his fist.

Peter heard the back of her head smack the wall. At once
she kicked the man in the shins with her heavy shoes and
ducked out of his way. Before she reached the window and
threw up the sash she was screaming at the top of her
voice. "Help! Robbers! They're trying to kill me! Police!"

The younger man glared at Peter as if he wished he had
time to finish him, then he ran for the door, digging a set
of car keys out of his pocket. "Stop them! Stop, thief!"
Peter's grandmother cried as the other man hobbled out,
and Peter wondered why she sounded more terrified now
they were leaving. Of course, she was afraid they would
come back.

He had to stop them. He lunged at the open window,
pushed her aside and clambered out. He almost lost his
footing in the muddy flowerbed, but slithered onto the
garden path and was out of the gate just ahead of them. He
wrenched at the sliding door of the van with the cardboard
license plates and heaved himself into the driver's seat, a
moment ahead of the thought, both panicky and ludicrous,
that perhaps this wasn't the thieves' van at all.

But it was. He just had time to grab the door and hold it
shut as the driver dragged at the outer handle, his face
reddening. Peter had to wedge his body between the seat
and the dashboard and hold onto the door with both hands.
He could do nothing when the passenger door rattled open
and the older man vaulted in.

"Give it up, son," he hissed, and punched him on the
back of the head. It felt as if he'd used both fists and all
his weight. Peter's forehead slammed into the nearside
window, which splintered. His hands were letting go of
the door, he seemed unable to stop them, but as the driver
reached through the opening to drag him out, Peter's
hands—somewhere in the distance, beyond the pain that
was pumping up his head like a balloon—clenched on the
steering wheel. The thieves wouldn't move him while he
could hold on.

He dug his nails into his palms when the men tried to

bend his fingers back. That pain was hardly noticeable beyond his swelling head, which felt close to bursting. The deserted street seemed utterly unreal, even when his grandmother ran out, still screaming for help, and began to pull the driver's unkempt hair. As the driver let go of Peter's fingers Peter saw, miles away at the end of the street, a policeman crossing.

He jammed the heel of his free hand against the button in the center of the wheel. The horn blared, so loudly he was afraid it must drown his grandmother's cries. The policeman shaded his eyes and stared toward the van, and Peter released the button so that the policeman could hear what she was screaming. But he was already running toward them.

The thieves scrambled away from the van, up the slope toward the common. A young man dashed out of a house and gave chase, as if the appearance of the police had been a signal or at least an indication of who was in the wrong. Peter heard shouts and a whistle up on the common, and closed his eyes. "Are you all right? Did they hurt you, the swine? God forgive them," his grandmother cried, until he managed to find her hand and lower himself from the van. Leaning on each other, they groped their way into the house and were sitting on the couch, trying to recuperate, when someone knocked on the hall door. Peter's grandmother screamed as two men came into the room.

They were from the ambulance that a neighbor had called. "I'm all right," Peter said, touching his enormous skull and finding little blood. "It's my gran," he said and, standing up, fell to the floor. It seemed easiest to lie there and let the men load him onto the stretcher, carry him into the ambulance, and out again into the hospital. His parents kept appearing in the distance by his bed to tell him the police had arrested the men, thugs, animals, savages, and that he had a concussion, that was all, just lie still now. Some days later he was home with no more pain than aspirin could deal with. It wasn't until he found that he was sleeping on a camp bed in the storeroom that he remembered his grandmother had come to stay because she was afraid to be on her own. He didn't mind, though he wondered where some of his magazines had gone. Everything seemed all right now, if distant. He would be fine so long as his headaches stayed that way.

Chapter III

JIMMY was trying to be fair. He wrote slowly and precisely, giving himself time to think. You couldn't blame Macmillan for having Eisenhower's missiles on British soil, not when Russia had invaded Hungary, but the Campaign for Nuclear Disarmament had the right to march to Aldermaston, it was British to let them march. You could understand their fears of fallout, especially now Russia had put Sputnik and a man into space, but where would the space race end? You might think there were more deserving places for man to concentrate his powers. Still, everyone was eager to spend now that rationing was over and the installment plan opened up, and you couldn't stop them going abroad for their holidays even if it hurt Seaward. Look at the examples they were being given, J. Paul Getty spending millions on paintings he never looked at yet making guests at his manor pay to use the phone, Lord and Lady Docker driving about in a gold-plated Daimler upholstered in zebra skin because "mink is too hot to sit

13

on''; no wonder everyone talked about ''when I come up on the pools'' and crime was on the increase. Jimmy tried to think how to round off his essay, but he still had Sunday for thinking. He went downstairs to the Nosebag.

Jessie Elsey and two other girls were sitting in the café with its round tables and red-and-white-checked tablecloths, its chairs that looked like giant chocolate candies. The girls were loudly sucking the last of their milk shakes through straws, but now they stopped to whisper. ''There's Jimmy Waters,'' one hissed.

''Jimmy waters the lawn,'' a girl with her beehive in a headscarf giggled.

''Jimmy waters his bed.''

''Jimmy pees in his bed,'' Jessie Elsey spluttered as if that were a brilliant improvement. He had to ignore them: customers were always right, even girls—silly, giggling, secretive creatures he'd never heard talk about anything worth hearing. He was glad when his mother came bustling out of the kitchen. ''Anything else, young ladies?'' she said briskly. ''Thanks, Jimmy, I can manage just now.''

''I'll go round to Pete's, then.''

''Don't be late for dinner. Stop by the theater on your way and bring your father if he's there,'' she said, almost casually enough.

The Nosebag was tucked among the small hotels at the far end of the North Promenade from the lighthouse, but people crossed town for his mother's cooking. Hotel awnings striped like deck chairs gleamed opposite the long, thin cliff-top park; sailing boats bobbed on the steely sea; seagulls wheeled through the May sunshine. Jimmy walked past the growing hotels until they gave out on the curve beneath the lighthouse. Bowling greens and tennis courts and Crazy Golf were laid out in the shelter of the point, and there was Steve Innes.

Steve was kicking half a tennis ball around the Crazy Golf course, through the traps watched over by plaster gnomes. "I must be crazy," he said with a wry grin that made a dimple to go with the dent in his chin. He had thoughtful blue eyes in a square face and curly black hair that he always tried to stick down with hair cream.

"Finished your homework, or thinking?" Jimmy said.

Steve's grin faded. "I know what I'm going to write."

"What's stopping you?"

"Not a damn thing when I'm ready. I've plenty to say about Getty and the Dockers and the rest of that mob. That's what Dizzy expects me to say," he said, beginning to stutter as he did whenever he was angry or upset, "and that's what I'll give him."

"No need to shout at me, it isn't my fault. You'll be saying what you believe, won't you?"

"Bloody right I will. Half the people with power want to buy the world and the other half want to blow it up."

"God, you're a misery. Want to come to the flicks tonight with me and Pete?"

"I'll go if you're going. Nothing else to do round here."

"It'll take your mind off things," Jimmy said, knowing half of this was bluff.

Peter lived in a street of small pebbly houses behind the hotels on the East Promenade, not quite high enough for a view of the sea. When Jimmy knocked at the front door, Peter's grandmother looked out between the front-room curtains. "Who is it?" she cried.

"We've come to see Pete."

"He's resting now. He doesn't want to be disturbed," she shouted as Peter appeared behind her. "It's all right," Jimmy saw him saying. "They're my friends."

"If you say so." All the same, she took her time about unchaining and unbolting the front door. "Don't stay long," she said and frowned at the CND badge on Steve's lapel. As soon as they were in the front room, which was full of her furniture and the Priests', she said, "They don't allow you to wear that at school, do they?"

"I only got it," Steve said and had to struggle, "last night."

"Better keep it to yourself. They don't want that kind of thing at school. I know Mr. Gillespie wouldn't. He and I go to the same church."

Gillespie was the English teacher, who seemed to dislike everything about Steve and to enjoy making him stutter in class. Jimmy changed the subject quickly. "Want to come to the flicks with us tonight, Pete?"

"I thought Peter might like to go to the theater with me," his grandmother said. "You know I don't like going out by myself anymore, Peter, especially at night."

"Can't my mum go with you? Then I will." He shrugged at his friends. "You understand."

"You mustn't let me force you to do anything against your will."

"I do want to come," Peter vowed, so vehemently that Jimmy tried to take the pressure off him. "My dad's in the theater," he said. "He's in the Seaward Players."

"More power to him for keeping it alive, so long as they keep it clean. They're lucky the theaters are owned by someone who can afford to keep both of them open." Steve's face hardly changed, but she demanded, "Don't you agree?"

"I don't believe in private property."

"I thought your father's business was selling houses."

"So?" Steve said, and Jimmy interrupted, "I think we'd better go." Either Steve didn't realize she wanted him to leave or that made him determined to stay. Jimmy left them arguing, for the mention of the theater had made him anxious to see that his father was there.

The Little Theater overlooked the Steps, a path that turned sharply back on itself five times as it descended the cliff at the far end of the East Promenade. A stray wind followed him into the red-carpeted foyer and fluttered the handbills stacked outside the ticket windows. "It's a bargain," a woman said to three actors on the bare stage, and peered down the small high auditorium at Jimmy. "You can't come in here," the producer said shrilly, and then, "Oh, it's you. Your father's gone. He isn't in this scene."

Jimmy's heart sank. "Gone home, you mean?"

The producer swept his hand over his forehead as if he'd forgotten he was bald. "Look, boy, I've enough trouble keeping these people in line on stage without wondering where they go afterward. You ought to know where he is if anyone does."

Jimmy was afraid he did. He hurried up a side street to the East Fork. Beyond the department stores and tea shops and Victorian arcades, the few pubs and betting shops were hidden in the side streets. Jimmy held his breath and made a wish as he went into the nearest betting shop, the furthest from the Nosebag, but he saw his father at once.

His father was holding his bowler hat in front of him and gazing up at an overhead speaker as if he were meeting royalty. A grin that pretended he hadn't turned guiltily spread across his broad face. "Come here, lad, stand here with me. You'll enjoy this."

"Here's trouble," said a man with inky fingers and no buttons on his jacket. "He's come to put the ring through your nose, Bill."

Because of him, Jimmy didn't speak until he reached his father, and then under his breath. "Dad, what are you doing? You promised mum you wouldn't gamble anymore."

"Don't let me down, lad, don't make a scene," his father whispered. "Trust me for once."

Didn't he realize Jimmy wished he could, more than anything else in the world? "You told me you needed all the money for the café."

"I'm here because we need the money, don't you understand?" He put an arm around Jimmy's shoulders and pulled him close. "This time it's a sure thing, Jimmy," he whispered as if he was afraid the others might hear.

"But you don't need to take the risk, dad. Mum says we'll be all right once the holiday season starts."

"Your mother doesn't want to face it, Jimmy. They'll all be going abroad now with all these package holidays. Anyway," he said with a kind of guilty triumph, "I've made the bet and I can't stop it now."

The commentator's voice above their heads slowed down from jabbering, the roar of the crowd faded to the sound inside a seashell. "Listen to that," Jimmy's father said, grasping Jimmy's shoulders in his large plump hands. "We've won."

He dug in the inside breast pocket of his pin-striped suit and pressed a pound note into Jimmy's hand. "Here, have another for luck. If we win the next race, and we will, we'll have won five hundred pounds."

Jimmy clenched his fist and tried not to feel as though his father's luck was in his hands. "You bastard," a gambler muttered at the overhead speaker and stalked out, tearing up his betting slip. A man whose lapels were covered with ash was squinting desperately at the tacked-up newspapers; over in one corner a gambler was surreptitiously fingering a rosary. "Come on, Lucky Devil," Jimmy's father murmured as the race began, and Jimmy urged the horse on too, silently but so fiercely he felt that everyone must hear. Five hundred pounds would keep them out of debt for years and, better still, was such a sum that his father would surely never bet again. Come on Lucky Devil, come on five hundred pounds. His arm was aching so hard he couldn't move it, and he thought that was because he was clenching his fist on the money until he realized his father was gripping his arm. "Come on, Lucky Devil," his father and several others cried, and Jimmy was about to add his voice to the chorus when the horse fell.

The cheers of the crowd sank to a groan that seemed to plunge through Jimmy's stomach. He bit his lip as his father bruised his arm and then let go. He was hardly aware that his father was prizing open his fist to take the money. "Just lend it to me, Jimmy, I'll give it back to you when I win. I always leave the last race clear so I can play a hunch."

He lost that race too. He jammed his bowler on his head and stared at the floor as he shoved Jimmy toward the street and muttered his goodbyes. "What about the other race, the one you won?" Jimmy protested. "Aren't you going to collect your winnings?"

"It was an accumulator, Jimmy. Either Lucky Devil won or I got nothing. Come on, lad, let's get out of here." As soon as they were outside he grabbed Jimmy's bruised arm. "Your mother thinks I was rehearsing. Don't tell her different, will you? No use upsetting her, she's got enough on her mind. Let's keep it a secret between us men."

"I won't tell her if you promise not to do it again. Really promise this time."

"I'll do my best, Jimmy. I can't say fairer than that, can I? You needn't think it's fun for me. I wish I didn't need to, believe me." They climbed the East Fork to the junction, and Jimmy saw the shadow of the town mounting the disused lighthouse, turning it black as a charred tree. "Don't worry, I didn't bet much to start with," his father said, and Jimmy heard how he was already persuading himself that it had been nothing at all.

Chapter IV

THE CURTAIN had scarcely risen on the Agatha Christie play when Peter's grandmother began to grow ill at ease, tutting under her breath. When the first corpse turned up she murmured, "I don't know if this is suitable for you."

"Mum and dad won't mind," he told her without thinking. "They let me read magazines from the shop." All that bothered him about the play was that it seemed too unreal to touch him, as much so as the winged bulls that dwindled up the walls of the auditorium, the bearded faces supporting the boxes on either side of the great proscenium arch. At the end of the play everyone bowed, the villain, who was after all only an actor, and the corpses too, none of which seemed more unreal than the audience that flooded into the foyer full of mirrors, studied smiles and conversation multiplying under glass. He couldn't help wishing he were with Jimmy and Steve at the Lux.

The Grand stood opposite Seaward Village school, among the houses clustered along the road that emerged from the forest near the museum. The afterglow held the silhouettes of trees like a glass slide. His grandmother was silent until they reached the dark hump of the common. As they started down the East Fork toward the floodlit hotels she said, "Peter, I wish you'd choose yourself some new friends."

He was enjoying feeling real again, the sea air chilling his face and his nostrils. "I've got friends," he said, not quite understanding.

"Of a kind, Peter. You're at the age when you must take care not to fall into bad company." Her bony fingers closed on his arm, for support down the slope or to make sure he took notice. "The Waters boy seems dependable enough. It's the others who worry me."

"Why?"

"I hope you really don't know, Peter. If you don't know what that girl is then I'm glad. You shouldn't know at your age."

"Who, Robin?" Of course he knew her mother wasn't married: his parents had told him so and that it made no difference, his mother had taken to Robin's mother at once when they had met at the bridge club. "She's all right. We have some good games."

"I'm sure you have." Her tone made it clear that she didn't mean their games of chess, not that his headaches let him play much anymore. "Or you will if you're not careful. Your mother's too ready with her pity. She ought to know better than to let you associate with that girl or your friend with the stutter."

"Steve can't help how he talks."

"God's way of making it harder for him to spread his Communistic ideas, if you ask me. He'll pay for what he's trying to do, you mark my words." She pulled him away from the quickest way home, a stepped alley, and made for a street with more lights. "Even if they don't influence you, you'll be associated with them in people's minds. Maybe you don't care about that now, but it won't be long before you're applying for jobs." She caught hold of his hands. "I'm worried for you, Peter. Say you won't see them again, for my peace of mind if you won't do it for yourself."

Her voice sounded close to shaking, the way it shook when she called out "Who's there?" if anyone got up during the night, but how could he promise? He and Steve had been friends for years; they'd swapped comics in the schoolyard, flown kites on the cliff, cycled along the coast to Great Yarmouth last summer and spent all their money on two Scottish girls whose boyfriends had roared up on motorcycles just as things seemed promising. "I can't not see Steve," he protested. "He's in my class at school."

"I'm sorry if you won't do it for me, Peter."

He wished he could promise with his fingers crossed, but she wouldn't believe him now. As soon as they were home he went upstairs so as not to. hear her telling his parents about him.

The smell of her furniture followed him to the storeroom. He sat on the camp bed and gazed at his star maps as if they might take his mind out of the small house that seemed to have grown smaller. Now and then a phrase floated up through the sound of the unseen sea, his grandmother saying "I wish you wouldn't let him" in that vulnerable way, his mother complaining "But mam" in a voice that made him wince as if she were turning back into a child. His father said hardly anything. "It isn't granny's fault she's like this," Peter said to himself so as to blot out the voices. "She can't help being nervous after what happened, you can't blame her for not wanting to be left in the house by herself; she does try to help in the shop, but you'd think she would go up to bed before mum and dad sometimes or let them go out for a walk by themselves. . . ."

He was talking so loudly that he didn't hear his mother until she marched into his room. "What have you been saying to my mother about us?"

This was so unexpected that he gaped at her. "Nothing."

"You little liar." She stood with her hands on her thick hips. "Don't you dare go telling her we let you read that rubbish in the shop. You know I don't approve. What do you think she'll think of me?"

"I only said it because she didn't want me to see the murders."

"I don't know what you're talking about, and I'm sure I don't care. You're not to read any more of them, do you hear?" She drew a breath that made her face turn red. "And you're not to have that Innes boy round here anymore."

"I can still go out with him though, can't I?"

"What did I just say to you? Won't you be satisfied until you upset everyone in the house? Don't you let me hear you've been with that boy again."

She hadn't told him not to see Steve, only not to be found out. He wondered if she had meant to give him that option, wondered if she was being fierce with him because she resented sounding like a child when she argued with her mother. He couldn't think, not with this growing headache. He was lying down and thinking of nothing—sometimes then his headaches went away—when his father came into his bedroom. "Don't resent your mother, Pete," he said, blinking at his glasses, which he was cleaning. "She's under a lot of strain just now."

"I know." Peter closed his eyes again. "But why does she have to be like that about Steve?"

"Parsy kew, Pete. Parsy kew, that's why." His face-tiousness sounded tired, self-conscious. "Women can be like that when they don't know what to do. I know you can't avoid Steve even if you wanted to, and so does your mother if she'd let herself admit it. Just keep it to yourself, all right? Just while your grandmother's here."

When Peter opened his eyes his father smiled encouragingly at him. "Past your bedtime, son," he said and went downstairs, where Peter's grandmother was saying "I wish you wouldn't let him sell them in the shop." Peter groped his way through his headache to the bathroom and the aspirin. All he could see was his father smiling fixedly as though he wondered if Peter's grandmother would ever leave.

Chapter V

JAYNE MANSFIELD and Diana Dors and Marilyn Monroe were on the beach that first hot dry weekend, or at least dyed blondes who were trying to look like them. Steve strolled along the pebbly beach, past girls spread out on beach towels, bikinied breasts aimed at the sky, and grinned as he remembered Jimmy saying that they looked like rude postcards come to life, frowned quickly so that none of them would call him Dimples. The beach stretched away for a mile in the direction of Great Yarmouth, until the cliff brought a row of cottages down to the seawall, but he turned away and made for the Steps. Without Pete Priest he felt exposed down here, on show.

At the top of the zigzag path the hotels shone like laundered sheets. Men in livery stood outside glass porches tall as cottages. The waste of space offended him, and so did the sight of the Elsey real estate agency on a street between two of the most expensive hotels. He scowled at the descriptions of houses for sale: heated swimming pool,

exclusive district, would suit large family. . . . Large
family of millionaires, he thought as Jessie Elsey came up
behind him. "What are you after, left-couch?" she
demanded.

"Buying your uncle out." When she flounced into her
uncle's office he strolled exaggeratedly away. She made
being left-handed sound like a disease, the way Gillespie
did. She'd made Steve think of the teacher when he was
trying to forget about him for the weekend, not that he
ever could for very long.

It wasn't only that the teacher seemed to loathe everything about Steve, so much so that he never lost an oppor-
tunity to show him up in front of the class. Worse than
that, he made him feel incapable of thinking freely, of
thinking anything except what Dizzy expected him to think.
It was people like the Elseys Steve objected to, not his
own father—the Elseys who had no time for anyone poorer
than themselves. Inexpensive properties would lie on the
Elsey agency's books for years while Mr. Elsey devoted
all his energy to selling the choicest houses. Steve might
have said as much to Peter's grandmother, but he'd ended
up saying what she seemed to expect to hear. That must be
why Pete was uncomfortable with him.

Steve's house was on the north side. The Georgian
street overlooked the bay and Seaward Forest, a few distant trees venturing down to paddle where the cliff became
a slope. Two neighbors wheeled their golf bags by as
Steve let himself into the house.

His mother looked a warning at him when he went into
the front room. Sunlight through the net curtains dazzled
him and glared back from the mounted photographs of
forest patterns, which his mother took between photo-
graphing houses for the agency, and then he saw that his
father had her toaster in pieces on the rug, next to a
manual he must have borrowed from the library. He would
never learn, Steve thought affectionately, even though whenever his father tried to do repairs himself he almost always

had to take them in and pay extra for the damage he'd done. Steve winked at his mother before he realized that his father was glowering at neither of them: someone was sitting in the window. It was Gillespie.

"Innes." The hint of a prim smile appeared at the corners of the teacher's thin lips. "I was just discussing your opinions with your parents. I think your father was surprised to hear what you think of his livelihood."

Steve's father sat back on his haunches and picked up his screwdriver. Even in that position he looked powerful, his face did, with its jutting chin and large, bright, close-set eyes, and so did his hands, with fingers that could have snapped Gillespie's in a handshake. "I'm a damn sight more surprised you felt you had to come and tell me."

"If Innes had said it in my classroom I would have dealt with it, I assure you." The teacher raised his graying eyebrows. "But he upset a friend of mine who is in no condition to be upset."

"He means Pete's grandmother. She wanted me to argue."

"Pigheaded and proud of it as ever. She wanted you to listen, Innes, listen respectfully and learn. Just as I imagine your parents would."

"We don't believe in indoctrination, Mr. Gillespie." Steve's mother was perched on the very edge of her chair, hands gripping her knees through her flowered dress. "Even if we don't always agree with his ideas, they're his. It does no good to squash them down. That's squashing him."

Steve often resented her treating his feelings as if they were a phase he was going through, but now he could have hugged her. "Did you really say your father was exploiting people, Steve?" she said gently.

"I did not. I said the Elseys," Steve said, so furiously that he had to take several runs at the name.

"Perhaps you'd have less trouble speaking if what you had to say was worth saying," the teacher said. "Mr.

Elsey and his brother are on the town council. Your elders and betters obviously think more of them than you do."

Steve's father spoke without looking up. "My son has a stammer he'll grow out of. I don't expect anyone who's being paid to teach him to try to make him look a fool." His suppressed anger made him drive the screwdriver into his hand as he tried to tighten a screw. "Damn and blast the bloody thing, it'll have to go back to the shop."

"It's all right, Norman. Come upstairs and let me put something on that. Was there anything else, Mr. Gillespie?" Steve's mother said as an afterthought, smiling sweetly at him.

"Nothing that I need say here." The teacher's face had gone pink. He was breathing heavily, touching his chest with one hand. "I must say your attitude surprises me." He pointed a finger brown with nicotine at Steve's CND badge. "If you have the impertinence to wear that anywhere near the school I shall confiscate it. I suggest you leave it at home with your attitudes."

Steve's father stared after him through the sunlight and net curtains. When Steve's mother tried to examine his hand he shrugged her away. "Is he like that with you all the time at school?" he demanded. "You never told us."

"I don't care, dad. Dizzy doesn't bother me." Worse than the threat of Gillespie's next class, worse even than coming home to find him here, was that now Steve's parents knew about the teacher despite all the care Steve had taken not to worry them. "He's like that with everyone," he lied, "nobody takes any notice," and smiled until his parents went doubtfully upstairs. He pulled the net curtain aside and closed his fist on the tiny figure at the foot of the slope, squeezed and grinned until just for a second he felt he had reason to grin. Then Gillespie walked out of his fist and away until Monday morning.

Chapter VI

"I'M GLAD you're staying home on Sundays now, Peter," his grandmother said.

It was a gloomy July Sunday. He thought she was getting at his father, who went out to the pub now that he couldn't have a drink with his meals for fear of upsetting her, until she said, "That Innes boy could learn from your example."

"I'd better let him see it then, hadn't I?"

"Don't try to be witty, Peter, that's the devil talking. There's too much of that already in this house. I think Mr. Gillespie made it clear what we think of your association."

"Who's we?" his father said sharply. "What do you mean?"

Peter turned away, blushing and tongue-tied, but she was proud to explain. Peter's father stared at her. "We've given in to you on quite a few things," he said. "No need to go sneaking behind our backs."

"I don't call looking after Peter's welfare sneaking."

"I wouldn't like to tell you what I'd call it. Pete can be trusted to choose his own friends."

"I wish you wouldn't call him Pete. Don't you like what Peter means? 'Upon this rock I shall build my church. . . .' Don't you care what kind of friends he has any more than you care what he reads?"

Peter watched his father's face and knew he was going to say everything he'd left unsaid. He couldn't believe it when his father muttered, "She's your mother, you deal with it. I'll be back when I am."

"Letting him go out drinking on a Sunday," his grandmother said as the front door slammed. "What do you mean by it. Bernadette?"

"But he needs to relax, mam," Peter's mother said, and he couldn't take any more—couldn't bear how his father's only catch-phrase now was "better hadn't," when he thought of a joke Peter's grandmother might fail to see and think dirty or blasphemous, or when Peter tried to talk to him about any one of several subjects they used to discuss openly. Why, he'd even given in to her about stocking the magazines in the shop, he'd told Peter they didn't make enough profit to be worth the trouble. Now Peter felt his father's failure to speak building up into the worst headache he'd ever had. "I'm going for a walk," he said, and went out before his grandmother could say anything to stop him.

Dark clouds came pouring over the horizon, thickening the muddy air. Families were strolling on the promenade and ignoring several Teddy boys who were fighting halfheartedly in one of the pebbly shelters. The clouds made the point appear to be rushing forward, the lighthouse to be tottering. As he reached the North Promenade a few raindrops that felt big and chill and lingering struck his forehead and made him flinch. He'd thought of going to Jimmy's, but now he found he didn't want to talk. He turned aside between the hotels and climbed the steps to the Lux.

Goldfish swam over a mosaic in the foyer of the cinema. An organ sank into the stage under the screen as the lights dimmed. Binoculars with hidden spikes put out a woman's eyes, a guillotine decapitated another woman as she lay on her bed, and Peter felt depressed, afraid of the thoughts that the film was driving out of hiding. As he made for Seaward Forest, he was almost running.

Where the cliff road became unsafe and was fenced off, tracks led between the trees. His headache drove him into the forest with some thought of shelter if the storm should break. He didn't know when he strayed from the track and stumbled among the pines, where the dimness felt like drowning. He had to avoid pools crawling with flies where the roots of fallen trees had lifted lids of earth. Whenever he came into the open, too briefly to be able to distinguish a path, the storm clouds seemed closer to the treetops, the trees looked charred, already struck by lightning. He thought he smelled burning, but couldn't make out what his senses were doing: the entire dim, pathless forest seemed to be crammed spikily into his head.

When he came out from under the trees at last, he was on the cliff. The cliff road had fallen away completely here, and he could look straight down to the bay. He stepped forward until he was a pace away from the crumbling edge.

The sky on the horizon was black glass that white fire kept cracking. A lone bird sang in the stillness between the shuddering crashes of thunder. He thought of being struck or falling to the stony beach, and found he didn't care, not when he considered the way his parents were changing. His grandmother would go on finding fault with them and the way they brought him up, his father would withdraw further into himself, his mother would grow more nervous and more unsympathetic to Peter, and he could see no end to it: it looked like the whole of his future. He shouted something, he didn't know what—a plea or a curse—into

the storm that was sweeping toward him, jabbing at the
black sea.

Absurdly, what sent him back under the trees was the
threat of being drenched. At least he might still be struck
by lightning. His skin was crawling with electricity, the
endless forest was exploding from the center of his brain.
He wished he hadn't shouted, for he felt as if he'd called
something that was rushing toward him, at his back now,
in his brain. Perhaps he was screaming as he ran, screaming at the headache his skull could no longer contain, or
perhaps that was the forest shrieking past him, the squeal
of wooden needles underfoot. Was that the forest road
ahead, the crossroads where highwaymen were buried?
Why did he want to be in the open if what was driving him
onward was only the storm? Yes, it was a crossroads,
though one he'd never seen before. He staggered out
between the roads, and the lightning struck him.

Or perhaps his skull had split open at last, for the light
seemed to be in him as well as outside him. Bare-knuckled
trees stepped forward, flattening. Everything had the sudden glassy clarity of a slide snapped into the holder of his
eyes, and he couldn't close them, for the light was behind
them too. It was lasting too long for lightning, but he
didn't care what it was; he welcomed it in a breathless
terrified way—he could do nothing else. The dimness and
oppression had gone, and so had his headache. The roads
around him looked floodlit, absolutely clear.

He must have chosen the right one, for the next he knew
he was hurrying, half-blind with rain, along the promenade. At home nobody was speaking to anyone else, hardly
even when his parents went with his grandmother to evening mass in the hope of a truce. Peter was uncomfortable
in church that day—he hadn't gone every Sunday by any
means until his grandmother had come to stay, and he
didn't feel as if he ought to be there now—but he kept
remembering the light at the crossroads. Though he couldn't
recall when it had faded, he felt he would see it again.

And so he did, a few days later when an anonymous envelope with a blurred postmark arrived for him. As he unfolded the single sheet of paper it seemed to brighten until he could hardly look, as if a floodlight had been switched on over his shoulder or inside his head. The sheet of cheap paper bore a London box number and six typed words: WHATEVER YOU MOST NEED I DO.

Chapter VII

"MAKE the most of your holidays," Robin's mother kept saying. "Don't spend all your time at the museum." But Peter seemed to be avoiding people now that the school term was over, and Robin's girlfriends seemed afraid to talk intelligently anymore in case boys heard them, to have committed themselves to boys, makeup, clothes, the Top Twenty, would Elvis survive the army, how could they sleep at night until they knew, didn't Robin care about *anything*? There was almost a gale that early August day, and so she went up to the museum. Perhaps she might find out what was troubling her mother.

The flattened grass streamed across the common away from the leaping sea, the trees on the common strained to stoop to the grass. Robin walked between the laughing lions and up the wide path, her long slim legs striding easily, her black hair blowing across her face, her large brown eyes, pale lips, freckles speckling the bridge of her long delicate nose. Waves of light and wind rushed through the spacious lawns as she stepped into the porch.

"Good morning, Miss Laurel," the doorman said, but now she felt as if her mother hadn't wanted her to come. Wide marble staircases overlooked by portraits curved up to the floor where her mother worked, but Robin turned aside into the museum. The man at the enquiry desk, a man with a large head and a graying beard that hid the knot of his tie, glanced sharply at her as if he knew her, though she had never spoken to him. She nodded to him, not caring what he thought of her, and strolled on down the long, high, sunlit room.

Here was the history of Seaward and this youngest side of Britain, in glass cases displaying fossils, a Lower Paleolithic pebble tool, Neolithic pottery, beakers and urns from the Bronze Age, Celtic shields, coins and fragments of mosaic from the Roman walled town near the signal station where the lighthouse was now. . . . All this and her knowing that her mother had restored some of these glimpses of history made her even happier to have come to live in Seaward, and she was turning toward her mother's office when an old lady holding onto the doorman's arm rapped on the enquiry desk. "Is this of any value?"

The bearded man squinted at the coin. "I shouldn't like to say, madam. If you'd care to take a seat I'll show it to my colleague who does most of our dating."

Robin felt proud, because he meant her mother. She followed him unobtrusively to hear what her mother would say. When she reached the landing she heard her mother's voice along the left-hand passage. "Why have you brought me this? You know quite well it's worthless."

"I just wanted to be sure."

"Yes, and we both know of what, don't we, Douglas? I thought I'd made myself clear enough even for you. I don't want to go out with you, I don't want to spend my lunchtimes with you, I don't want to see you at all except when it's professionally necessary. One walk in the forest was quite enough, thank you very much."

"You shouldn't have told me so much about yourself if you weren't going to be friendly."

"Threatening me now, are you? Do you know what the law calls forcing your attentions on a woman, Douglas? The word is rape."

"Don't be silly." His voice was dropping as hers rose. "Anyway, I could say you led me on, telling me your secrets."

"Rape, I said. You come anywhere near me and I'll have Mr. Talley up here in a flash."

"Keep your voice down or you'll have him up here before you want him. Don't be threatening my reputation, Emily. I could tell the board a few things about you if I weren't a gentleman."

Robin had had enough. Eavesdropping made her feel she had something to hide. She went quickly along the passage, but hesitated with her hand on the doorknob twice the size of her fist, for under the notice that said CONSERVATOR it said MRS. LAUREL. Her mother had never been married. Suddenly she knew what secret the bearded man was threatening to reveal. She wasn't going to be made to feel ashamed, there was no reason why she should or why her mother should either. "I said *if* I weren't a gentleman," the bearded man murmured as Robin flung open the door.

Her mother's bench and microscopes were between him and her mother, who was standing against her shelves of chemicals and soft brushes and the rest of her tools. Both of them turned as Robin came into the book-lined room. Her mother's long fingers flew to her pale lips; whatever his mouth was doing was hidden by his beard. "I don't care what you say about me," Robin told him, "but you leave my mother alone."

"I thought you were the daughter. You have your moth-

er's eyes. You're sure this is of no value?" he said to
Robin's mother. "Then I'll leave you alone."

Robin's mother ran to her as he closed the door behind
him. "How much did you hear, love?"

Robin couldn't help being stiff as her mother took her
face in her hands. "Enough."

"You'll forgive me, won't you? I did mean to tell you,
I just didn't know how. You'll always be my Robin, you
know that."

"You told them you were married."

"Widowed. I had to, Robin. I never told you, but I'm
sure I failed the other interview because I told them the
truth."

"But if you didn't want them to know about me, how
did that man downstairs find out?"

"Of course I want them to know about you, Robin. I
want them to know you and admire you as much as I do.
You're the best thing in my life, I hope you know. It's not
your fault I wasn't married, you musn't ever think I blame
you. It's just that some people are so Victorian still,
especially in a place like this. They'd turn me out into the
storm if they knew about me," she said, trying to smile.

Robin wanted to take her hands but couldn't quite.
"You still haven't said how he found out."

"I told him when I thought I could trust him. I was
wrong. Men are like that. You be careful." She risked a
smile. "Listen to who's telling you. And I mentioned it to
Mrs. Priest because she's been so friendly. I only hope she
keeps it to herself. I was lucky to get this post, you know.
Past forty and some interviewers don't want to know at
all."

Robin hugged her so hard they felt like one body. "Oh,
mummy, you're getting yourself into a state for no reason.
They should be glad to have you. There aren't many
people with your qualifications."

"Perhaps you're right, love, perhaps I worry too much.
Sometimes I wish I had your poise." She disengaged

herself gently so as to look into Robin's eyes. "Just keep that one thing to yourself until I say it's all right, will you? I know you understand."

Robin had told nobody in Seaward she was illegitimate, simply because it was her mother's secret more than hers, but now she felt as if her own existence was putting her mother at risk. "Let me get some work done now and we can walk home together," her mother said. "Don't let Douglas bother you. I think we sent him packing."

"I shouldn't have come when you told me not to. I'll see you at home," Robin said and left her with a quick kiss. Douglas glanced speculatively up the stairs as Robin hurried out, and she wanted to make sure he wouldn't trouble her mother, but how could she? She wandered into the forest, feeling helpless and wordlessly furious, too much so to enjoy the tumult of the pines, and had walked miles when she met Peter.

His long oval face with its protruding ears looked preoccupied, unsure how he was feeling. "Hi, Robin, I must come up to yours for a game some evening when you aren't busy," he said vaguely, then he blinked at her. "What's wrong?"

"I wish I could tell you."

"That bad, is it?" His gray eyes gazed at his thoughts for quite some time before he said, "Whatever it is, maybe I know what to do."

Chapter VIII

PETER had been carrying the letter in his pocket for most of
the school holidays and wondering how to respond. At
first the promise in the letter made him feel powerful, able
to solve everything if he had to, but as his mother gave in
more and more to her mother for the sake of their nerves
while his father hardly spoke to anyone, he realized he was
afraid. Who had sent him the letter, and what might they
do if he asked for help? How had they known he needed
it? Now, rereading the letter made him afraid that he
would be compelled to respond; sometimes even thinking
of the letter set him composing a response. He was wandering the forest, searching for the floodlit clarity he'd lost
before he could judge what it was, when he met Robin.
Suddenly he knew he wouldn't be afraid if he wasn't alone
in responding.

When he showed her the letter she looked disappointed,
almost insulted. "I should take it back to whichever joke
shop you bought it from and tell them you've been cheated."

"I didn't buy it." He pocketed the letter before the wind could snatch it. "It just came in the post one day."

"Who sent it? Why should they send it to you?"

"One way to find out."

"Don't, Peter. I don't trust it. If I were you I'd tear it up right now." She walked home with him and tried to persuade him, and smiled as if she couldn't care less that he wasn't inviting her in because of his grandmother. "Come round soon and we'll have a game," she said. "You throw that letter on the fire. Things aren't that bad."

That only made him think they were for Robin too, though he hadn't been able to find out what was wrong. He had to share the letter. That evening he went round to Steve's.

"I'd give my right arm to see Gillespie vanish," Steve admitted with a wink. "Go ahead, say you've a friend who's interested, see what happens. You ought to ask Jimmy too. They could use some luck."

He wasn't taking the letter or his trouble seriously, not while Gillespie and the autumn term were weeks away. Jimmy seemed worth approaching once Steve explained how Mr. Waters was running the family into debt, though Peter didn't say that to Jimmy, only wondered if Jimmy had any problems the letter might solve.

"I wouldn't have thought this was your kind of rot, Pete. Bit beneath you, isn't it? You'll be seeing ghosts next if you aren't careful." Nevertheless, he copied the letter painstakingly into a notebook, box number and all. "I might be interested at that, if you're really going to answer it. They shouldn't be allowed to work on people's troubles like this. I'd like to see what they send you."

Peter borrowed the typewriter his mother used to make up the accounts for the shop. As he posted his letter that said four of them were interested, he had a moment of panic: suppose his parents or his grandmother opened the reply by mistake? He was still nervous the night he went to

Robin's, a suite of rooms with enormous fireplaces and echoes. Halfway through a game of chess she said, "You didn't write to that box number, did you?"

"Yes, I did."

"You fool. What happened?"

"Nothing yet."

"I hope nothing does. You shouldn't get involved with things like that." She moved a knight recklessly, risking three pieces. "If you hear anything you can let me know."

"What's wrong, Robin? Can't you tell me?"

"I can't tell anyone who knows me, and Terry Tebbitt's no bloody use." She glanced toward the kitchen to make sure her mother wasn't listening. "I'd write to anyone if I really thought they had something to offer."

Terry Tebbitt wrote the advice column in the local paper. As soon as Peter was home he went into the shed and began to sort through the old newspapers his parents saved to take to the shop for wrapping. The only likely letter he could find was from "Love Child, Seaward," whom Terry Tebbitt advised to tell her mother to report the man to her employers and throw herself on their mercy. He was wishing he could help Robin himself when his grandmother came to see why the light was on. "Come here quickly, Bernadette," she cried. "Will you look at what he's up to now, grubbing in the rubbish like a tramp." Her cry startled his mother so much that she dropped the Dresden teapot, part of the set that had been her parents' wedding gift to her. Peter heard her crying brokenly as he went up to bed, as he lay not knowing whether the feeling in his head was the threat of a head-ache or the beginning of a light behind his eyes. "Come on," he muttered, "help me, I need you now," and the next morning a thick envelope addressed to him was propped up on the breakfast table.

When he put it under his chair in the hope they would forget it his mother said, "Well, what is it?"

"A new chess magazine."

''Let's have a look, then,'' she said, staring at him until he had to pick up the envelope. He tore the flap so slowly that his mother gave an angry sigh, just as his grandmother protested, ''Don't have him reading at the table, Bernadette. It's the height of bad manners.''

Being grateful to her made Peter feel guilty, and so did his father's hurt look. ''I could have got you a discount. I'm still a shopkeeper, you know.''

Peter went up to the bathroom as soon as he could and turned on the taps to muffle the sound of taking out the contents of the envelope, four identical photocopied sheets. Most of each sheet was blank, not even bearing the box number. WHAT I MOST NEED IS, a line of typescript said, and left several inches of space before the dotted line above the words *Without a signature this form is invalid*. There was one more sentence. *The price*, it said, *is something that you do not value and which you may regain*.

He hadn't thought about a fee, but in any case it seemed it didn't matter. Now that he was close to asking for what he needed he wondered if he could; however carefully he worded it, what might he be asking, and of whom? Persuading the others to meet took his mind off wondering. Perhaps once they were together he would find it easier to ask.

They met on the common that evening. Red spikes of sunset probed the forest, a few fishing boats from Shipham bobbed on either side of the point that divided the horizon of the sea. Jimmy was the last to arrive, in muddy football gear, and seemed resentful that Robin was there. She and Steve were arguing, first because she'd told him his hair would look better if he let it be natural and now about the Earl of Seaward, who'd presented the common as well as his mansion to Seaward on condition they were made available to the public. ''They shouldn't have been his to give,'' Steve said.

''I thought it was girls who were supposed to be illogical.''

"You don't seem so much like a girl," Jimmy told her, and wondered why she looked both appalled and amused. "Thank you so much," she said, and Peter thought it was time to hand out the forms.

The sunset had drained into the ground between the trees. It must be the afterglow that made the forms easy to read. Steve laughed shortly, Robin drew a loud impatient breath, Jimmy pinched his brows and pored over the last line. "Regain how?" he said.

"I don't know. Does it matter?"

"Didn't think we'd ask that, eh Pete?" Steve might be laughing at himself for having hoped. "You made the whole thing up, didn't you? Got the idea out of the back of one of those magazines your dad used to sell."

"I don't know where these forms came from. I told you how it happened, how the letter came." Peter's head felt close to aching; the form in his hand flickered like lightning. All at once he felt sure that unless they all responded, his wish wouldn't work. "Say I wrote them if you like. Then there's no reason for you not to fill yours in."

"I don't mind if it'll make you feel better. Calm down, Pete, it's only fun, isn't it? It isn't as if I'd be wishing anyone dead, only out of the way."

Robin shrugged and nodded. "Don't get yourself into a state, Peter, you'll be giving yourself one of your headaches," she said, and began to scribble on her form.

Jimmy borrowed Peter's spare pen. "I don't want anything for myself, but I'll ask for something. I want to see how far this will go." Now they were all writing but Peter, whose fingers had begun to ache with the memory of clinging to the wheel of the thieves' van. How could he put his grandmother at the mercy of whoever had sent the forms? But there was no room for her at home: his parents could hardly stand living there now, hardly stand each other. He couldn't help it, he regretted being brave enough to face up to the thieves. He wouldn't be wishing her any

harm, he told himself. WHAT I MOST NEED IS my grandmother to go away, he scrawled, and signed the form as
the others signed theirs.

At once he could no longer see the form, though the
afterglow was still visible behind the trees. "What are we
supposed to put for the fee?" Steve said, climbing the
common toward the lighthouse to see if there was more
light higher up. All four of them were standing near the
lighthouse, where they could still not make out the forms,
when a sudden silent gust of wind snatched the pages out
of their hands.

Peter cried out, Steve turned away and slapped his
forehead, Jimmy leapt for his form and lost his footing,
slithering down the grass. Only Robin watched impas-
sively as the pages swooped over the sea. "If anyone reads
it I'm glad," she said. "I'm sick of pretending. What I am
is who I am."

The pages lost momentum suddenly and plunged together into the dark sea, and Peter felt intensely relieved.
He dragged the original letter out of his pocket and held it
above his head until a wind carried it out to sea. "You
were right, Steve; it was only fun," he said.

He hugged his grandmother when he got home, so hard
that she peered suspiciously at him. She'd been subdued
since his mother had broken the teapot; perhaps while she
was susceptible he ought to ask someone to talk to her
about the effect she was having. He would have if he
could have thought of anyone, but all at once it was the
last week of the holidays and still he hadn't thought what
to do. Maybe he could ask Robin's advice now that she'd
determined to live with her own and her mother's troubles.
He hurried through the streets in a sunlit interlude between
two rainstorms, and was turning the corner of her street
when he saw her coming toward him.

She faltered when she saw him, then strode forward.
"Were you coming to tell me some news, Peter?" she said
in an odd stiff voice as soon as she was near enough.

He found himself stammering like Steve. "I just wanted to talk."

"Then tell me something first. Was Steve right? Did you write that letter and those forms?"

"No, I told you." His head was beginning to throb like a bruise. "I don't know where they came from."

"Then I don't like it, Peter. I wish I hadn't let you give me one. I asked for a man my mother works with to stop pestering her, and yesterday he was run over outside the museum."

"It must have been an accident, don't you think? People are always being run over. My grandmother's afraid to cross the road." It must have been only a coincidence when it was so much more than Robin had asked for. "I don't want granny to be harmed," he said over and over each night until he fell asleep, "please just let her go away," and felt so relieved each morning when he heard her and knew she hadn't been harmed that he thought he might be sick, until he realized that neither had she gone away. Would she if his father told her to? Peter might suggest that to him if he could catch his father in an approachable mood. Nothing else would happen, the accident outside the museum had been a lucky coincidence. But on the first day of the autumn term he learned that Steve's bugbear Gillespie had had a stroke and would no longer be teaching, and on the fourth day Jimmy's father won the pools.

Chapter IX

THE LOOK on Jimmy's face as their eyes met across the classroom told Peter what Jimmy had wished. He'd wished his parents out of debt, and now they were. Peter felt as if a rod were boring through the top of his head and into his spine. He sank onto his seat and closed his eyes as if that would make the world go away.

"Well, Waters," Mr. Meldrum said, "I suppose we must allow you that as an excuse for singing in the corridor," and with a ponderous attempt at humor, "Don't let it occur again." Peter heard Jimmy walk to his desk, heard the creak of the seat, the squeal of the desk lid, the thump of a book on wood; the shivering of the windows as the wind rushed the school made him flinch. He heard boards creaking under Mr. Meldrum's feet, nearer and nearer. "Aren't you well, Priest?" the teacher's voice said in his ear. "Do you want to go home?"

"No, sir." Peter knew the teacher meant to be kind, but he could hardly have said anything crueller. Peter forced himself to stare at the boy still on the burning deck, the words flickering and trembling. He stared as if that might stop time, keep him here forever. It was too much to wish for time to run backward and erase what he'd written on the form, but he spent the afternoon pretending to work and promising to do anything he had to do if he could only take it back.

The sound of the bell for the end of the school day jerked his head on his spine, and then he saw Jimmy and Steve converging on him. They wanted to talk about the forms. He grabbed his satchel and elbowed his way blindly out of the classroom, ran down the stone stairs and out of the school.

He stumbled down to the North Promenade. Beyond the cliff the world was tossing, crumbling into spray. Flags that the wind had ripped from the markers lay like underwear about the golf course, a hotel porter was sweeping up birds that had flown into the sheets of glass around a swimming pool, pensioners with raw faces huddled in promenade shelters. He must go home, because then he might be able to protect his grandmother, watch out for whatever was coming. By the time he reached the front door he couldn't swallow for the metallic taste of fear.

He looked in at the window first, but the room was empty. He had to force himself to knock on the front door. His stomach flinched when he saw his mother's face, for she had obviously been crying. She said nothing, and he didn't dare speak. It was almost more than he could do to walk along the hall to the back parlor rather than flee upstairs to his room.

His father was sitting at his grandmother's mahogany table, which had ousted the dining table that stood up-ended against the wall. He was staring into a mug of tea and stirring it obsessively. Peter prayed he was wrong to think he knew why his father didn't want to look up, and so he was. When he stepped into the room he saw his grandmother was at the table too.

She gazed levelly at him. "You don't want me here either, Peter, do you?"

He tried to swallow as he realized she'd said "either." She couldn't read his mind, she didn't know about the wish. "At least I'm glad to see you find it hard to lie," she said. "All right, Peter, I'll let you off. I know I've outstayed my welcome."

His mother shook his father to make him look up. "Answer your granny, Peter. I've never heard such nonsense. You know we don't want you to go, mam, after all you went through."

"You've been letting me use that as an excuse, Bernadette. You won't be able to stand the sight of each other soon if I don't give you room to move, and then Peter won't have a proper family. I won't have that on my conscience." She turned to Peter. "It's all settled. I'm going to live with a friend who has some apartments in Cromer. I hope you'll come and see me sometimes."

"Of course I will, granny. When will you be going? I mean, when can I come and see you?"

"I'll probably go this weekend. My friend will be phoning tonight when she gets home to let me know. You'll be able to put up with me until the weekend, won't you?"

He didn't know what to say. "Come here," she said, and hugged him. "I shouldn't be getting at you of all people, after you saved me from those thugs. You used to say you'd fight devils for me when you were little."

"I would too." He disengaged himself as soon as he could and went up to the storeroom, not so much because he was embarrassed by her gratitude as because he felt light-headed with relief. His grandmother hadn't been harmed and yet she was going away. He lay on the camp bed for a while before he changed out of his school uniform, hopped about the room to put on his out-of-school trousers. He was thinking of calling on Jimmy and Steve to apologize for avoiding them and tell them it was all over, when suddenly he groaned and shuddered and sat down on the bed.

"Please, no," he moaned. "It can't be." His wish could hardly have made her decide to leave, it must have been the broken wedding present and the atmosphere in the house. His wish had yet to be granted. Surely there would be no need since she was leaving, surely nothing else would happen. He was still sitting with his head in his hands, his fingers squeezing his skull as if they could squeeze out his headache and the poison of his thoughts, when his mother called him down to dinner.

He couldn't taste what he was eating. "I do believe you're sorry I'm going," his grandmother said, looking at the food he'd left on his plate, and he was suddenly so close to tears he could only nod.

"We all are," his mother said fiercely. "Don't you even think of leaving until you're sure it's what *you* want."

His father cleared his throat. "I've got to finish putting up those shelves. Will you give me a hand, Pete?"

"I've got a headache."

"I'll help you," his mother said with a look that warned his father the discussion wasn't over. "You don't mind if we leave you alone for a while, do you, mam?"

"I'm past all that silliness. You two go along and have a few hours to yourselves. Peter and I will see to the washing up." When they'd gone to the shop she said, "I'll do it. You rest your headache."

"No, I'll help." He was afraid to let her out of his sight in case it happened then, whatever was coming, though surely nothing was. He dried the slippery plates as she filed them in the drainer, and more than one plate almost leapt out of his hands. Surely she would be safe once her friend confirmed she had room. "When's your friend calling?" he said, and closed his eyes.

"Not just yet, Peter. Soon." She sounded hurt but forgiving. "If you've a headache you ought to go and lie down."

"No, I want to stay with you." He had to, at least until the call came, however much his head throbbed. "I want to," he told himself aloud.

"That's nice, anyway. Shall we listen to some music?" She looked disapproving when he didn't stand aside for her to go into the hall, but he wanted to switch on the light; the house was darkening as rain closed in. She tutted and switched it off as she went into the front room. Rain that looked like spit thumped the window, and he turned nervously to see what was there, wondering how he could protect her when he didn't know what was coming. "Don't do that," she said sharply. "You'll have me as bad as I was."

There was nothing she liked on the radio. "Close your eyes and I'll sing to you," she said. "Remember which record we liked best?" She sat down opposite him and began to sing "Keep Right On to the End of the Road," her voice wavering as it competed with the downpour at the window. But she had only reached the line about what would be waiting there when she cried, "What is it, child? What's the matter?"

Peter jumped up, his head pounding, and snatched open the door to the hall. He was sure he'd heard the front door close stealthily. He groped in the dimness for the light switch, so desperately that at first he couldn't find it. When he did, the hall and the stairs were deserted. "I thought I heard someone," he said.

She ran to the door and peered along the hall, then she turned on him. "How could there be? Do you want me upset again? Leave me alone if you're going to play tricks on me. I'll be gone soon, no need to frighten me away."

"I don't want to. I'm trying to protect you," he cried. "Shall we play a game?" he said, all he could think of to calm her.

"I can't now, you've got me so on edge. Just sit quietly and perhaps I'll be able to." She sat back in the easy chair, put her forearm over her eyes, breathed like sighing.

She was beginning to sound as if she was going to sleep when she demanded, "What did you say?"

Surely he hadn't said any of what he was thinking: that he was beginning to feel sure that before the stealthy closing of the front door he'd heard a slight but perceptible increase in the noise of rain. "I didn't say anything," he mumbled.

"Who did, then? Someone who's crept into the house to murder us? God forgive your father for letting you read those magazines." She marched out of the room, daring anyone to be there, but he saw her fists were trembling. "There's nobody," she said, "he's just trying to scare me," and hurried upstairs to the bathroom.

He followed her as quietly as he could, to search upstairs. Nobody was hiding in his parents' room, nobody was in the storeroom that was his room now. He didn't mind sleeping in there, didn't mind the lack of space; he'd stay in there if he could only take back his wish so that nothing could happen to her. He was just opening the door of his old bedroom, hers now with its smells of scent and old cloth, when she came out of the bathroom. "What are you up to now?" she cried. "Waiting to jump out and give me a heart attack?"

"I was just seeing if all the lights work."

"Why, were you hoping they wouldn't so you could scare me that way? What are you trying to do to me?" She stood in the hall, hands on hips, while he searched the kitchen and the parlor, made sure the back door was bolted. "I'll tell your parents about this when they come home," she cried. "Stop it this minute or I'll get the police to you."

Could he call them? What could he say? At least if they came she might be safer. He stared at the phone and tried to think until she shouted, "What are you scheming now, you devil? Go and sit where I can see you or I'll go out of this house right now. Perhaps if I get pneumonia you'll be satisfied."

That made him panic. He might have wondered if she would be safer out of the house, assuming someone had sneaked in, but he would only have to follow her. He had a vision of her running from him in the rain, running in front of a car that couldn't stop in time. He went and sat in the front room at once, closing his eyes and trying not to think until his headache eased, opening them narrowly when he seemed to hear stealthy footsteps, peering surreptitiously at his grandmother to see if she'd noticed. "I can see you," she cried. "Stop looking at me like that, you devil. Stop it, do you hear? You'll pay for what you're doing." All at once she clutched her stomach and doubled over. "Oh, you little swine," she wailed, and ran up to the bathroom.

He mustn't follow her. The rain had abated, and she would hear him. At least now he would be able to hear if they weren't alone in the house. Surely the noises he'd heard before had been the storm. He'd searched the house and found nobody, the back door was bolted—and then he realized the front door was not. Could he bolt it before she came down? The toilet flushed as he pushed himself up from his chair, and he was about to tiptoe quickly to the door when she cried, "What are you doing up here now? I can hear you."

Whatever she could hear, it wasn't Peter. It took him a moment to realize, and then he was racing breathlessly into the hall that was grubby with shadows of rain, and grabbing the banister so as to leap stairs. She came out of the bathroom just as he reached the landing, which was deserted. "Let me be," she screamed at him, "get away from me," and shoved him aside so as to flee downstairs.

Just as he saw how the stair carpet had come untacked from the landing, the carpet tripped her. He made a grab for her that wrenched his shoulder, and missed. She fell sideways, her wrist thumping the wall and shattering the crystal of her gold watch. Her nails scraped furrows in the wallpaper as she tried to hold on, but her head struck the hall floor with the full weight of her body. He heard her neck break.

He almost fell as he ran down to her. She was gazing at him with a look that said You wanted this. "No, granny, I didn't," he pleaded, "you'll be all right," as she went out of her eyes. He seized her wrist and felt wildly for a pulse, and noticed with a clarity whose disinterest appalled him that the breaking of her watch had jarred it forward several hours. For a moment he thought he heard her breathing, but it was only the sound of the sea. There was no life in her wrist, and nothing in her eyes. Come back, he cried, I didn't mean it, I loved you really, we all do. He was gazing desperately into her eyes, and beginning to shiver with the thought of how his mother would react, when he thought he heard the front door close stealthily behind him. Then, too late, the phone began to ring.

Now

Chapter X

"MUMMY, the rain feels lovely," Francesca called from the edge of the cliff. "It feels like bathwater."

"So it does." Tanya was unpacking the haversack onto the picnic table. "Come back here and feel it, love."

"I'm all right here. I won't fall."

"Just the same, do as you're told. You know why."

"Because he'll imitate me."

"I won't. I'm five now. I go to school as well as you." Russell stuck out his tongue at his sister as he emptied his pockets onto the table: the top of a bath tap; the propellor from a toy boat; the badge from the miniature policeman's uniform he'd been given for his third birthday. "I can climb higher than you, anyway."

"Well, I can read more than you. I can do lots of things you can't. Five imitates seven, doesn't he, mummy?"

"Now just you stop it, you two," Jimmy said. "Stop pretending you don't know how to behave."

The picnic area overlooked the bay, the north slope of

Seaward, the railed-off area where the lighthouse used to be. The sprinkling of rain was already fading under the scalloped shell of cloud that filled half the blue May sky. Francesca dawdled backward from the edge—"Shush, mummy," she said when Tanya hurried her, "I'm listening to my imagination"—and sat down next to her father on the rough bench. She had Tanya's silky ash-blonde hair and her unself-consciousness; he hoped she would always have both. Russell had Jimmy's round face and heavy eyelids and a tinge of his red hair, and didn't talk half as much as Francesca, though Tanya tried to make sure he was given the chance. "Just eat your sandwiches and see if you can go five minutes without talking," she said to Francesca now.

She had blonde down on her high cheeks, eyebrows that turned silver when the sun caught them, very pink full lips, a wide mouth, and the darkest eyes he'd ever seen. Jimmy had met her when he was at college, met her in a pub where she'd heard his Norfolk accent and said how much she liked it, and he felt now as if that moment had led inevitably to their marriage. He squeezed her hand to tell her so, and she smiled at him as if she knew what he was thinking. He let go when three loud young Londoners came out of the forest and sprawled around the far table.

He'd kept his family away from cities, but sometimes the city came to Seaward. The youths were scratching their stubbly scalps, drumming their boots on the benches, flicking cigarette butts over the cliff. Francesca watched them with a mixture of envy and contempt, then said loudly to Russell, "Mummy's a dentist, you know."

"No she isn't. She has parties at the bird place."

"She doesn't *have* parties at the sanctuary, she *shows* parties of people round. He's silly, isn't he, mummy? Anyway, she is a dentist. She puts fillings in sandwiches."

She grinned at the groans and whistles from the far table. "Don't show off, Francesca," Tanya said and frowned as the Londoners repeated the name incredulously, sniggering. "You can play while you eat if you like. Just stay away from the edge."

Russell planted the plum stone he'd unearthed from his pocket, then he and Francesca skimmed a Tupperware dish to each other while Tanya and Jimmy lingered over another drink from the wine box. Eventually Russell shied the dish under the far table, and one of the youths leaned down to grab it. "What's this? What do you call these fucking things?"

"It's a fucking—you know, one of those fucking things, a fucking—what do you call the fuckers?"

"Frisbees," Francesca said.

"Fucking right, fucking Frisbees." He held out the dish to her. "Fucking Francesca's fucking Frisbee."

Jimmy had had enough, even if they weren't aware what they were doing. "Will you moderate your language, please."

The youth flung the dish at Francesca. "Who the fuck says?"

"I do." Jimmy drew a deep breath as he stepped forward. "And I'm a police officer."

The three youths swung themselves down from the table, metal toecaps scraping the benches. "Where's your fucking uniform then, mate?" one sneered.

"Never you mind about that. Here's my warrant card." As Jimmy flashed it, five-year-old Russell clenched his fists and came to stand beside his father before Tanya could stop him. Two of the youths snickered, and Jimmy thought that this was it at last, the moment when he'd be attacked because someone didn't care that he was a policeman or perhaps for being one. But the third youth was staring at the warrant card. "Come on, let's fuck off," he muttered. "I don't want to be put back inside," and after a few seconds of silent glaring at Jimmy the others followed him, whistling.

"Daddy," Francesca complained, "I can feel my blood shaking." Jimmy hugged his family while his own heart slowed down, and when he felt sure the youths would be well out of the way the four of them made for the forest, where the walks were marked with colored arrows on posts. "Red sounds shortest," Russell said. Jimmy and Tanya strolled hand in hand, Tanya telling Francesca the names of plants, Russell climbing trees to see if he could bash the sky yet, until a boy of about Russell's age skidded round a bend in front of them. The miniature Honda he was riding sounded like bees trapped in a tin can. "Are you with somebody, son?" Jimmy said.

The boy's grandfather appeared, puffing. "What's the problem?" he demanded truculently, then saw Jimmy. "I told you to be careful, Dominic. Do as Inspector Waters says or he'll lock you up. You can't tell them anything these days," he confided to Jimmy and Tanya.

"Can't you?" Tanya said innocently, and he turned to Jimmy. The flesh of his neck, into which his chin melted, twisted like dough. "Any news on the drug problem? Can we say arrests are imminent?"

"Not just yet, Mayor Elsey." Jimmy felt uncomfortable trying to impress him in front of Tanya and the children. "We dealt with the bikers before they could take over. I'm sure we'll deal with this."

"I hope so. All the more so now we've our reputation to maintain as a convention town. At least we can be glad we have some expert help."

Two men from the London drugs squad had been seconded to the force to determine whether Seaward was being used for smuggling. "That's so, isn't it?" the mayor said, a little sharply.

"We can always use extra manpower."

"No reflection on you, inspector. It isn't your fault you lack experience of that kind of crime. A tribute to our town that you do, wouldn't you say? Come along, Dominic," he said, then turned back to Jimmy. "One thing while I think of it. The council isn't happy with the way the Grand is being left to rot. I spoke to old man Innes but could get no sense out of him.''

''I don't think there's much that can be done legally.''

''Not directly, perhaps. All the same, if he and his client can't take care of the building, they must be persuaded to give it up to someone who can. Dominic's father tells me you and the son were friends at school. I'd like you to have a friendly word with him.'' He started after Dominic, trousers smoking with the exhaust, then turned back once more. ''Not too friendly.''

''How I dislike that man,'' Tanya murmured. ''What does he expect you to do, threaten to close down the agency?''

''Maybe send in our friends from London, or Dominic.'' Jimmy called the children back to the path. ''Listen, if you see anyone going near the Grand tell your teachers, all right? You know it could be dangerous.'' When Francesca bit her lip and nodded he said, ''What's wrong?''

''Diane said I was a telltale because you're my daddy. Last week the teacher told her to behave or you'd lock her up.''

''Your teacher ought to know better. If children got into the Grand they might be hurt, love, do you see? You tell your friends that if they say anything to you.''

Russell was tugging at her hand, but she shook him off. ''Do you mind if I finish my conversation, please?'' she said in the tone of a parent at the end of an especially taxing day. ''Daddy, please may I go to the Star Trek convention? Diane's going. It's in the summer holidays.''

''We'll see.''

''He means yes,'' she told Russell, and lingered. ''Daddy, Jennifer in my class says her mummy and daddy smoke special cigarettes, and stuff in a pipe.''

''Tell your friend Jennifer not to tell tales about her parents. This way home, Russell,'' Jimmy said.

Forest shade was spreading into Seaward Village. A white Volvo cruised away from one of the antique shops.

Tanya's rock garden was blooming in front of their tall wide house. After dinner the children raced to be first in the bath—"I've emptied myself" Russell cried as he pulled off the last of his clothes—and then Jimmy rubbed them dry. "Cuddle me too," Francesca demanded, and he sat with both of them wrapped in a towel, warm little heads snuggling under his chin. He heard them read, Russell in a halting robot voice, then he tucked them up in bed, kissed their closed eyes, listened outside their door to Russell singing sleepily "Crocodile baby on the treetop." When he went down to tell Tanya they were waiting to be kissed good night he found her talking to Helen, their baby-sitter.

"I can still bring my boyfriend," Helen was saying, "can't I?"

"You know you can," Tanya said. "Why, has anything changed?"

"Only that I want to keep Henry away from some people. They wouldn't dare come near your house."

"Sit tonight if you like. We could go up to the Smugglers. And if you or Henry ever need to talk," Jimmy said, "you can always come to me."

Jimmy's parents ran a pub now, the Four Smugglers. Seawarders called the pub and the forest crossroads where it stood the Four Villains. By the time Jimmy and Tanya walked there the pub was crowded with admirers of his mother's cooking.

"Here's the family," Jimmy's father wheezed. His large frame was stooped now, his round face was baggy, but he could still serve faster than the barmaids and squeeze Jimmy's and Tanya's hands between taking orders. Jimmy's mother came out of the back room to give them both a brawny hug, bustled them to a table and brought them drinks, mouthed "No" at Jimmy's father when he gazed wistfully at the fruit machine that a gambler had left full of money, said "Never mind" as a girl with rainbow hair won the jackpot with her first coin. "Shall we see the children again soon?" she asked Jimmy and Tanya.

"There'll be no more teaching them to play cards for money, I promise you."

"Of course we'll bring them," Tanya said. "They look forward to coming."

"They're my darlings. I wouldn't like to think anything might rob me of that pleasure," Jimmy's mother said, glancing at his father behind the bar.

On the homeward road that was zebra-striped by moonlight Tanya said, "I don't think your father does them any harm, do you? You didn't turn out too badly yourself," and stroked his arm.

"I had an example of how not to live," Jimmy said, and was glad his father couldn't hear him. At home they made love gently and drowsily, and then Tanya fell asleep. Soon Jimmy was asleep too. The prospect of confronting Steve Innes troubled him hardly at all.

Chapter XI

THE OLD LADY lifted her spectacles on their cord. "Be quiet, Hercules," she said as the poodle on her lap began to whimper, and rested the folder on its back as she leafed through. "Ah, this is the flat I viewed last week. Do they keep their dogs on the lead round there?"

"I'm sure they do, madam," Steve said.

"Never be sure of anything, then you won't be disappointed. I saw one big dog that wasn't. And this is the flat near the hotels. Dear me, the hotels used to be select, but now they're opening their doors to all these conventions." She let her spectacles drop. "May I let you have my decision by the end of the week?"

"Do please take your time. We'd appreciate hearing as soon as you've made your choice."

"If there are people queuing up to buy then you must say so," she said pointedly as he held open the door for her and her wriggling armful. "I hope to be able to patronize you. I don't care much for your competitors."

Down on the edge of the North Promenade kites sank for lack of wind. The hot day felt slow even for Seaward. Twenty years ago he wouldn't have believed he could enjoy the pace of life here, Sunday all week, and neither would Maggie, his wife. When they'd dropped out of university together they'd agreed to make enough money to set up something really radical—the sixties had seemed brimming with possibilities—but he had never bargained for enjoying working with his father. Even before he'd been made a partner he'd known he couldn't leave, not when his father had both high blood pressure and the Elsey real estate agency to contend with. The Elsey agency had more than high-powered sales techniques on its side, it had Mayor Elsey and his sister on the council to nod through grants and planning permissions. At least the Elseys' reputation was beginning to turn people such as the old lady with the poodle against them, Steve thought, and Maggie seemed happier in her new job. He was closing the door when he saw the policeman coming toward him. "How are you, Jimmy?" he said.

He'd hardly seen Jimmy for years, not since he'd handled the sale of Jimmy's house in Seaward Village. The sight of a policeman heading for the shop hadn't made him feel at all uneasy but, oddly, realizing it was Jimmy had. "Fine, and you?" Jimmy said, and they asked after each other's families as they settled down in the mock-leather chairs by the display window. "What can I do for you?" Steve said then.

"I just wanted to have a word with you about the Grand."

"What's that about the Grand?" Steve's father flung open his office door and stood there breathing heavily. "Good God, what's wrong now?"

"Don't worry, Mr. Innes, there hasn't been a break-in or anything like that. It's just that the members of the council are a bit concerned about how long the theater is going to be left unoccupied."

"Mayor Elsey is, you mean. Wherever there's a pack of damn fools you'll find a leader. So he sent you to put the frighteners on, did he?"

"He asked me to speak to Steve, and I thought you'd want to be aware of the kind of thing the council must be saying."

"Oh, it's you, Jimmy." Steve's father mopped his forehead and leaned on the counter. "Well, tell him from me that his brother's welcome to take over the Grand whenever he's ready."

"I'm afraid you'd have to tell him that yourself," Jimmy said, smiling, "but I don't think it would be awfully helpful, do you?"

"Go ahead then, tell me what would. You know damn well Elsey wouldn't touch the Grand because it's too much trouble. The owner won't sell unless it's to be used as a theater and even if the law could get round that there's a preservation order on the building and interior. The council could buy the place themselves and reopen it, but that's always voted down. Any little thing the Elseys can think of to make life harder for us they'll do."

"Now, dad," Steve said, but Jimmy interrupted. "If you've any evidence of illegality please tell me."

"You know as well as I do the buggers are too clever. Going to run me in for using offensive language?"

"Not unless you insist, Mr. Innes. Can you get in touch with the owner and let him know how things are?"

"If his mail ever catches up with him. He's hardly ever in the same country two days running."

"We did manage to contact him earlier this year," Steve said. "He sent in some builders from out of town to see to anything that needed doing. They boarded up the theater again before we had a chance to look in, but we've a written guarantee."

"So long as the building is safe," Jimmy said. "That's all that concerns me, frankly. Vandals love a disused building, and it's very close to the school."

"Then it's time you and the teachers got to work, isn't it?"

"We had the boards on the front reinforced last week."

"Thanks for telling me, Steve. We'll keep an eye on things, Mr. Innes, believe me. I have children at the school myself."

"Sorry if I offended you, Jimmy. I know you have to do your job," Steve's father said and went back into his office.

"We must get together for a drink sometime," Jimmy said, standing up, and Steve responded, "Maggie and I don't live far from your dad's pub," willing Jimmy to leave. When Jimmy had gone Steve let out a breath that felt as satisfying as the first drag on a cigarette used to. The very sight of Jimmy had made him feel he'd forgotten something he would rather not remember.

Chapter XII

THE HEAD of Video Universe wore cuff links and a tiepin in the shape of videocassettes. He leaned conspiratorially over Maggie's desk, baring his small even teeth in a smile, and Maggie wished she could laugh. "By lady entertainers you mean strippers," she said.

"Too right, if you can lay them on. I knew as soon as we made eye contact we understood each other."

"I'm afraid I don't know of any strippers locally."

"Maybe you could bring them in?" He was ogling her as if she might offer herself, ogling her large breasts, slim body, tapering face, snub nose. "Well, don't feel bad about it," he said. "My instincts tell me you can come up with something in the females line. I want to give fifty video retailers a weekend they'll remember. Can't do that without girls."

By now she knew that her job of convention coordinator entailed, or was assumed to entail, stranger requests than this, but none that made her feel so suddenly like giving up the job. "There are no escort agencies round here that I'm aware of."

"Maybe you should start one. Could make you a lot of money." He winked at her. "If your husband goes away on business you must know how it is."

"He doesn't need to go away."

"I knew you were a liberated lady. Maybe you've got friends who'd be available?"

"In Seaward? You must be joking. I can only suggest you ask at the hotel if anyone can help," she said, hoping they would tell him where to go. "And by the way, all I meant about my husband is that he's never needed that kind of thing."

She would have added that she was closing her office now, except that she could tell he would linger and try to buy her a drink. She pretended to be working late until he went away; she leafed through the glossy Seaward brochure they were soon to send out to thousands of business addresses and brooded about Steve. She couldn't believe he was seeing other women. That couldn't be why he was no longer the Steve she'd married.

Perhaps in order to grow up he'd had to realize that he couldn't change the world, even if he still wore his CND badge to work, but he seemed more and more like his father without his father's fieriness. The Steve who used to say that compromise financed dictatorships and let tobacco companies and chemical waste poison the world would never have been able to bear the thought of spending the rest of his life in Seaward. For years they had been going to use their money to make people more aware, but somewhere among the years that ambition had slipped away unnoticed. She felt life settling around them, and wasn't sure that Steve realized it was. If he was so unaware, what could be preoccupying him?

She slipped the proofs of the brochure into her briefcase to be checked at home and walked out of the gray corridors of the town hall. As she drove home she caught sight

of people she'd known since school: Jean, who'd wanted
to be a nurse but ran a hairdresser's instead; Nancy, who'd
founded the Weight Watchers of Seaward. She grinned
wryly at the thought of their being available to the conven-
tioneers, then her grin faded as she realized that at least it
would be something unexpected. All the same, she would
far rather that nothing in her life was ever unfamiliar again
than that Steve should be.

She drove along the forest road and parked outside their
house among the trees. Steve's parents had let them choose
the house from the agency's list, had paid the deposit on
the mortgage as a wedding present. She loved the view of
the sea from their bedroom window, but now the May
leaves had closed in, and she wouldn't have that view
again until winter, another year gone. The spacious rooms
were painted blue, the chairs were blue with clusters of
green leaves, and she'd always looked forward to the way
they looked in the light through the growing foliage. Only
this year she was beginning to feel as if they were
underwater.

Steve was in the kitchen making pizza. He smiled at
her, then hugged her quickly as if his dimples still embarrassed him even now when there was a trace of gray in his
curly hair. "Sell anything today?" she said.

"Found a young couple a flat. They were very anxious
to let me know they'd be getting married, which I thought
was rather sweet. And an old lady's gone away to think."
He patted her bottom abstractedly and slipped the pizza
into the oven. "How about you? Sell anything?"

"Almost myself."

"I hope you told them you were secondhand." He
frowned when she didn't grin back. "Why, did someone
turn nasty?"

"He treated me like a pimp."

"Well, you know you aren't and I'm sure you let him
know. Let's enjoy the evening. I'll tell you what I'd like to
do while we're waiting for the pizza—smoke that dope."

She couldn't help smiling at how middle class that seemed now—once he would have attacked it as bourgeois self-indulgence. Friends of hers from Edinburgh had left it last summer while visiting. Suddenly she wasn't smiling but wondering if he needed it because something was troubling him. When he passed her the joint she said, "What else happened today?"

He lay back on a beanbag to gaze out of the window. "Jimmy Waters came to the office."

"Why should you say it like that? Oh, you mean on official business?"

"On the business of your friend the mayor."

"He isn't my friend." This kind of undercurrent was one reason she'd applied for the new job, to get out of working in the mayor's office. "He never tried to use me against you or your father, did he? Never said anything to me about you."

"That's what I mean—your friend the mayor." He gave her an apologetic look. "Ignore me when I'm like this, won't you?"

"I want to know *why* you're like this. What did Jimmy want?"

"Just to tell us Elsey the mayor has been bitching about the Grand. It's not as if my dad can do anything except try to catch the owner. Dad tries not to seem bothered, but I know he wishes he'd never offered to look after the place."

"Business isn't doing his health much good either. You know what we should all do, don't you? Move."

"Never trust perfect solutions."

"I mean it, Steve. You and your parents could open an agency somewhere else, couldn't you? And we'd get a good price for this house."

"If you want to try persuading my dad to move, good luck to you. I don't think even you could." The joint seemed to be slowing him down rather than relaxing him. "I've told him I'll keep an eye on the Grand, take the pressure off him. It won't bother me."

"What has been?"

Perhaps he hadn't heard her, or perhaps he didn't want to; there had been more than one occasion recently when she hadn't been sure which. When she repeated her question he said, "What do you mean?"

"Something's been worrying you."

"Observant, aren't you?" He leaned back so as to look away. "Maybe I wish Elsey had come to the office himself."

"Why?"

"Seeing Jimmy." He was beginning to stutter. "Reminded me of something we once did."

"Are you going to tell me?"

"No need to sound as if I'm keeping secrets from you. I never used to tell my parents everything either, you know. It was so stupid, what we did. Seems even stupider now. Maybe that's why it bothers me, thinking I could be that stupid." He grimaced and shook his head and eventually muttered, "He wished for luck and I wished someone out of the way, and it came true for both of us."

"When was this?"

"My God, it must be—" He closed his eyes to help him remember. "Twenty-five years ago."

"Is that all? Steve?" She waited until he looked at her, and realized that he seldom called her by name anymore. "Is that all?"

"Isn't it enough? Christ, what else would you expect after twenty-five years?" He smiled at her to show he had dismissed the question and headed for the kitchen before she could reply.

It wasn't enough, especially when her question had obviously bothered him. Whatever the trouble was, it couldn't be anything so trivial and, as he'd said himself, so stupid. She felt resentful that he assumed she would believe him.

They didn't talk much over dinner; she couldn't remember when last they had. Later they made love, warm breezes carrying the murmur of the trees through the open bedroom window, and she almost managed to persuade herself that Steve didn't know himself what was worrying him. It was only afterward she realized that they had never once looked into each other's eyes that night while making love.

Chapter XIII

As ROBIN turned off the North Fork toward the surgery she saw a man in a tattered suit with his hands in the wastebin on the corner of her road. Two women emerging from the hairdresser's glared at him to make sure he stayed away from them. Robin was shocked by how young and desperate he looked: she knew drug abuse was on the increase in Seaward, but she hadn't realized it was as bad as this. He stuffed his prize into his pocket and dodged into the crowd, and was out of sight before she would have been able to park and see if she could help.

She drove the car into her garage and locked it in. A salty breeze wandered up from the bay, then the overcast heat settled again. She had a few minutes before afternoon surgery, and so she hurried past the glassed-in porch to the side door, to see how Raquel, the new receptionist, was coping.

She heard Anglia Radio before she opened the door. No wonder her mother had come through from the body of the

house to ask Raquel or her boyfriend to turn the volume
down. She limped quickly over to Robin. "Are you home
now, Robin? I was beginning to worry, you were such a
long time."

"Yes, mother, I'm home. We had trouble finding a bed
at the hospital. Turn that down, please, Raquel, and remind your friend not to sit on your desk."

The boyfriend lolled off the corner of the desk, where
she was stamping prescription forms with the surgery address. "You've done enough for one day," Raquel scolded
him, and Robin was about to deal with the issue of visitors
at work once and for all when her mother said, "Come in
the house a minute. I want a word with you."

"I've surgery at four." Nevertheless Robin followed
her, wondering if it was about Raquel. "What is it,
mother?"

"Don't hurry me. Have a little consideration and give
me time to sit down." She led the way into the living
room and sat down gradually, groaning, then she hitched
herself forward to stare at Robin. "You didn't do it, did
you? You didn't have Mrs. Starr taken into hospital."

"I'm afraid I did. If it's any consolation, I believe she
half wanted to go."

"Because she's half-witted, you mean? Don't you try to
tell me that. She's as compos mentis as I am. That's why
her children want her out of the way, because she can see
what they're up to."

"That simply isn't true, mother. They wanted her to
live with them, but she wouldn't go. For heaven's sake,
this morning she set fire to herself."

"No wonder, the way you and her brats have been
nagging her. How could you let them hoodwink you,
Robin? Would *you* like to be put away there? You said
yourself it's not a hospital. A maze where nobody knows
what anyone else is doing, that's what you said."

Three local hospitals had recently been amalgamated
into one, where wards were being closed now for lack of

staff. In-patients were being sat in chairs all day to free their beds for day patients, consultants insisted on keeping their patients in bed so that rival consultants wouldn't grab the space. By now, consultants had to send scouts through the wards to find beds, and today Robin had had to find a bed herself and refuse to leave until they admitted Mrs. Starr. "It's the best we have to offer," she said.

"No, Robin, the best is your own family. That's the only care worth having. I don't know how you dared put her away when you knew she was my friend. I'll tell you this, I'm going to visit her, and the moment I think she's well enough to leave, out she comes."

"I haven't time to argue." Robin stood up. "I want a few words with Raquel before surgery."

"Don't be too hard on her in her first job. You promised her parents you'd give her a chance. I don't often ask you to do favors for my friends. If I'm not here after surgery," she said as Robin reached the door, "I shall be at the library conducting my research."

At least that kept her happy, reading the books and magazines Raquel's father ordered for her, staying abreast of new developments as if she were still working at the museum. Robin went to her desk and buzzed Raquel to bring in the prescription forms, one pad of which was too haphazardly stamped to use. She tore it up carefully, to make sure the forms couldn't be forged and for Raquel to see. "When I asked you not to use my phone to call your friends," she said, "I didn't mean you should have them visiting instead."

"He's my boyfriend, miss."

"All the same, no courting while you're at work." When Raquel stared cowlike at her, Robin said, "Will you ask him to leave or shall I?"

Raquel flounced out, and Robin heard her giggling in the waiting room. When Robin buzzed her she spluttered, "He's just going, miss."

"Will you send in my first patient," Robin said, "and

please try to remember to call me doctor.'' She hoped it wouldn't be long before Jo had her baby and came back—much more of this and she'd find someone else to fill in.

People lived longer in Norfolk than the British average and visited their doctors less often, and there were fewer patients today than usual. She had time to chat with Mrs. Coyne, who complained tonelessly, ''It's my bloody ankles now, doctor, my ankles and my bloody ears and bowels,'' and had time to reassure a pregnant teenager who had just joined Robin's list after leaving Dr. Fenner's. Fenner had upset virtually every expectant mother on his list and had little to offer for sexual problems except disapproval. Surgery over, Raquel tidied her desk and the files before strutting out to her boyfriend, leaving Robin to turn off the radio. Robin sat down for a few minutes to listen to Terry Tebbitt's Teatime Talk-In—broadcasting reduced to the level of pub arguments and lending them a spurious authority—and was about to switch off in disgust when she heard her mother.

''I want to talk about the way elderly people are treated. Is it a crime to be elderly nowadays, Miss Tebbitt? Drug addicts are left to roam our streets while people are being locked up for no crime except their age.'' Though callers didn't give their full names on the air, Robin knew it was her mother, and couldn't help being shocked: not so long ago her mother had scoffed at the program—speak your mind by all means, she would say, but first make sure it's worth hearing. Terry Tebbitt let her have her say and thanked her, adding, ''There's another topic for discussion: are we doing enough for our old folk?'' Robin switched her off and wondered if she even grasped the issue that as more people retired to Seaward, the problems were bound to get worse.

Robin's mother had left dinner half-prepared again. Robin finished the preparations and hoped that wouldn't provoke another argument. She could hear her mother arguing with the radio in the living room, where she must have plugged in the domestic phone. "What do you mean, *our* old folk? We aren't chattels, you know, you can't just put us away when you think we're worn out," she declared, and then, without warning, she gave a cry. "Oh, what's that? Robin, where are you? Don't leave me alone with this."

Robin ran into the living room. "What's wrong, mother?"

"There's a spider in here, a huge one."

Robin began to search where her mother was pointing, on the brown carpet between the black armchairs. She hoped the spider hadn't hidden among the fossils that her mother had collected since leaving the museum, which were arranged on shelves around the room. "Pass me your cup and saucer," she said, and was draining the dregs of coffee so as to be able to drop the cup over the spider when her mother cried, "There it is, by your leg."

Robin whirled, almost dropping the cup. All she could see was the shadow the sunlight was casting of her mother's hand. "Where?"

"There, can't you see? There!" She pointed at the shadow, vanishing it in the process. She shrieked. "Oh, where's it gone now?"

"That was your hand, mother."

"Don't be ridiculous. What do you take me for? Are you trying to tell me my hand looks like a spider?"

"No, mother. Just the shadow of it."

"How can the shadow of my hand look like a spider if my hand doesn't?"

"It doesn't." Robin was beginning to feel like the straight man in a misconceived comedy duo. "Neither does, not really."

"I can't even see what my own shadow looks like, is that it?" Her mother stamped her foot, shaking the fossils. "What exactly are you trying to say about me?"

"Nothing, mother," Robin said wearily, thinking: it isn't the first time, it was bound to come sooner or later, it could have been later than seventy years old, but there's no point in wishing.

"Don't, either. Don't you dare treat me like one of your patients." She stooped painfully and began to peer under the furniture. "I'll find it and show you, just wait and see, since I don't suppose you've the patience to let me finish making dinner."

At dinner she was sullen, perhaps because she hadn't been able to produce the spider, but as they washed up afterward she grew gentler. "You'll let Mrs. Starr come out of hospital as soon as she's healed, won't you?"

"That's out of my hands now, mother."

"Then I'll speak to the hospital." She controlled her momentary anger. "Don't let anyone else use you against their parents, Robin. Don't do anything you may live to regret. I know what that's like."

"Mother, you've no reason to regret anything, really." Robin took hold of one dry wrinkled hand. "Hardly anyone would think the worse of you these days. In fact, I think some of my patients find it easier to talk to me freely because they know you weren't married."

"I wasn't talking about that." Her mother changed the subject abruptly, and Robin didn't pursue the matter. Later they drank gin and played chess. Robin was pleased when her mother won a game—she wouldn't have admitted to herself that she felt relieved. All the same, she found it hard to fall asleep that night for wondering what her mother regretted. By the time she found out, everything else that had happened that afternoon was beginning to close in.

Chapter XIV

PETER buttoned his jacket despite the heat as he climbed the side street from the East Fork and tightened the knot of his tie. First impressions were important, and first interviews were often the most difficult, especially in a case like this. He threw back his shoulders as he stepped off the pavement toward the large house.

Both the house and the lumpy barren garden beside the cracked path were haphazardly whitewashed. He rang the bell, or at least pushed the button that was drooping on its wire. He was wondering if it worked when a curtain shifted at the left-hand window and a child shouted, "It's a man with someone else's hair."

Thank you so much, Peter thought, bracing himself for worse. The Marvles had already proved too much for one of his colleagues, which was why Peter had taken over the case. But when the thin woman with prematurely gray hair opened the door she seemed less hostile than harassed. "Are you the social worker?" she wanted to know.

"The name's Priest, Mrs. Marvle. I believe we have an appointment for eleven o'clock."

"What time is it now?" she said hopefully, giving up hope when he showed her his watch. "I suppose you'd better come in, seeing as you wanted them all here. You'll have to forgive the mess."

The sagging furniture in the room to the right of the hall was occupied by car engines and fragments of engines. The family was crammed into the left-hand room, on half a dozen unmatched chairs. Peter almost tripped over a hole in the carpet as he followed her in, and Maria, who'd announced him from the window, started giggling. Nobody else even smiled, least of all the young man with bad teeth and bitten lips who was glaring at Peter over his shoulder. Peter ignored him for the moment and sat down in a fractured easy chair next to a young woman. "You must be Hilda."

"That's who she is," the young man said, having glared at him all the way to the chair. "And she wants to be left alone."

Mrs. Marvle gestured nervously at him. "Let Mr. Priest have his say, Roger."

The man who was sitting in the furthest corner of the room and staring at his knuckly hands was unaccounted for. "This is my friend Sid who's staying," Mrs. Marvle said awkwardly. "He's just a friend, just staying for a few days, aren't you, Sid? You won't let them take Hilda away again, Mr. Priest, will you?"

The lurch of subject startled both men. "I hope to help her stay with you," Peter said.

"Then do it by leaving her alone. We know best what she needs."

"Roger," Mrs. Marvle pleaded. Peter suffered his glare as he went through the history of the case, while Maria stood on her head and wouldn't be told to go out and play, and Sid gazed at his hands as if he'd never seen them before as his face grew redder and redder. Hilda's father had had access to her after Mrs. Marvle had remarried until, when she was just thirteen, he'd seduced her. Twelve-year-old Roger had found them and run for the police, and Hilda had been taken into care for psychiatric treatment, at the insistence of Roger's father, a lorry driver who was frequently away for weeks and who might not be Maria's father. Now Hilda was nineteen years old and home again, and Roger seemed to be the problem, following her everywhere to make sure she was safe, allowing her no friends of her own choosing or time by herself. "Have you had any thoughts about finding a job, Hilda?" Peter said.

She sucked her lips and shook her head. She hadn't said a word to him, though he'd addressed himself throughout to her. Interviewing her at home hadn't been such a good idea, it seemed, but he knew from his colleague whom Roger had driven off the case that Roger would make his presence felt even if one managed to get Hilda by herself. "I'll arrange an interview for you at the employment office, shall I?" Peter said.

"You leave my sister alone. We all know what you're after."

Peter wasn't sure if he was being accused of planning to seduce her or to put her back in care. "Would you like me to arrange the interview, Hilda?"

She took her time about giving him a timid nod. "Excellent," he said. "I'll call by later today and let you know when." He went out feeling he'd already achieved more than his predecessor, however tentatively. He unbuttoned his jacket and strode up to the town hall at the junction of the Forks to make the appointment for Hilda, then he went upstairs to take lunch at his desk.

After lunch he strolled out to the law courts next to the town hall. He was to give an independent report in a dispute over fostering. Peter's colleague and the foster parents were conferring on one side of the aisle that divided the paneled room. The natural parents glared across the aisle at Peter, and so did the overweight man, presumably a relative, who was sitting with them. Peter sat down by himself and waited for the hearing.

He'd been favorably impressed by the foster parents. He couldn't imagine that the natural parents would win custody when they'd neglected the children for years and now wanted only one of them back. He would have felt absolutely at ease except for the way the overweight man had begun to stare at Peter as if he recognized him—but here was the judge.

The judge heard the case worker's submission first, then called Peter. All that was required of him was a disinterested view of the fostering, in case his colleague had become too involved, yet he'd spoken for hardly a minute before he started to falter, for the overweight man was staring at him now almost as if waiting to be recognized. Peter was sure he'd never dealt with him. He stumbled through his report and hoped he hadn't weakened the case for fostering.

At least the natural parents were weakening their own case by putting it themselves. "My father will tell you," the woman kept saying, pointing a crimson fingernail at the overweight man, until the judge intervened. "I think you had better realize it would be inappropriate for you to look to your father for a guarantee of character in this court."

"I've given up all that," the overweight man said, looking found out, trapped. Peter wondered idly what his history might be, and then he knew. He ground his knuckles into his lips to keep in a gasp. He remembered the man as thinner and shabbier, not dressed in his best suit as he was now. He remembered his threat: "Do yourself a favor, son. Pretend you never saw us. . . ."

The man glanced at Peter and saw that he knew. Before Peter could control himself he flinched and looked away from the man. He'd only terrorized Peter's grandmother; it was Peter who had wished her dead, even if he hadn't

meant to. Sweat broke out on Peter's forehead, and he
stared at the floor, his eyes burning.

He'd thought all that was over, the sleepless nights and
the uncontrollable grief, but suddenly he felt as he'd felt
then, recoiling in the first moments of sleep from dreams
he couldn't bear, having to find somewhere to hide at
school or in the street or during his first years at work
when, without warning, he would remember his grandmother and what he'd done to her and burst into tears.
Now his job was helping people not to grow as desperate
as he had been when he'd made the wish, but suddenly he
felt again as though he couldn't help himself. He listened
to the judge and tried to ignore the overweight man, he
heard the judgment given in favor of the foster parents and
stumbled out of the court as soon as he could, his temples
aching like teeth. He was in the town hall and heading for
the refuge of his desk when he remembered Hilda Marvle
and his promise.

Roger answered the door. "She isn't in," he said, one
eye blinking.

"Then may I leave a message with whoever else is?"
Peter slipped in, having heard Roger talking to someone,
and found it was Hilda. When he told her he'd made her
an appointment for tomorrow she smiled timidly, which
was something. That was all he could do here for now,
and he wanted to be out of the house, whose clutter
suddenly reminded him of the way his grandmother's furniture had invaded his parents' house, especially the jum-
ble of furniture and car engines in the right-hand room.
"Don't you be nosing in my dad's room," Roger said,
then peered narrowly at Peter. "What are you scared of?"

"Nothing."

He shouldn't have replied, even though the young man's
insight had startled him. "You bloody are," Roger said
triumphantly. "I'll find out too, just you wait, if you don't
leave my sister alone."

It was an empty threat, Peter told himself. The skin of

his forehead felt stretched almost to splitting. He went back to the town hall and typed up his report on the Marvles, then he swallowed three aspirin tablets. He was still waiting for them to work when the chief social worker came over to knock on his desk so that she could close the office. "Waiting for a lady friend?" she said, and he jumped up, blushing.

He almost forgot to collect his radio alarm clock from the repair shop by the Lux, which was a supermarket now. He climbed the stepped pavement to his building at the top of the street, and then the stairs to the second floor. Mrs. Corner, who cleaned his rooms twice a week, was just leaving. "You'll be all right now, Mr. Priest, will you? You're sure you don't need anything?" He saw her out at last, then he lay down to give the aspirin a chance to work. Eventually his head felt soothed, though fragile, and he was sitting up to adjust the alarm when he heard Mrs. Corner come back.

He went into the hall, which was lit by large moony wall lamps. It was deserted, and so were the kitchen, the bathroom, and the main room with its plain, dark brown easy chairs. He opened his door and called down the wide stairs, but when he went back to the main room and glanced out the window he caught sight of her down by the Lux. He couldn't have heard her return after all. He finished setting the alarm, then he turned on the oven, where she'd left a homemade pie for his dinner.

Later he completed the *Times* crossword and started reading a detective story, but found he couldn't concentrate on the plot: it was just words on paper, not worth the threat of a headache. He sat at his window and watched the bay darkening until the water seemed to turn into black ice. He musn't let his encounter in the courtroom upset him, he told himself, he was doing his best to make up for his grandmother's death by helping people who needed help. All the same, his rooms suddenly felt as large as loneliness, and he was afraid to go to bed in case one of those visions that were more than dreams was waiting for him at the edge of sleep. But when eventually he stumbled half asleep to bed, he slept for hours until the alarm woke him.

It was far too dark. When he peered bleary-eyed at the luminous hands, he saw that it was almost three o'clock in the morning. That woke him fully, his scalp crawling. Somehow the alarm must have retained the setting at which he'd left it while he'd gone to look for Mrs. Corner—and it was the time he'd seen on his grandmother's broken watch as he'd searched vainly for her pulse.

He tried to reason with himself as his limbs clenched, tried to lull himself back to sleep before it left him alone in the dark. The courtroom encounter had revived his guilt, that was all, and his guilt had made him set the alarm for that time without realizing; he'd known guilt to make people do stranger things. He knew he would always feel guilty, and so he should. If you can hear me, he said silently, I didn't mean to harm you.

"I can hear you." He not only heard the voice in the dark, he felt teeth and dry cracked lips against his ear. "And you did."

Chapter XV

"I HOPE to have news of your furniture soon," Jimmy said.

The retired couple thanked him wistfully and put their arms around each other as they hobbled back into their house, and he hoped he could do more than hope. This was a kind of expert crime he particularly disliked, thieves sending the old couple tickets to a show and parking a furniture van in front of the house while they carried out the antiques. Of course the name on the van had been false. He'd circulate descriptions of the stolen property and run a computer search for gangs who worked that way, and hope the couple would be among the lucky ones whose property was recovered. You had to believe in luck sometimes.

The June sky was opening as he went down to the East Promenade. Perhaps with so much money in parts of Seaward robberies were inevitable—at least one burglar made a habit of robbing properties where an alarm was already sounding—but that was no excuse. Crime was a matter of choice and weakness, and he'd no time for people who felt that inequality entitled them to rob. He'd earned everything he had, except for the money his parents had given him as a wedding present to help buy the house, the last of the pools win his father had frittered away. He wouldn't have accepted if his parents hadn't put the money in trust for that sole purpose.

He went into the Royal, the largest hotel. Stragglers from the Future Media convention were leaving, grown men with armfuls of comics and the kind of magazine Pete Priest's father used to sell. A man with a mane of white hair was waiting for the garage attendant to bring his car round, a white Volvo. "Haven't I seen him before?" Jimmy said to the hotel receptionist.

"Maurice Fox? He writes science fiction. All these sci-fi conventions invite him." She showed him a Maurice Fox novel, apparently a love story set in another galaxy, and gave him an address for Francesca to write to in order to join the Star Trek convention. He passed the Volvo as he jogged up to the police station near the law courts, to keep himself fit. There was a message on his desk that Robin Laurel had phoned.

Hearing from her after so long made him feel odd. He called her twice but found the line engaged. Five minutes' striding took him down the North Fork to her house.

Her mother opened the door. Her face and bare arms were even more freckled than he remembered. "Oh, dear," she wailed, and flurried away down the hall, leaving him to show himself in. "It's another policeman," she cried.

She clearly didn't recognize him, but Robin did. "Jimmy, thanks so much for coming."

She looked better than ever—long legs, black hair cut shorter now, a speckling of freckles across her nose—except that her smile seemed unable to gain a hold. "I gather someone's already been to see you," he said.

"Yes, but—" She glanced over his shoulder. "Would

you excuse us, mother?" she said, and waited until her mother left the living room, reluctantly. "I wouldn't have called you except I didn't know who else to turn to," she said to Jimmy then. "I only thought of you because we used to be friends."

"I hope we still are."

"Even so, I probably shouldn't be asking you." She took a deep breath. "Just give me your advice if that's possible. The police who were here earlier more or less accused me of pushing drugs."

"Are you?"

"No," she said without resentment. "Someone's been forging prescriptions using my forms."

"How could they have got hold of them?"

"All I can think of is that they must have been stolen from Raquel's desk. She says she doesn't know anything about it, and I don't think she could be involved in that kind of thing."

"And the men who interviewed you—"

"If they're colleagues of yours I'm sorry, but I thought they were nasty pieces of work, not our kind at all. They as good as told me they knew I was guilty and nothing would persuade them different. Do *you* think that's necessary?"

She wasn't merely angry, for he could see her shaking. "I shouldn't have thought so," he said. "What were their names?"

"Dexter and Deedes."

"I thought they might be. They've been seconded from London to look into drug smuggling. Maybe they've got tired of watching the boats. They shouldn't be on a case like yours."

"Were they just trying to frighten me, Jimmy?"

"I'm sure they were, but I can't see why. Raquel is your receptionist, is she? Perhaps I could just have a word with her."

As he stepped into the hall Robin's mother came out of

the kitchen, her hands and chin white with icing sugar. "You're supposed to be her friend," she said, having recognized him. "Tell her not to get mixed up with drugs, for God's sake. I was always afraid she would."

"I don't believe she is, Mrs. Laurel. I think it's a misunderstanding."

"You would say that, being her friend," she said fiercely, and turned her back on him. He interviewed the receptionist, a girl with a flat, sullenly hostile face and large breasts, who said she always left the forms on her desk ready to be taken into surgery. No, she didn't know she'd been told not to, and that was all he could get out of her. "I'll have a word with our friends from the drug squad," he told Robin, and went back to the police station.

Tanya had called without leaving a message. He phoned home, but she must be on her way to collect the children from school. He went next door to the office Dexter and Deedes were using. "I hear you interviewed a friend of mine today, Dr. Laurel."

"Complained to you, did she?" Dexter, whose shaved face looked bruised by scraping, said.

"She felt she was being treated like a criminal."

"How do you know she isn't one?" Deedes said out of his small face, its features crowded together in the middle of his large head. "She was criminally negligent at the very least, or someone she employs was. That's reason enough to put the fear of God into her."

"We need to get fear back," Dexter said. "The swine we have to deal with aren't afraid of anything these days."

Some people call us pigs, you know, Jimmy thought, and that isn't much help either. "I really don't think you can prove criminal negligence. Treating her like a pusher will do none of us any good."

"You'd be surprised what we can prove," Dexter said.

"I wouldn't advise you to try it on any friend of mine who's committed no crime. She's a respected local figure with a reputation to maintain."

"Close friends, are you?" Dexter sneered, and Deedes intervened, "You've got children, inspector. What kind of world do you want them to grow up in?"

"I hope," Jimmy said mildly, "not a world where the innocent are treated like hardened criminals."

"None of us are innocent, inspector, though too many of us think we are. If fear is taking the place of religion, so be it. Something worthwhile has to." Deedes held his cupped hands toward Jimmy. "What if it comes down to either treating some people that way or having pushers go after your kids?"

"I don't think it needs to be either."

"Maybe you don't think, but we know," Dexter said. "That kind of thinking may get you by round here, but it wouldn't be worth shit where we come from."

Perhaps policing cities made you feel that way—one reason Jimmy stayed in Seaward was that he preferred not to find out what he might be forced to do in order to deal with urban crime—but he distrusted anyone who identified so closely with their job they forgot that they were dealing with people, that they were people themselves. "If Dr. Laurel is still under suspicion I'll put one of my men on the case," he said. "It certainly isn't the sort of thing you're here for."

"Let her wet her knickers for a while," Dexter said.

"Tell me what we *are* here for," Deedes complained. He seemed to feel the rumors of drug smuggling were false, perhaps even a means of diverting attention from where the drugs were being brought into the country. Jimmy left the two of them complaining and told the desk sergeant that he was going up to the school for a few minutes.

The school was emptying as he drove past. By the time he'd parked the car, the last few children were running to their parents, displaying reading books and paintings. There was no sign of Tanya. She must be on her way home, he thought, and was heading in that direction when he saw

Russell and Francesca across the road. They were standing
by themselves outside the Grand.

The street crossing guard held up the traffic for him.
Jimmy's anger was growing, for the boards nailed across
the entrance to the theater had been torn down, the doors
were standing open. "You were told to stay away from
here," he said as calmly as he could, "and never to cross
the road without me or your mother."

"Mummy's in there," Russell cried, his lower lip
trembling with the unfairness of the accusation. "I'm not
teasing, I'm realing."

"She is, daddy. She heard someone crying inside. She
told us to stay here and not let anyone except grown-ups
go in."

"Good girl. You're good too, Russell. Stay here,"
Jimmy said, and ran up the grubby marble steps. He
hardly heard Francesca say, "I didn't think it sounded like
anyone crying."

The light from the open doors illuminated most of the
lobby. Winged bulls guarded the staircases that curved up
to the balcony entrances; the dusty ticket windows looked
like slabs of slate. He turned as someone stepped out of
the shadows beyond an archway, but it was himself in a
cracked mirror as high as the arch. "Tanya?" he called
and stepped between the second pair of open doors, into
the auditorium.

It was much darker in there. At first he could see
nothing but a dim glow beyond the ranks of seats. "Jimmy,
is that you?" Tanya said from high up in the glow, and he
went quickly forward down the central aisle.

She was up on the stage somewhere. The glow came
from the flashlight she always carried in her handbag, the
flashlight upturned now at the foot of a ladder attached to
the wall at the back of the stage, beyond a left-over
pasteboard cloud. He was peripherally aware of the great
blind stone faces that framed the stage as he peered up in
search of her. When he caught sight of her he didn't
believe at first that it was Tanya, hoped it wasn't her at all.

She was thirty feet or more up the ladder, almost at the top. She looked small and precarious and much too far away. "The doors were open and I think a child got in," she called to him. "I'm sure I heard them up here," and as she looked up, moved no more violently than that, the ladder came loose from the wall.

He heard metal grind in stone as the screws jerked loose. The ladder gave a rusty screech as it began to totter. A screw fell from the top to the stage with a thump that echoed through the empty theater. "Hold on," Jimmy shouted and dashed forward, praying there was nothing in the dimness that could trip him.

His footfalls felt ponderous as if trying to run underwater. Boards sprang under the carpet, which he could tell was rotting. He realized with a dull fury that the interior hadn't been made safe, whatever Steve Innes might think. He was driving himself faster, coughing with the rasp of dust in his breath, and peering to find the steps to the stage. Tanya wrapped her arms round the ladder in a desperate attempt to hold on. With a groan of metal and a rain of screws, the ladder tore itself away from the wall completely, and fell.

"Throw yourself clear," Jimmy cried, too late. The moment froze him, hands reaching out as though he could will her into them and catch her. Then the ladder broke her against the edge of the stage. It carried her into the orchestra pit, and the flashlight rolled toward him, blinding him then showing him the steps to the stage before it clinked against the disused footlights. He ran up the steps, controlling himself tightly, to get the flashlight so that he could see into the pit. He was already afraid to shine it down there, for Tanya was making no sound at all.

Chapter XVI

MAGGIE phoned Steve as soon as she heard from her friend in the mayor's office that someone had been hurt at the Grand. Steve drove up from the agency, silently cursing the vandals and fearing the worst he could think of. When he saw the ambulance outside the theater he realized he'd meant his fears to be worse than the truth. The thought of finding out was drying up his mouth.

He parked round the corner from the school. As he hurried back, a woman was leading two children out of the schoolyard. Decency made him look away as he heard what they were saying. "I don't want mummy to die," the little boy pleaded. "She won't die, will she?"

"How does granny know?" his sister said furiously, then put her arms round him as he burst into tears. "Don't cry, Russ, I didn't mean to be nasty. Don't cry, there's a good boy. Can we just see her, granny? Just for a moment. Just to see she's alive."

"Not now, Francesca. Let your daddy and the ambulance men look after her now. You come home with me," she said in a determinedly level voice, "and I'll give you both a special drink in the bar."

Before Steve could force himself to look at them to confirm that he knew who they were, Jimmy appeared at the top of the steps to the Grand. The ambulance attendants carried out a stretcher as he held one door. Steve couldn't see the face of the person on the stretcher, and was afraid to think why. "Come along now," Jimmy's mother said briskly, "they don't want us here getting in their way," and hurried the children, both of whom were crying now, up the road toward the forest. Steve's palms began to sweat as he made himself cross the road.

Jimmy looked up from keeping pace with the stretcher. His face was carefully expressionless, and froze that way as he saw Steve. At least Tanya's face was partly hidden by her ash-blonde hair and not, as Steve had thought for a dreadful moment, by the sheet. "What happened, Jimmy?" he said.

"As you see, your boards weren't as secure as they ought to have been." Jimmy's voice was as stiff as his face. "She called me to tell me. She should have waited till I got here."

"Why didn't she? Why did she go in?"

"You think it may have been her fault, do you?" Jimmy's eyes brightened dangerously. "She thought she heard a child in there. She must have been mistaken—nobody came out this way, and the other doors are boarded up. Maybe you're right, it was her fault for thinking a child was in danger."

"I'm sorry, Jimmy," Steve said, hating the inadequacy. "Is there anything I can do?"

"Find whoever was responsible for leaving the place in this state. The work you told me had been done hasn't been. The place is a death trap. As you see," he said, nodding at the ambulance, clenching his teeth.

"We have to get going, inspector," one of the attendants said.

"How is she, Jimmy?" Steve managed to ask, having sensed a hint of hope.

Jimmy swung himself into the back of the ambulance. "She may live."

Steve watched the ambulance dwindle, its siren blaring, and then he realized that the woman who'd been standing patiently near him on the steps was a reporter from Anglia Radio. He told her the truth brusquely, then he called Seaward Security from a nearby phone booth and went into the Grand. There was no doubt that the theater had been left unsafe—that most of the guaranteed work hadn't been carried out at all. He began cursing until his echoes were so loud that he fell silent.

When Seaward Security arrived he went back to the agency and found the written guarantee. He made himself calm down before he reached for the phone, but he might as well not have bothered: the builders were no longer at that address, and the firm who'd moved in thought they were no longer even trading.

He was explaining to his father what had happened when Maggie came in. "I thought you must be here, since you weren't at the Grand. Don't worry, love," she said, but now he had his father's reaction to worry him too: he'd never seen his father so downcast before. "Nobody's ever been hurt on one of our properties," his father said. "Maybe I'm getting past it. Maybe it's time to shut up shop."

"Don't you let them make you think so, Norman," Steve's mother cried, and Steve joined in, "It wasn't your fault, dad, it was those buggers who were supposed to have done the work. No wonder they didn't give us time to inspect it."

"I should have insisted." He seized his jutting chin with one large hand as if he had to use it to lift his head, and gazed at Steve. "This won't do the old firm any good, you know. If you and Maggie want to think of moving I'm sure there are plenty of agencies that would take you on, and I'll do all I can to help.''

''We wouldn't dream of it, would we, Maggie?'' Steve said, and waited until she murmured negatively. He cabled the owner of the Grand at several addresses to contact the agency at once, and clasped his father's hand when they'd locked up for the night. ''We'll stick with you,'' he said, and repeated the promise fiercely to himself the next morning as he cleaned the graffiti off the display window before his parents could see them. GET OUT OF SEWARD NEGLIGANT BASTERDS, the dripping spray-painted letters said.

Chapter XVII

"NOW here's the news but don't go away, will you? I'll be seeing you in a few minutes," Terry Tebbitt said in her usual way. Robin had sat down, having finished surgery and making dinner, to enjoy a large gin and tonic while she listened to the news, when her mother marched in. "Waiting to hear if they've found out about you yet?" she cried. "For your own sake, Robin, give up this business with the drugs before it's too late."

Robin was too tired to reopen the argument. "Won't you even deny it now? Take notice of me, I'm older than you," her mother pleaded, and threw up her hands in desperation as Robin sat back, closing her eyes. She had to sit up wearily as her mother made to turn off the radio. "You aren't listening to this, are you, Robin? I want to say something to you."

"Just let me hear this." It was a report about the accident yesterday at the Grand, rumors of which she had been hearing all day from her patients. The victim's name was Tanya Waters—why, that was Jimmy's wife. "You don't need to hear this," Robin's mother interrupted. "I've something important to tell you."

"Oh, mother, please be quiet for a few moments." Now she'd missed hearing how Tanya was, and the newsreader was introducing a telephone interview with the owner of the Grand. Would he say that negligence had caused the accident? "Not by me," he said, with an accent that sounded Canadian but might be made up from the places he'd lived. "I was assured that the building was being kept up."

"Shouldn't you have checked personally?" the brash young reporter pounced.

"I'm so seldom in Britain it would have been next to impossible. You're lucky to have caught me here now. Anyway," he said, "I wonder what the lady thought she was doing in a building that was closed to the public."

"She went in to save a child she thought she heard."

"Wasn't there one?"

"Apparently not." The reporter tried to regain the advantage. "Surely you must accept some responsibility for what happened."

"I'd have expected my agent to keep an eye on things and let me know when work needed doing."

"You mean the estate agent."

"Since you ask me, yes, that's who I mean." He went on to say he would sell the Grand to anyone who would take it off his hands, he'd had enough of being blamed for trying to preserve the heritage of Seaward, and Robin's mother kept sighing impatiently, so loudly she almost blotted out his voice. When it was clear that the news wasn't going to refer again to Tanya, Robin turned it off. "Am I allowed to speak now?" her mother said.

"Don't be unreasonable, mother. Surely you don't mind if I listen to the news."

"Are you sure you weren't just trying to avoid hearing

what I had to say? I wish you had a father, Robin. You'd listen to him."

Robin took a deep breath rather than disagree, and her mother went on. "You wouldn't have got mixed up with drugs either. I know, it's my fault too for letting you grow up without a father."

"Mother, I've told you my only involvement with drugs is prescribing them. Perhaps I should remind you I'm a doctor."

"Yes, you've told me, and I might believe you if I weren't your mother. Oh, Robin, we've always been too close to be able to lie to each other." She dabbed quickly at her eyes as if they'd taken her unawares. "I don't like to think of you left on your own when I've gone."

"You aren't going anywhere, so stop that kind of talk." Robin went to her and took her hands. "You'll be around for a long time yet, take my word as a doctor."

"And I'll be all the more trouble to you." Her mother pulled her hands away to dab her eyes again. "Aren't you ever going to find yourself a husband, Robin? At least then you'd have someone to share your burdens. Believe me, they get worse as you get older."

"I don't need anyone, mother," Robin said and forced a laugh.

"Of course you do. I can't keep an eye on you all the time. If you had a man he wouldn't have let you get mixed up with drugs." She clapped her hands, her eyes brightening. "What about your friend the policeman? He certainly wouldn't. I'd like to see you cultivate him."

"Mother, he's married. It was his wife who got into the theater."

"What's her career to do with it?" When Robin explained, her mother was more impatient still. "Well, you ought to look around for someone like him. Someone who'd keep you on the right path."

"Mother . . ."

"Just try listening for a change instead of always arguing. You've made me forget what I wanted to say. Sit down and let me be quiet and think."

That gave Robin time to think too, to remember the students who'd either found her intelligence threatening or been involved with someone else. After university and seven years of medical school she'd worked 140-hour weeks for six months all over a large hospital, then she had gone into practice, feeling exploited and vulnerable, inevitably making mistakes that the doctor who'd reluctantly taken her on as a partner seemed to regard as points he was scoring. Setting up her own practice had come as a relief, but what she had once been told at medical school was only too true, that you spent your career trying to recover from all you'd had to undergo in training. No wonder she'd never had time to become seriously involved with anyone, she thought, as her mother said, "Robin, I'm going to tell you something I've never told you before."

"I'm listening."

"You or anyone else. Just listen and let me say it and don't make it any harder for me than it already is. Perhaps when you've heard it you'll feel like telling me the truth about what you've been doing. Don't start arguing," she cried, though Robin had only been taking a breath so as not to do so, "or I won't be able to."

She stared at her hands, turned them over and stared at them. Eventually she said, "Do you remember Douglas?"

Robin had to think. "Wasn't he the man at the museum who made life difficult for you?"

"That's how he seemed to me then. When it was too late I realized he was a much finer person than I'd taken him for. I wish now—I wish I hadn't treated him the way I did."

"Was that what you meant the other day when you said you'd lived to regret something? Oh, mummy . . ."

"No, that isn't it. I haven't told you yet." Her impatience sounded desperate. "You know he was run over.

Outside the museum, in the car park. A car backed into him and broke his legs.''

Robin didn't like how tense her mother was growing. "I didn't know that was how it happened, but all I can say is they should both have looked where they were going."

"Robin!" It was almost a scream. "I'm trying to tell you. Can't you listen? It was me, Robin. I did it. I pushed him under the car."

Robin looked gently at her and wondered if she were more afraid that her mother was telling the truth or that this was the first sign of paramnesia, false memory. All she could think of to say was "Are you sure?"

"Do you think I'd misremember something like that? What are you trying to say about me?" Robin's mother jumped up and hurried into the surgery, hobbled back. "Just making sure that girl isn't still here. Perhaps you'd like me to be overheard. That would make it easier for you to get rid of me so that you can carry on selling your drugs."

"You know I don't want to get rid of you," Robin said, gritting her teeth.

"I know nothing of the kind. But I'll tell you what I do know: I know I pushed Douglas under that car. I don't know what he said to make me do it, I can't remember. As God is my witness, I wasn't thinking what I was doing. Something came over me. Perhaps you know what I mean."

"How could you keep it a secret? Surely Douglas must have talked."

"He never did," her mother said, too simply to be inventing. "He could have had me prosecuted, but when he came out of hospital he found a job elsewhere. He did that for me, Robin."

So it wasn't paramnesia, but Robin was beginning to feel that she might have preferred it to be. "I should have gone after him. He was the kind of father you needed," her mother said, then suddenly her eyes sparkled. "You *can* cultivate the policeman, you know. He must be a widower now."

Robin looked away. Her mother was growing old, that was all. Too often that involved losing touch with the proprieties. "We don't know that, mother. That was why I was trying to listen to the news, to hear how his wife is," she said, and made for the kitchen before they became entangled in another argument. They were halfway through dinner when the phone rang.

It was Jimmy. "I just wanted to let you know I don't think you need worry any further about the men who came to see you."

He sounded subdued and tense. "They aren't going to press charges, then," she said, postponing what she had to ask.

"They've no charges to press, Robin. They were just going to let you stew for a while, but I wasn't having that."

"I appreciate it, Jimmy. It was very sweet of you to think of me when . . ." She felt not only touched by his thoughtfulness but ashamed of having given him her problem to deal with. "I heard the news. I'm so sorry, Jimmy. How is she?"

"She's in the new hospital. Lumbar fracture and a ruptured spleen. They've taken her spleen out the last I heard from them. She ought to be able to recognize me soon, shouldn't she? They seem to have her on so many tubes and transfusions and God knows what else. I keep telling myself she'll be all right. It's just the stories you hear about that hospital."

"I'm sure she's in good hands," she said, hoping. "Would you like me to visit her one evening? Maybe then I could put your mind at rest."

"I'd be most grateful, Robin. Say you're a friend of the family. Let me know when you're going, will you? They only allow two visitors at a time."

As soon as Robin put down the phone her mother said, "Well?" She looked frustrated and impatient when she heard Tanya was in hospital. She tried again to persuade

Robin to confess, and was obviously furious that she'd
confessed herself to no avail. "We can all be tempted,"
she said, but that only reminded Robin of things she'd
thought she had dealt with and forgotten. It was partly the
pressure of unresolved memories that made her call Steve
Innes that evening.

His wife answered the phone. "How are you, Maggie?"
Robin said.

"Who's speaking, please?"

"It's Robin. Robin Laurel. We met once when I was
buying my house."

"Oh, do you remember that? You must have a long
memory. If you're after Steve, he isn't here just now. Can
I take a message?"

"Only that I heard the news and wanted to tell him I
thought they were trying to lay all the blame on him and
his father."

"I expect you would."

"I'm sure other people will make allowance for that
too."

"Not the people who've been writing about him on
walls."

"People like that aren't worth taking notice of. Someone's been doing that, have they?"

"Oh, I thought you were saying you'd heard. Yes, on
the shop and some of the sale boards as well. That's where
Steve and his father are now, checking the properties.
Shall I ask Steve to call you when he comes in?"

"Don't bother. I mean, don't have him call unless he
wants to," Robin said. There was an undercurrent to the
conversation she couldn't quite define and hadn't time to
ponder. She left her mother watching television and went
out for a stroll, to think.

Breezes ruffled the edge of the cliff and touched her
bare arms, twilight crept into the sea. She'd thought she
had come to terms with whatever had happened twenty-
five years ago. She was a doctor now, not a vulnerable

adolescent. She was in control of her life—had been ever since she'd been able to deal with the suicide at the gun club without flinching, the man's jaw sitting all by itself on his neck. If a wish had come true for her a quarter of a century ago, what did it matter now? But it certainly did if her wish had been carried out by her mother.

Had her mother been brooding over her guilt all these years? Was it the guilt that had been wearing her down so much lately? Of course she had seemed desperate enough to push Douglas under the car, yet Robin couldn't take advantage of that explanation. As a child she'd often felt she had lost her mother a husband, Robin's father—had lost him for her by being conceived, for that had driven him away. Now she felt as if she'd lost her mother more than that, by wishing—her mother's self-control, her sense of herself.

Perhaps now her mother had confessed she would grow to feel better. Perhaps it would bring them closer, bring her mother back to herself. Robin went home as the streetlamps came on, and found the house in darkness. Her mother was dozing, and Robin let her sleep in the armchair until she was ready for bed herself.

She ought to have wakened her mother when she came home, though she would have been even grumpier. At three in the morning Robin woke to hear her wandering through the house, refusing to believe the clocks, demanding out loud why it was so dark outside. Robin managed to convince her of the time and tucked her up in bed, then lay awake for more than an hour, blood pumping in her ears, listening to hear if her mother got up again.

It was just old age. She could help her mother adjust to the way her body clock was altering, if only her mother would let her. She drank black coffee throughout morning surgery, Raquel sulkily refilling her cup, then she made her house calls. Driving home, she resolved to call Jimmy without letting memories loose. She locked the garage and strode into the house, and was so intent on reaching the phone in the living room that she didn't notice the men from the drugs squad until they stood up.

She might have asked what was ailing them if they hadn't looked both grim and smug under their professional masks. "What seems to be the problem?" she said, refusing to let them see they'd taken her aback.

"You'd almost believe she didn't know," the policeman with flecks of blood on his shaved face said. "Or her friend the seaside bobby would."

"I'm afraid this time your friend won't be able to help you," said the policeman with the small crowded face. "Not now that we have an independent witness."

"What are you talking about? A witness of what?"

"Of the fact that you issued the prescription forms you claimed had been stolen from you." The policeman's small lips closed primly, opened with a tiny dry sound. "I mean the chemist who called you this morning because he was suspicious of the signature and you assured him it was yours."

Chapter XVIII

WIND swept across the tousled sea and squeaked the hanging signboard of the supermarket that had been the Lux, and Peter patted the top of his head automatically as he came out of his building, to make sure of his hair. In almost ten years of wearing a toupee he hadn't managed to convince himself that it was safe on a day like this. He was still resting his fingers negligently on the brushed bushy surface as he reached the corner of his street and glanced up at the Innes Real Estate Agency board outside the house for sale, and then he halted, gazing at the new words on the board. NEGLIGANT BASTERDS, the ragged letters said.

He stood and drummed his fingers on his cap of hair. First there had been the radio interview with the owner of the Grand, now this, but why should those things make him nervous? What could they have to do with him? The householder glared out at him until Peter went away, wondering what he had almost realized. He was still wondering when he reached the town hall. He made for the switchboard room to see how Hilda Marvle was coping with her new job.

She was wearing a dress somewhat too large and too young for her. She swiveled as he came in, and lifted one earphone away from her ear. "How's it going, Hilda?" he said.

"Everyone's being kind to me." He didn't know how to take that until she said, "I want to keep this job, Mr. Priest, I really do."

"Roger?"

"He keeps phoning to try and get me flustered so I won't be able to stay."

"Would you like me to have a word with him?"

"Oh, would you, please?" She smiled as if she were trying out her protruding teeth. "I like coming to work, it makes me feel like someone for a change. I like talking to people and being with people, I keep telling him so. I'd be able to grow out of my past if he'd only give me a chance."

It was a remarkably long speech for her, and all the more impressive because she continued to operate the switchboard while talking. "One moment, please. Putting you through now," she said as though she'd been doing the job for years. Then her face changed, lips hiding her teeth quickly. "There he is."

"I'll speak to him." Peter leaned close and heard Roger in one earphone. "When are you coming home, Hilda? You've got me and mother worried sick. You're going with a man there, aren't you, that's why you won't let me see you at work. I'll know if you have been, I'll smell him on you."

Peter seized the mouthpiece that stood in front of Hilda. "I'm here, Roger, Mr. Priest, and I advise you to leave Hilda alone. Making calls like yours could be an offense, you know. Especially to an official switchboard."

"Got your hands on her, have you? Is she paying you

back for finding her a job?'' His voice dwindled as she
turned her head and the earphone away from Peter in
shame. "You can't fool me. I'll find out what you're
scared of if you don't leave her alone and let her come
back where she's safe from the likes of you.''

"I warn you this kind of call could be a matter for the
police,'' Peter said, but Roger had gone.

"I'm sorry about what he said, Mr. Priest,'' Hilda said,
blushing. "He's only trying to do what he thinks is right.''

"We all try to do that,'' Peter said, and made for the
door, where the supervisor had a murmured word with
him. "I wish I could have more trainees like her,'' she
said. "She'll be fine so long as she's left to get on with the
job. I'm keeping an eye on this business with the brother.''

"Keep me informed,'' Peter said, and went up the wide
stairs. Most of the desks in the office were empty, his
colleagues out on cases. Several messages were waiting
for him: one of his alcoholics had got drunk last night and
beaten up his wife; a shoplifter was due in court again; an
old lady who refused to admit she was housebound wanted
Peter to go back to see her, she didn't say why. She lived
two streets away from where Peter's grandmother had
lived.

The window beside him shivered a little, a ventilator
squealed at the far end of the long room that smelled of
typewriters and stale paper. It hadn't mattered where the
housebound lady lived when he'd visited her to offer her
the services, and it mustn't matter now. What he'd heard
and felt the other night had just been the edge of a guilty
dream. He made himself go to see the housebound lady at
once.

The streets of pebbly houses were so sunlit they looked
unreal. Wind kept tugging at his shoulders. Of course that
was why he felt as if he was being followed, watched. He
marched up to the white Victorian house, which was very
like his grandmother's, and rang the lowest bell.

Mrs. Alden, the housebound lady, shaded her eyes as

she opened the door. "Who's that?" she demanded, and seemed at first to be looking beyond him. "Oh, it's you, Mr. Priest. Thank you for coming. Don't say anything out here, I don't want the neighbors listening."

Her apartment was on the ground floor. Chairs faced the corners of the main room, a fallen window curtain was draped over the settee. Books were piled on the mantelpiece as high as she could reach. "I'm sorry I was short with you last time you called," she wheezed, clinging to her stick as she lowered herself onto the settee. "I thought the neighbors could hear."

"May I take it you've had second thoughts about our services?"

"I won't have them bringing me meals. I won't have the neighbors seeing that and thinking I can't look after myself. You said I could have a home help. I'll be telling the neighbors she's a relative, so please make sure she's of good character."

It had been her neighbors who'd called Peter in to visit her. "All our home helps are, Mrs. Alden. I'll set the wheels in motion for you today."

She insisted on accompanying him to the front door. If he hadn't had to match her pace he might not have glimpsed Roger across the road, through a sliver of clear glass in the frosted pane beside the door. No wonder Peter had felt he was being followed. Roger folded his arms defiantly as Peter strode out to him, and then Mrs. Alden called, "Where's the lady who came in with you?"

It must be one of those delusions solitary people had sometimes. Nevertheless he halted in the middle of the road as if she'd grabbed him by the neck, and Roger saw his face. Peter turned quickly. "Nobody did, Mrs. Alden."

"You'll pardon me, someone did. An old lady who looked a bit like you. Just you take her with you. I've no room for lodgers." She limped away down the hall and eventually reappeared. "She's gone, or she's hiding. I wouldn't have let you in if I'd known that was your game.

Forget what I asked you before, I'll manage on my own,"
she declared, and slammed the door.

He might have tried to make peace with her if it hadn't
been for Roger, who came and stood so close that Peter
could smell his bad teeth. "So it's an old lady you're
scared of, eh? What did you do to her?"

"I've no idea what you mean," Peter said, stiff-faced.

"I'll find out what you did if you don't leave Hilda
alone." Roger danced ahead of him as he hurried back to
the office. "There she is, behind you," he kept yelping,
while Peter suppressed an urge to lash out at him and tried
to ignore him, told himself that Mrs. Alden had only
imagined she'd seen someone. "Go on, hit me, I can see
you want to," Roger muttered, dancing close. "You're no
better than the rest of us. You've no right to interfere in
other people's lives."

The security guard stopped Roger at the doors of the
town hall, and Peter hurried upstairs without looking back.
He sat at his desk and pressed his temples as if they might
restrain his growing headache, pressed them until they felt
as if they might crack. Time passed before he was able to
reach in his desk drawer for the aspirins.

Later he went to see the alcoholic. The man's wife had
taken pity on him again, and all Peter could do was make
him promise to go back to Alcoholics Anonymous. "I
swear on my mother's grave this is the last time," the man
said, holding up his hands as if to display their shaking.
Peter put his file away for review and walked home under
an overcast sky.

He bought a take-home salad in the Lux and ate it while
he listened to the radio, Terry Tebbitt's Teatime Talk-In
filling his large room with voices. One call condemned the
Innes agency for letting the Grand decay and the council
for agreeing to restore it now, another wanted to know
why the community health council didn't keep a closer eye
on doctors, one of whom was abusing her power to prescribe drugs. "I'll have to stop you there, caller," Terry

Tebbitt told her briskly, "in case people guess who you mean."

Until she'd said that, Peter hadn't realized he could—it seemed so unlike the Robin he remembered to harm anyone, however little she'd cared what people thought of her. He switched off the radio and walked to the jagged fenced-off hump where the lighthouse had been, the land rearing up and blotting out miles of sea. Early stars glittered above the fishing boats, fewer boats than there used to be. Perhaps he was seeing stars that had died long ago; couldn't hearing a voice that no longer existed be natural too? He wished he hadn't thought of that, wished he'd kept on believing it had been a dream.

He was almost home when he stopped and stared. The board with the graffiti had been taken down; the Elsey agency was selling the house now. He went to bed feeling that the day had been full of clues or threats. Perhaps that was why his sleep was so uneasy, why he dreamed of visiting his parents as he did every Sunday, his father staring grimly at him and saying, "Time to go to your grandmother's."

He woke in a panic, his heart and his skull pounding. When he switched on the light his bedroom looked gloomy and cluttered and cramped, wholly unfamiliar. He stumbled to the bathroom for a glass of water to wash the sour taste out of his mouth, and was peering stupidly at himself in the mirror when he heard a movement in the main room.

He saw his face flinch. He wanted to flee back to the bedroom, switching on the moony wall lamps as he went. Nobody could be in the main room, he told himself, nobody. He made himself go into the dark hall and turn toward the darker main room, switching on each light as he came to it. He didn't need to switch on the overhead light in the main room, for the glow from the last of the wall lamps reached as far as the opposite end of the table, where his grandmother was sitting.

She smiled as she saw his terror, and her cheeks seemed to fall in. As she sat forward, her long nails clicking on the table, he saw that her nostrils were ragged, one of them considerably larger than the other. Her voice sounded even closer to him than she was, though what was left of her mouth seemed hardly to move. "You'll pay," she said. "You'll pay just as your friends are paying."

Chapter XIX

AS STEVE went into the town hall to meet Maggie for lunch he heard her in the switchboard room. "What are you playing at, you stupid girl? That's the second time I've lost that call."

"I'm sorry, Mrs. Innes. Someone keeps ringing up and getting me flustered and won't go away."

"Calls like that come with the job, girl. If you can't handle them you should call the police."

"I don't want to do that. I know him."

"I thought as much. I won't have your troubles with your boyfriend interfering with an important phone call. I'll be speaking to your supervisor when she comes back."

Steve had never heard her talk so harshly, and didn't like it much. "You're new here, aren't you?" he said to the toothy girl. "Don't be too hard on her, Maggie. Don't go losing her her job."

The girl gave him a timid grateful smile. Maggie didn't speak to him until she'd collected her handbag and locked

her office and they were on the way down to the East
Promenade, through streets that looked sunbleached under
the bluest sky so far that year. "I hope you realize you
humiliated me in front of that girl Hilda," she said then.

"I was only trying to save you from yourself. I know it
can't be easy for you either just now."

"You know that, do you, Steve? It's the first I've heard
of it. It'd be a lot easier for me if you talked to me
occasionally."

"Look, Maggie, I didn't come out to lunch just to be
reminded of what's waiting when I get back. You wouldn't
want to be reminded of your problems at work, would
you?"

"I wouldn't mind talking about them if I thought you'd
listen. I know, I know, you've heard it all before. Just
don't make me look a fool at work."

A few businessmen perched on stools in the long bar of
the Hotel Excelsior. Steve and Maggie ordered lunch, and
at a table overlooking the sea he said, "Tell me about it if
you like."

"Tell you about what, Steve? About the way you inter-
fered? My status there is low enough as it is. If one more
convention organizer gives me the wink I really believe I
may spit in his eye. I told you you'd heard it all before."

"I'm sorry. Here, let me get you another drink." He
came back to find her staring sadly at him. "Maggie, what
else is wrong?"

"More to the point, what's wrong with you, Steve?"

"What's wrong with *me?* My God, I let Jimmy's wife
almost get killed, for a start. Someone's writing insults
about me and my folks all over town. And people have
started taking their houses away to the Elseys."

"And people blame us for living where we live while
the Grand was decaying."

"Oh, you heard they're saying that, did you?" he said
uncomfortably.

"Yes, but I had to hear it from someone else."

"I just didn't want you to be upset when you didn't have to be." He fell silent while the waiter brought their food, then he took her hand. "So that's all, is it?"

She let her hand lie limp in his. "Is it, Steve? You tell me."

"Why, what else would there be?"

She didn't answer directly. "Have you called Robin Laurel back yet?"

"God, no. Thanks for reminding me. It was kind of her to call."

"Especially after all this time."

"Exactly. Why do you say it like that?"

"Wouldn't you say it was odd that she did?"

"If it'll keep you happy."

"And even odder that you haven't returned her call."

"There's a reason," he said, wanting to coax the tone of polite hurt disbelief out of her voice. "If you must know, she was involved in that business twenty-five years ago."

"Oh, Steve." Now she sounded disappointed too. "Why didn't you say she was when you told me about it?"

"Either I forgot or I just didn't want to go into detail. I wouldn't have mentioned it now except to put your mind at rest. I mean, I can do without being reminded of it in the midst of everything else. You understand that, don't you?"

"Steve, you're hiding so much of yourself from me these days I don't think you believe I'm capable of understanding you at all."

"Maybe I don't like being understood, did that ever occur to you? Go ahead, understand that I did something stupid when I was a kid and I've been ashamed of having done it ever since. Will that satisfy you?" He leaned across the remains of their food, his voice low and angry. "Just tell me this: why are you giving me all this crap about Robin Laurel when you know what I'm going through?''

"Forget it, Steve. Not here."

"You shouldn't have started it here then, should you? What's the matter, do you think I'm having it off with Robin?"

"To tell you the truth, Steve, I don't know what to think."

"Then think what the h—'' Infuriatingly, he began to stutter. He saw in her eyes how that confirmed her suspicions. "Think what the devil you like," he said, so low he could barely hear himself. "No doubt we'll continue this at home. I'm supposed to be looking at a house and I'm already late."

As soon as he was out of the hotel he wanted to go back. Maybe he was trying to sit on too many of his problems: no wonder Maggie felt he had something to hide. At the same time he was worried about his father, who hadn't seemed at all well that morning. He'd phone Maggie from the office when they had both had a chance to think.

The house for sale was one of the half-houses, a terrace of small buildings near the common, disproportionately large and steep staircases taking up much of the space in each front hall. He valued the house, and was touched when the owner said, "Tell your dad he's still got friends if he needs them. He won't remember me, but I used to carry his golf clubs."

"Why, that's old Dennis," Steve's father said when he heard about it. He smiled moist-eyed at the memory, but perhaps he was realizing that the man mightn't have offered the house to the agency otherwise. When Steve had come into the office just now his father had looked beaten, the look that came over his face these days when he tried to mend something and couldn't put it back together, and old. If only Steve could do more than wait to hear how Tanya was! He clasped his father's hand and went to his own desk. When the phone rang he couldn't help growing tense, all the more so when he heard Peter Priest's voice. "Steve, I know what's happening to you," Peter said, "and I know why."

Chapter XX

OF COURSE it had been Robin's mother who'd pretended to be Robin on the phone. The men from the drugs squad had had to accept that Robin couldn't have told the chemist she had signed the prescription form when at the time of the phone conversation she'd been making a house call. They checked that, and then they interviewed her mother, who insisted that she didn't know who could have answered the phone and pleaded with them to stop Robin from peddling drugs. "She got the idea from you in the first place," Robin told them furiously as they went away at last.

It was her mother who spoke to Terry Tebbitt about her. For days she wouldn't admit to having done that either, not until two of Robin's patients asked to be transferred from her list. "They didn't want to leave you, I could tell, but they had to look out for their children," her mother said then. "You'd understand that if you had children yourself. I'm sure they would come back if you showed them they could trust you."

"Showed them what? That you've been telling a pack of lies about me? My God, you're even broadcasting it now."

"Oh, Robin, don't try to deny it, not when I've known you all your life. Known you and looked after you and held you in my arms when you were little and you used to tell me all your secrets. You don't think I like speaking ill of you, do you? I wouldn't if there were any other way. I'm only doing it for your own good."

"Mother," Robin said in a voice that hurt her throat, "all you're doing is ruining my reputation."

"Well, you didn't care about ruining Mrs. Starr's by making everyone think she couldn't look after herself, did you? Now you know how it feels." Her mother stood up, wincing. "I still haven't been to visit her in hospital. You said you'd take me but you never did. If you won't take me I'll go myself right now."

"I'll take you." It wasn't worth pointing out that she hadn't previously said so. She phoned Jimmy's house first, but there was no reply. She could at least look at Tanya. She held the car door open for her mother, who climbed in as if she were doing Robin a favor by riding in the car.

The car park was too small for the hospital, which sprawled amid miles of flat land and winding roads. Robin had to park on the road, several hundred yards away from the gates. Her mother complained as she limped through the maze of paths with their bunches of signs for departments of the hospital. Visitors stared at signposts and tried to make out where they had lost their way.

Patient Information consisted of three house phones in the unmanned lobby of the main building. "I'll find out where she is for you," Robin said. Tanya was one floor up from Mrs. Starr, a tired hoarse distant voice told her eventually, in Margaret Thatcher Ward. "You've told me it's the second floor," her mother said when Robin made to walk up with her. "I'm still capable of finding that myself. She won't want to see you after what you did."

"She is my patient, mother. Besides, I want to look in on someone else."

Halfway up the green stone stairs that smelled of antiseptic Robin's mother seemed ready to turn back. She brightened when they reached the ward and she saw Mrs. Starr sitting up in bed, waiting for visitors. "You look as good as new," she cried. "You'll be out of here in no time."

Apart from her bandaged hands and forearms, Mrs. Starr's burns had almost faded. "Thank you for taking care of me, doctor," she said to Robin. "I don't know what I would have done without you. I didn't realize how much I needed looking after."

"Don't you let them tell you so, Ada. You don't need it any more than I do."

"I hope you never will, Emily. You know I used to feel I didn't either, but I haven't felt so contented for years. There's a lady who comes round the wards who's going to take me to a home when I'm well enough. They say I can stay a few days to see how I like it. I really think I might be happy there."

Robin caught sight of the ward sister at the end of the aisle and went to her. Yes, Mrs. Starr was improving steadily, the sister told her; now if only the hospital would. . . . She'd lowered her voice to continue when Robin's mother came hurrying. "What are you talking about?" she demanded, so loudly that every head turned that could.

"Just about how Mrs. Starr is mending, mother."

"Don't lie to me. Why should you be talking about her?"

"I told you, mother, she's my patient."

"She certainly is now, isn't she? You've got her just how you want her, believing everyone knows what's good for her except herself." She turned on the sister. "What have you been giving Mrs. Starr to make her like this?"

"Nothing, Mrs. Laurel, I assure you. Please keep your voice down, you're disturbing my patients."

"No, you don't want them to hear the truth, do you? You've got them locked up safely, why should you care if they hear?" Her eyes narrowed. "Oh, I see. It's the visitors you don't want to hear. They're liable to go repeating what they've heard."

"Mother," Robin said tightly, "please stop this or we'll have to leave. Just talk to Mrs. Starr for a few minutes while I look in upstairs."

"I've seen her. I've seen all I want to see. Sweet Jesus, that's why you were so eager all of a sudden to bring me, isn't it? Because you've got her how you want her at last and you thought she might be able to work on me."

"Then don't talk to her." On second thought, leaving her mother in the ward wasn't such a good idea. "Wait downstairs for me. I'll only be a few minutes."

"Oh, no, you won't get rid of me so easily. I won't be left alone in this maze of a place." Then she gave a gasp that was almost a scream. "Of course, that's what you've been up to all along. You brought me here to leave me, knowing I'd never be able to find my way out. You nearly tricked me, God forgive you. You want to leave me here because I know too much about you and your drugs."

"Mother, just go downstairs and wait for me," Robin murmured, her voice sticking in her throat. She ran up to the next floor, hurried down the corridor with its glistening green walls to Margaret Thatcher Ward. She felt breathless, helplessly angry, oppressed by the heat, which was even more relentless in the hospital. She wasn't wishing her mother would go away, she must never wish again. Surely in time they could sort out their differences.

The ward sister was rolling back a screen from around a bed at the far end of the ward. Jimmy had been sitting beyond the bed, outside the screen, and so the supine figure full of tubes must be Tanya. Both Jimmy and the surgeon who'd been examining her looked up as Robin opened the doors into the ward. At that moment her mother hobbled into the corridor. "Don't you dare try to leave me," she cried. "I'll kill myself if you leave me in here, I'll throw myself down these stairs."

"Mother, just wait here. I'm going in this ward for a few minutes. There's no other exit, I can't get away," Robin said, feeling all at once close to hysterical giggles, and turned to find the surgeon barring her way. "Dr. Laurel, isn't it?" he said. "I want you to hear this and take notice. Sister, I don't want Dr. Laurel admitted to my wards under any circumstances. As for you, Dr. Laurel, with your reputation I'm surprised you dare show your face in here at all."

Chapter XXI

JIMMY squeezed Tanya's limp hand that he was holding and stood up. "I won't be a minute," he said, wondering if she'd heard him or could feel the pressure of his hand, and hurried down the aisle between the beds.

The surgeon was blocking the doorway between him and Robin. Jimmy meant to intervene, tell the surgeon she was a friend of the family, until she looked at him and shook her head. "I'd just like a word with my friend Robin Laurel," he said.

"So long as you understand she is not to come into my ward." The surgeon waited until the sister nodded, then he stalked along the corridor, gray hair bristling on either side of his bald head.

"I'm sorry about this, Robin," Jimmy murmured.

"Good Lord, it isn't your fault."

He felt as if it were, felt as though the police as a body, himself included, were to blame. "How is she?" Robin said.

"Seems a bit better," he said, reminding himself of the moments when her eyes had opened and seemed aware or she'd spoken drowsily. "The surgeon thinks she's improving."

"You can trust him, Jimmy. Don't let our confrontation influence you. I can't really blame him. He's a good doctor," she said with some bitterness.

Jimmy was trying to think what might lift her spirits when the sight of her mother limping along the corridor stopped him. "What are you plotting now?" she demanded, then peered narrowly at Jimmy. "You're the policeman, aren't you? Why are you skulking around here out of uniform?"

"I'm here visiting my wife, Mrs. Laurel."

"I thought she was supposed to be dead."

"Not by me," Jimmy said, feeling his lips stiffen and his face grow hot as Robin looked a fierce apology at him. As he retreated into the ward, which seemed the safest course, her mother said, "Don't you believe he's here to see his wife. He's tailing you, Robin, that's why he's in plain clothes."

Tanya hadn't moved. Her hand that he'd been holding ever since he'd arrived lay on the sheet as he'd left it, limp as her hair, which a nurse had brushed and spread out silver on the pillow. Her wide full lips were turned down as though in helpless protest at the tubes that ran from her left arm and nose and crotch. Her face was so thin and pale it looked too fragile to touch. He reached out and stroked her lips gently and stroked her unresponsive hand. "I'm back," he said.

Her eyelids fluttered momentarily. She had the darkest eyes he'd ever seen and yet he could scarcely remember how they looked. "What was I saying?" he said, telling himself he mustn't hope too much for a response, the slowness of her recovery meant it would be permanent. "I remember, I was telling you about the kids."

Her hand moved then, gave his the ghost of a squeeze.

"As I was saying," he said, almost babbling now that she'd responded, "my folks have them tonight and then they'll be home for the weekend. They want to come and see you, but I think it's best to wait until you can talk to them, don't you? Helen will have them while I'm visiting. She couldn't have been more helpful, especially now she's left school. I told you she'd got a place at college, didn't I? We'll have to look for another baby-sitter when she goes."

The pressure of Tanya's hand had faded. He told himself fiercely that he'd felt it anyway. "She's still going out with Henry," he went on. "Presumably she managed to keep him away from whoever it was she disapproved of. He's been helping with the kids too—takes them for drives in his taxi sometimes. Took them to Yarmouth last week."

This time the pressure of her fingers was unmistakable, and her eyelids fluttered too. Of course, she wanted to hear about the children; what else would she want to hear? It didn't matter that he was repeating himself, having run out of news but not knowing if she'd heard him the first time. "Do you know who's been particularly good with them? My father. Keeps them away from the fruit machine even when the bar's shut. You were right, I should have trusted him," he said, and felt his guts twist with the thought that it had taken Tanya's accident to show him. "Remember he could never tell an oak from an ash? Just the other day I found him studying a heap of library books about trees and botany and wildlife. Russell wants to know what everything in the forest is called now, you see."

Russell had become interested since Tanya had gone into hospital and he was spending more time in the forest. Her grasp on Jimmy's hand tightened, momentarily so strong that he was both heartened and disconcerted: she must have realized she was missing how the children were developing. "Francesca has some pottery to show you when you're better," he said. "It's terrible, but my parents love it. She gave them one that looks like a garden gnome after a bad night. She insists it's Father Christmas. Maybe that's how he looks this time of year.''

He touched her lips—he would have given a great deal just then to see her smile—and then he froze. Suddenly she'd grasped his hand so hard her nails dug between the tendons. She was clinging to him as if she were dragging herself to the surface of consciousness. Her eyelids flickered, and then she gazed straight at him.

She looked more like herself than she had for days. He was starting to smile at her when she managed to speak. ''Up the ladder,'' she said.

''You're all right now, love. The ladder gave way. You're in hospital. Don't try to move too much.''

She tried to shake her head, but winced. ''Up the ladder,'' she repeated in a voice that was already exhausted, and took a breath that obviously hurt her. ''Said,'' she got out, just recognizably, and had to close her eyes and swallow. At last she managed to pronounce ''And the children.''

''I don't understand what you mean,'' Jimmy said. Her eyes were falling closed, her lips drooping. Her hand lost its grip on his as the ward sister came quickly to the bed and took her pulse. ''I should leave her to sleep now,'' the sister said. ''We mustn't rush her. I'll let you know at once if there's any change.''

''She'll be all right, won't she?''

''Bless you, yes. Don't fret yourself. She's making good progress. Time is all it takes.''

All the same, he sat by the bed until after the bells had rung for the end of visiting. What had Tanya been trying to say? How many words had she pronounced only in her mind? Either she was imagining that something had happened up the ladder or too much of her message had failed to reach her lips. He couldn't help brooding over it, so much so that he was barely aware of driving home, of slowing down when he reached Seaward Village, slowing

still more as he came abreast of a man with a mane of hair
as white as the Volvo he was unlocking.

It was Maurice Fox, the science fiction writer. No doubt
he'd been browsing in the antique shops that were multiplying in the village, yet it occurred to Jimmy that Fox
visited Seaward surprisingly often for such a small town.
Fox climbed into the driver's seat and reached to close the
door. That was when he saw Jimmy. His face stiffened,
and he looked away at once.

He'd recognized Jimmy. He must have remembered
seeing him in uniform at the hotel. Why would that bother
him? The white car seemed to brighten as if the sky had
cleared or someone had turned a floodlight on the car.
Jimmy felt as if he were close to an insight that might
solve more problems than he dared hope.

He watched the Volvo turn in his driving mirror and
speed away. Suppose Fox came into Seaward so that his
visits would eventually be taken for granted? Jimmy was
beginning to realize what that might mean as he let himself
into the empty house, the realization growing so bright and
clear in his mind that he hardly felt the aching of the
emptiness.

Chapter XXII

STEVE saw that something was wrong as soon as the widower came out of his father's office. "You do understand how it is, Mr. Innes," the widower said hopefully, and Steve's father gave him a nod and a shrug before closing his door with a firmness that made the man wince. The widower came over to Steve, who was changing the display of photographs in the window. "I did try to explain to your father, Mr. Innes. I've a chance of somewhere smaller and I need to sell my house quickly."

"You're leaving us?"

"I'd have been happy to let both you and the Elsey agency try to sell my house. Only your father pretty well made it clear I had to choose, and in that case I'm afraid it has to be your rivals. I'm buying my new place from them."

"Perhaps they'll let you move in before they've sold your house," Steve said, instantly regretting his sarcasm. He opened the door for the widower, then he went in to

129

see his father, who was tearing the photograph of the widower's house into smaller and smaller pieces. "Carry on if it makes you feel better," Steve's mother said. "It wasn't one of my best pictures anyway."

His father looked up and smiled lopsidedly. "You never change, do you, old girl? Thank God for you, and you as well, Steve. But don't go thinking I'm open to persuasion," he said as she made to speak. "If you want to share with that gang of crooks you can retire me first."

"As if we ever would, Norman. But really, I don't think it helps to lose your temper."

"I've no choice when I think of that mob. Who do you think always voted against taking over the Grand? Mayor Elsey and his cronies, that's who. I know that much from our one friend on the council. Of course they're happy to buy it now they've made us look negligent and they can get it for a song. And of course they'll tell the taxpayers they were just doing their best to save the town some money."

"Maybe they'll find out that people aren't so easily fooled. I don't blame you for feeling this way," Steve said, though he didn't like the hints of paranoia in his father's speech. "Let's hope nobody else wants us to share with the Elseys. By the way, I spoke to Jimmy today and he says Tanya is improving. I know the Elseys have been using people's feelings about what happened at the Grand, but maybe they won't be able to much longer."

"I'm surprised they can bear to let our boards stand next to theirs. You wait, it won't be long before they have people believing they'll sell quicker if they just go with the Elseys. They won't say it straight out, of course. They won't be happy until they see us closed down."

Steve left his mother calming him and went out to finish changing the display. At least it was almost time to close the office, and his father could go home and drink and doze and, Steve hoped, relax. Steve was slipping the last

new photograph into its plastic envelope when he saw
Peter Priest crossing the road.

He stepped back without thinking. He'd made an excuse
when Peter had phoned, he'd told him he would call him
back but never had. He had a good idea what Peter had
meant by saying he knew what was happening to Steve
and why, but he was already troubled enough; it would be
pointless to exhume that business. Peter had caught sight
of him, and he opened the door. "You were going to
phone me," Peter said.

His toupee wasn't quite straight. His eyes looked too
bright, and baggy with shadow. "Life's been hectic,"
Steve said, and found he was stuttering. "You know how
it is."

"Oh, I do, believe me." Peter's mouth began to form
what might have been a wry smile, then gave up. "You
must be nearly closing. We can go for a drink, can we?"

"I haven't time now, Peter. Maybe we can get together
next week."

The brightness in Peter's eyes flickered like distant lightning. "I need to talk," he said.

Steve sensed how desperate he was, and couldn't refuse.
"I'll have to call Maggie."

He barely caught her as she was leaving. "Peter's here
at the office. He wants a chat in private. I'll try not to be
too late."

"No doubt you'll find me waiting," she said, so coldly
that he wished he could ask what was wrong. He couldn't
in front of Peter, especially when Peter looked so nervous.
"I'll see you," he said, and hung up.

The shadowless street smelled dry as sand. Peter led the
way down to the Victoria Hotel, whose windowless bar
was the largest bar in Seaward. Feeble indirect lighting
splayed upward from behind sketchy murals of ships. A
couple who looked surreptitious sat staring at their drinks
in the darkest corner, and Peter glanced at them as though
they had stolen his place. He bought drinks and led Steve

to the other corner that was furthest from the door, and sat with his back to the wall. "How's business?" he said.

Steve felt as if he was missing the point, as if the question wasn't as inappropriate as it seemed. "Pretty much as you've been hearing," he said and then, to get it over with, "You said on the phone you knew what was happening."

"Someone's still defacing your properties."

"Oh, yes, they're having fun, the bastards. I'd love to catch them at it just once. I've been going by the houses at night, but I've never yet seen anyone. Nor have the police, of course."

"Strange to hear you getting so worked up about other people's property," Peter said, avoiding his eyes. "I'd never have thought when we were at school you'd end up working for your father."

"We've all changed, Peter. There'd be something lacking in us if we hadn't. Imagine lubbering about like teenagers all our lives." The laughter he was forcing faltered. "What's wrong?" he said, for Peter's mouth had begun to work.

"You're right, we've changed. You and me and Jimmy and Robin. That's what we didn't take into account, don't you see?" He was staring at Steve so intensely that his eyes began to stream. He glanced about quickly and muttered, "I'm scared."

"Of what? I'll help you if I can."

"Of what's happened and what's going to happen, but that isn't the point, that isn't what I'm trying to tell you. You aren't listening." Peter stared fiercely at him and dabbed his eyes. "Don't you understand what I'm telling you? I'm *scared*."

"Well, to be honest, Peter—"

"Oh, God." He thumped the table with the side of his fist, making the empty ashtray clatter on the black glass top. "I'm scared, you're worried about what's being done

to your properties, Robin's losing her reputation, Jimmy's
lost his wife. See now?''

"I don't think he's quite *lost* Tanya, has he?" Steve had
to clench his teeth before he could get her name out in one
piece. "He hasn't, has he?"

"All right, not lost her. As good as lost her. She'll
never be the same, you'll agree to that." He seemed to
have forgotten that Steve had been involved. "But you see
what I'm saying now, don't you?"

"I'm not sure if I do." Nor was Steve sure if he wanted
to. He might have used Maggie as an excuse to leave, but
he would only brood about Peter's theory, perhaps wish
he'd made Peter explain. Then Peter tried to swallow,
clapped a hand over his crumpled mouth and ran for the
men's room.

The heat seemed to gather about Steve while the air
conditioning creaked above him. A young man with bitten
lips came into the bar and carried a glass of ale to one of
the unoccupied corners. Steve was remembering why he'd
avoided Peter and the others after that business twenty-five
years ago: above all, to avoid conversations like the one he
was having with Peter.

The barman and the surreptitious couple and the new-
comer stared at Peter when he came back, his face splashed
with water. Steve had realized why he felt at a disadvan-
tage: Peter was assuming they both knew what he was
talking about. "You're talking about those forms you
handed out on the common that day," Steve said.

Peter obviously felt that Steve was being deliberately
and cruelly slow. "About what they were supposed to
do," Steve went on.

"They did, Steve. You know they did."

"I knew Gillespie had a stroke and couldn't pick on me
in class any longer, and that was just fine. That was as far
as I ever wanted to think."

Peter sat forward, his eyes and a trickle of water on his

forehead glittering. "Don't tell me you never wondered what the price would be."

"To tell you the truth, Pete, sometimes I wondered if you'd typed the forms and photocopied them yourself."

"My God, how could you think that?"

"Maybe it was the way you seemed so anxious for the rest of us to fill them in, because otherwise yours wouldn't work. I only said I wondered, Pete. I'll admit I did worry sometimes about the price." Momentarily, but disconcertingly, he realized how much easier it was to discuss this with Peter than with Maggie. "But remember, it was supposed to be something of no value to us," he said. "If it wasn't just a series of coincidences that would have happened anyway, if we're seriously arguing that we made them happen by wishing, then I'm sure we must all have paid the price by now and never noticed."

"I used to think that too. You see it now though, don't you?"

"I don't think I do, Pete."

"Christ, can't you give me any help at all? Why are you making it harder for me?" He lowered his voice, for everyone had stared at him; Steve thought the young man with the bitten lips still was, and grinning. "We're paying it now, Steve, all of us."

"Are you talking about what's happening to the properties I'm selling?" Steve was suddenly furious with Peter, since there was nobody else. "Are you trying to make out that's of no value to me?"

"It wasn't when you filled in the form."

Steve opened his mouth and found he had nothing to say. "You didn't care for property, Robin didn't care about her reputation, Jimmy had no time for girls," Peter said. "And people used to go on about how brave I was while all the time I was wishing I hadn't been. And now I'm scared."

Steve discovered that he didn't want to know why. "This is all pretty ingenious, Pete, but I really think—"

"Who do you think called Jimmy's wife into the Grand?"

Steve felt as if he had himself. "I don't know, and I don't see what it has to do with—"

"Nobody called her. Nobody anyone could see. If there had been anyone in there they would have been seen leaving. You must know that, you were the agent for the place."

"You don't need to remind me. Look, if we're talking about ghosts now, I have to tell you that I don't believe in them. I think the supernatural is just something people invent as an excuse for what they do or want to do themselves."

"All right, leave that subject alone," Peter said, so harshly that Steve realized he'd touched Peter's fear without knowing. "We've got to talk about the other thing, the rest of what we signed. You remember, don't you? The price was to be something of no value to us then, and . . ."

He nodded his head for Steve to complete the sentence, glared at him as if Steve were pretending not to remember. At last Peter said resentfully, "And which we may regain."

"Regain how?" With a shock Steve remembered Jimmy's question. It looked as though he was going to have to ask it himself, but first he had another question. "Who's that over there who's watching you?"

Peter screamed—at least, it would have been a scream if his knuckles hadn't dug into his lips and pressed the sound back into his mouth. He stared wildly at the dark corner. Steve saw that, disturbingly, the sight of the young man with the bitten lips came as a relief. "Go away, Roger," Peter muttered. "Leave me alone."

Steve could tell his voice wasn't meant to carry, but apparently the young man heard. "I'll leave you alone," he said loudly, "when you leave my sister alone."

He picked up his glass of beer and made for the table next to theirs. "He's the brother of one of my cases," Peter gabbled in a whisper. "We can't talk in front of him. I'll give you another call and we can meet to talk this out."

By the time he reached the door of the bar he was almost running, having peered about at all the dimmest areas of the room. The young man called Roger left quickly, and Steve sat and gazed at his drink. Eventually he drained it and walked toward the forest, where he found he couldn't think, didn't want to. By the time he came to himself he realized he should have been home hours ago.

Chapter XXIII

AS SOON as Jimmy mentioned Maurice Fox he regretted it, and couldn't think why. There was no question that the writer was involved in something he wouldn't like the police to know about—that much had been clear from his face when he'd recognized Jimmy. He was up to no good in Seaward, and Jimmy was convinced that could mean only one thing: Fox was one of the people Dexter and Deedes were looking for.

It was a matter for them, not for Jimmy, not while he was worrying about Tanya. Never mind that he'd protected Robin from them; people like Fox deserved them, people who were bringing down the price of heroin and the ages of the addicts deserved the worst the law could do to them. If by some chance Fox proved to be a different species of criminal then Dexter and Deedes would find that out too. Jimmy didn't understand why he should feel such a compulsion to investigate Fox himself. Ordinarily he would have followed the investigation through, but not now, not while Tanya filled his mind.

He pointed out to Dexter and Deedes what the computer showed: that Fox had been heavily fined last year for trying to smuggle Thai cannabis back from America. They went down to London to watch Fox's house, and Jimmy was waiting to hear of the arrest when he learned they weren't coming back to Seaward. It had been decided that their lack of progress in the area showed there was none to be made. They were being seconded to Birmingham, and presumably Fox would have to wait.

Jimmy felt frustrated and somehow responsible. Maybe he would take up where they'd left off, once he was sure Tanya was completely out of danger. Irrationally, he felt as if he'd become responsible for her condition too. He made himself hope instead, hope that tonight Tanya would be open-eyed and talkative, that he would be able to take the children to visit her at last.

Helen had brought them home from school and made them toad in the hole for dinner. "Turd in the hole," Francesca giggled, though it looked just like sausages in batter to Jimmy. "Francesca," he said warningly, his nerves tingling with impatience.

She hushed until he began to talk to Helen. "It isn't yummy, it's yuck. Turd in the hole, turd in the hole," she whispered to Russell, who made a face and put down his knife and fork. "He doesn't seem very interested in his dinner. Shall I finish it?" she called.

Both children had been behaving badly since Tanya had been taken into hospital. Jimmy had tried to make allowances, but he wouldn't have her showing him up in front of Helen. "Carry on like that and I won't be taking you to see your mother in hospital," he said.

"Are we going tonight?" Francesca cried, and Russell began to bounce up and down in his chair. "Tonight," he shouted.

"Not tonight," Jimmy said, cursing himself for having been so thoughtless. "Soon."

Francesca looked close to tears. "Oh, when, daddy?"

"I've told you, soon. The very first day mummy's well enough to see you, I promise. Now eat up Helen's lovely dinner like good children and then you can read to me so I can tell mummy how well you're doing."

Francesca read almost a whole chapter of her school library book to him before she began to weep. "You wouldn't really not take us to see mummy, would you? I feel as if I'll never see her again."

"Of course I wouldn't, love. I only said that because you made me angry. I'll ask the doctor at the hospital how soon he thinks you and Russell can go, all right?" He held her and stroked her hair until it was time for him to drive to the hospital. By then he was determined to take the children to visit as soon as he possibly could.

He'd kept them away from the hospital in case they found the sight of Tanya distressing. It hadn't occurred to him that her total absence from their lives might be at least as harmful. He mustn't hope for too much too soon, musn't go in expecting to see her waiting eagerly for him and the children; better to pretend to himself that he expected to see her exactly as she had been last night. All the same, as he parked the car near the hospital gates he couldn't help feeling there had been a change. He hurried through the grounds and ran lightly up the stairs, and had one hand against the lukewarm strip of metal on the door to the ward when he faltered. Tanya wasn't in her bed.

Unless they'd moved her to the bed that was concealed for the moment by a screen, she wasn't in the ward. Whoever was on duty must be behind the screen. He'd wait outside the screen or perhaps ask one of the other patients where Tanya was—not knowing made him feel hollow and fragile, suddenly afraid. He was pushing the door open when a nursing auxiliary tried to slip past him. "Are you looking for someone?" she said.

"Mrs. Waters," he said rapidly. "Where is she?"

For some reason she looked relieved. "She didn't need

to be in this ward any longer. They've moved her to another ward.''

"Which one?"

"I'm not sure. I'm new, you see. They'll tell you at Patient Information. Do you know where that is?''

He thought of insisting that she ask whoever was behind the screen, but he hadn't time to be impatient when he could be seeing how Tanya was. He ran downstairs to the phones in the lobby and grabbed the nearest, drummed his fingers on the plastic ledge in front of him while the phone rang eleven times. "Patient Information," an Asian voice said abruptly. "Can I help you, please?''

"My wife's been moved out of Margaret Thatcher Ward and I want to know where she is now, please. Mrs. Waters.''

"I'm checking for you.'' She seemed to be chatting to someone, at such length that Jimmy let out a loud breath for her to hear. Eventually she came back. "Mrs. Porter, did you say?''

"I said Mrs. Waters.''

"According to our computer it was Mrs. Porter who was moved out of Thatcher Ward this afternoon. She's in Nightingale Ward now. Was your wife transferred here from the Twilight Rest Home?''

"My wife's name is Tanya Waters. She's recovering from an operation for a ruptured spleen. She was injured at the Grand, if that means anything to you.'' Jimmy had begun to thump the shelf with his fist; the wall phone shuddered. "Where is she?''

"Please excuse me one more moment.'' Again the rapid muttered conversation, which her hand over the mouthpiece didn't quite muffle. Jimmy strained to hear but couldn't make out a word. The hand left the mouthpiece, and he heard the thin penetrating notes of a computer keyboard. "You are James Ernest Waters and your wife's names are Tanya Clarissa,'' the Asian voice said.

"Exactly. You've got her now. Where is she?''

"I'm extremely sorry, sir, to have to tell you this. I was hoping we had the name on our information wrong. I'm very much afraid that Mrs. Tanya Waters died half an hour ago."

"No, that can't be right. You must be mistaken." Jimmy let go of the plastic shelf, having realized that he was levering it away from the wall. "I just came from the ward, and they told me she'd been transferred."

"I do apologize, but our computer—" the voice said before he slammed the receiver into its cradle, bruising his fingers, and ran for the stairs. He was halfway up the first staircase when the sister from Margaret Thatcher Ward met him.

As soon as she saw him her face filled with sympathy, and he was suddenly so cold in the midst of the heat that he began to shiver. He held onto the banister and waited for her to speak. "I can't tell you how sorry I am, Mr. Waters," she said. "The girl you spoke to is very new."

"She got the names mixed up."

"It's never happened before in all my years of nursing." She let him glimpse how furious she was. "Will you sit down somewhere? Can I get you anything?"

His eyes felt like cinders. "Can you get me my wife back?"

"I wish I could, Mr. Waters. At least I can tell you it was very peaceful. She started rebleeding, and the transfusions couldn't keep pace. She wasn't conscious at the end."

"Wishing won't help, will it?" Jimmy had the thought, so dreadful that he couldn't swallow, that once it might have. "I don't want to sit down. I don't want anything from this excuse for a hospital or anyone connected with it."

She blinked but didn't respond. "There will be forms to sign, I'm afraid," she said after a while. "They can wait until tomorrow."

"They can wait until I'm good and ready," he said,

feeling ugly and stupid, and turned away blindly, trudged out of the hospital. Forms and wishing, he thought because he couldn't stop himself, and for a moment had the unbearable notion that he'd missed a chance to save Tanya, that he'd failed to notice what it was. He climbed into the car, which seemed hardly real, and drove away, feeling nothing yet but rage—with the hospital, with Tanya for having gone into the Grand that day, with himself for wasting time over the children's squabble when Tanya must have been conscious for the last time. He remembered what he'd said to Francesca, and had to slow down as his hands clutched the wheel. All the rest of the way home he was praying that Helen had put the children to bed, so that he wouldn't have to tell them until tomorrow.

Helen came out of the living room as he closed the front door. One look at her reddening eyes told him the hospital had phoned. He interrupted her before she could speak. "Have you told them?" he said in as low a voice as he could control.

"I haven't said anything, I didn't think you'd want me to, but I think—" She bit her lip and took a step toward him so as not to be overheard, and then Francesca came running out of the room. "Oh, daddy," she cried, "please say it isn't true."

"Oh, Francesca," he said hopelessly, and she burst into tears at once, stood there digging her fingers into her cheeks and her temples so hard that he saw the skin reddening. He went to her and knelt down to hold her. Russell appeared and began sobbing too, though he didn't look as if he knew why. Jimmy hugged the children to him, their heads burrowing under his chin, and felt his cindery eyes flooding. Part of him wished this could go on forever, their embrace and their grief. At least then nothing worse could happen.

Chapter XXIV

"COME ON, Pete," his father said, "and we'll have some fun while your mother makes lunch."

It was Sunday, and hotter than ever. Overhead the sun seemed to expand when you glanced at it, molten metal burning through the blue chrome of the sky. Peter drained the glass of his mother's homemade lemonade and crunched an ice cube as he stood up from his canvas chair in the front garden and followed his father down the slope.

An arc of haze walled in the sea, which looked as slow and metallic as mercury. Children trooped down the steps to the beach. A few families, overdressed for the July day, were heading for church. Peter's father set the pace along the promenade and stopped at all the displays of postcards, slapped his thigh and chortled at the naughtiest, bought one to show Peter's mother. He challenged Peter to a game of pinball on a machine that growled threats in a blurred mechanical voice; he growled back at it while the old lady in the change booth frowned at him and Peter glanced warily at the gamblers pumping the fruit machines. When Peter's turn came he couldn't keep the ball in play for glancing around at the cluttered arcade, the corners that seemed too dim. He was suddenly afraid his father would ask him what was wrong. Apart from Peter's mother, his father was the last person he could tell what he'd done all those years ago.

His father said nothing until they were outside, and then he said casually, "How are you finding living by yourself these days?"

For a moment Peter felt as if his father had seen past his immediate fear and looked deeper. "Oh, much the same as usual, you know," he said with a laugh that he hoped didn't sound like a shake in his voice.

"I don't know if I do know, Pete. How might that be?"

"How would it be? Why do you ask?"

"All right, I won't press you. You've a right to your own life. It's only that your mother has been worried about the way you've seemed lately, and to tell you the truth, so have I."

"I wish I'd known. You shouldn't be worrying yourselves for no reason."

"I hope we are, Pete. Just remember you can always count on us if you have a problem and need to talk to someone." Perhaps he sensed that didn't help, for he turned toward the sea and looked up as if he could see over the haze. "Actually, your mother was saying to me that she'd love to have you come back to us for a while if that would help."

"That's very sweet of her, but . . ." Peter couldn't think what else to say.

"Just for a week or two to see how it worked out. You'd still have your flat to go back to, of course. We wouldn't want you to pay us anything. Think of it as an extra holiday, a prize or something." He was looking anywhere but at Peter. "It might put your mother's mind at rest. You know how women are, making too much of things."

Peter thought of the fear that grabbed him by the stomach every time he went into his flat or from room to room. He thought of lying awake listening for sounds, jerking awake as dreams that didn't seem like dreams came at him, sleeping at last and wakening in the nightmare dark. "Perhaps I could give it a try for her," he said.

"Good man. I knew you'd do it for her." His father was clearly delighted, for all his pretense that they were doing it for Peter's mother. Peter found that he felt enormously relieved. He'd been given a solution he never would have thought of.

"Bernie," his father called as he opened the front door, "what do you think? Pete's agreed to come to us for a while."

"That's lovely." His mother came beaming out of the kitchen, wiping her hands on her Charles and Di apron. "I was wondering where the two of you had got to, but if that's what you were chewing over I'm glad you took your time. Hurry up now," she said to Peter, "I've made your favorite, brisket and Yorkshires."

He stepped into the house as she held out her arms, he hugged her fiercely to get rid of his momentary nervousness. "It'll be like twenty years ago, having you here again," she mumbled into his shoulder. "Just what we need to keep us young."

So long as it wasn't like five years before that. He let her shoo him into the dining room, where he sat holding his breath while his father struggled to open a bottle of red wine from the Lux. The cork popped out as his mother brought the meat on its flowered oval plate. "Give him plenty," she told his father. "We have to make up for all those bachelor dinners."

Could his diet be all that was troubling him? Mrs. Corner left him a meal on the days when she came in to clean, but he hadn't the patience to cook properly for himself. Certainly he'd dealt with people living on their own who ended up hallucinating because of some deficiency in their diet. "More than that," his mother said as she brought in the bowls of vegetables and the tray of little Yorkshire puddings, and Peter made himself a promise to eat as much as he could.

"That's more like it," she said as he set to. "You've been looking like a ghost lately, if you want to know." She must have seen that he didn't, for she went on, "Don't mind me. The shop's on my mind, that's all."

"Why, what's up?"

"Oh, nothing very terrible. Just the way life carries on, I suppose. We don't see so many of our old customers these days, and the new people favor the Lux. We're closing earlier, of course, we like to rest in the evenings now. Well, it's not as if we need the money anymore."

She blinked at him until he looked away from the door to the hall. He couldn't have heard anything, or if he had, it must have been a door upstairs in the adjoining house. "But what would you do if you didn't have the shop?" he said, and piled food into his mouth.

"We thought we might keep it open as a charity shop selling good, cheap, secondhand stuff. Some of the pensioners aren't as fortunate as us. It was you who put us in mind of it, you helping people while we do nothing but sit on our bums all day and wait for customers," she said, and blinked more quickly. "What's wrong?"

He must have heard a door open, for now he'd heard it shut, too quietly to have been audible if it were in the next house. "Is there anyone here besides us?" he blurted.

"Of course there isn't. Don't be saying things like that. My nerves aren't what they used to be."

He tried to calm down, tried to look as if it had just been a misguided attempt at a joke. "What do you think, then?" she said.

"Of your idea? I think you should give it a try if that's what you want to do." He filled his mouth before he realized that she must have wanted his professional opinion whether such a shop was needed locally. All he could do just now was eat, faster and faster, as though that could distract him from the sound of soft uneven footsteps coming slowly down the stairs or even make them cease to be, make them never have existed at all.

He swallowed the last mouthful and put his hand over his mouth to stifle a gasp that must have looked like a belch. "You *were* hungry. I knew you were," his mother said. "Give your plate here if you want seconds."

"No, I'm fine, thanks." He couldn't hear the footsteps now. Perhaps the food had worked, but he felt stuffed and rather sick.

"Well then, what do you think we have for afters?"

It had to be his favorite. "Apple pie and cream," he said as enthusiastically as he could manage.

"You'd be disappointed if I said no, wouldn't you?" She went out smiling and came back with the pie and jug of cream on a tray, returned again with dishes. "Here you are, all for you," she said, serving Peter a wedge. "I'll just clear some of these things away."

"I'll help you." His father followed her into the kitchen, carrying the remains, and either they started washing up or lingered in the kitchen to talk about something—Peter, he suspected. He wanted to go to them, for the room seemed gloomy and cluttered, crowding him so that his breathing grew louder and louder, as if it had nowhere to go. He dug his spoon into the pie in case eating could overcome this feeling too. Two mouthfuls he could barely swallow and then, thank God, the door opened; at least he wouldn't be on his own. But it was his grandmother who came padding into the room.

He tried to push his chair back and dodge out of her way. His head was throbbing wildly, a throbbing that swelled his eyes. He couldn't move, not even his mouth; he wasn't sure he could breathe. This close, and in daylight, there was no doubting she was real.

He heard her long discolored toenails scratching the carpet as she padded to the table and sat down next to him.

Her dull gray eyes seemed hardly capable of seeing him, and now he realized why: they were covered with a thin coating of dust. He knew deep down that she didn't need to be able to see him in order to find him.

He heard her ragged lips part, saw the upper lip leave a fragment of its skin on the lower. What was left of her voice seemed more penetrating than before. "I'll be waiting here for you. I'll be wherever you go."

He managed to look away from the remnant of a face, toward the sounds of his parents in the kitchen, but not for long. "Shall I tell them what you did?" the voice said close to him.

"Yes, tell them." His throat was so tight he could barely speak. "Let them see you."

"You'd like that, wouldn't you? No, you're the one who did it and you've got me all to yourself." She reached most of a hand toward him, and still he couldn't move. "And this won't help you."

Before he realized what she meant to do she had picked up his spoon and lifted a piece of the pie from his dish into her mouth. The mouthful of pie lay on her blackened tongue, cream dribbling from the corners of her lips. She wavered to her feet and leaned her face into his. "I told you you'd pay," she muttered, spattering his face with food. "And you'll go on paying."

He sat helplessly as she padded toward the door. He was praying that his father would come out of the kitchen and see her—God forbid that his mother should. But her footfalls dwindled beyond the door and were gone before his mother rejoined him. "That's the idea," she said, nodding at his plate. "Were you very hungry? You've got some on your face. Just finish up this last little bit." Picking up the spoon, she lifted a piece of pie from his dish to his mouth.

All at once he could move, so quickly that he almost overbalanced the chair and himself. "I think I've eaten too much," he babbled. "I'm just going out for a stroll."

His mother tried not to look hurt. "We'll come with you if you wait a few minutes."

"I mean I have to get home. Not stroll really. I'm on call this weekend," he lied. "I forgot to tell you and I knew you'd already have made lunch," and almost ran out of the house.

He wasn't going home. He ran down the slope to the promenade, praying that he knew what to do. He felt as if his entire body was shrinking from the heat; his head was hottest of all. Once he was past the hotels at the end of the East Promenade he had to stop to be sick in the grass at the edge of the path.

The path led past the church and the graveyard. Further on, where the path sloped down to the seawall, a row of cottages was wobbling. He closed his eyes and stood panting while his dizziness subsided. His body still felt unstable, shaky as his legs, but he swallowed hard and went into the graveyard.

Flowers in vases on the graves stirred in a feeble breeze, headstones gleamed through the haze. Though he hadn't been here for twenty-five years, he knew exactly where to go. He knelt in front of the stone with his grandmother's name, moisture seeping through the knees of his trousers at once. "I'm sorry I wished you dead," he said, and cleared his throat, because he couldn't hear himself. "I killed you, I know that, but I never wanted you to die, I swear to God I didn't. Tell me what you want. Don't just torment me. Whatever you want, if I can do it I will."

"So that's what it's about," Roger said, having tiptoed behind him on the grass, "and you've the cheek to try to tell other people how to behave. Did you tell them you'd killed someone when you went to apply for the job? Special qualification, was it?" He dodged out of reach. "You stay out of our lives or I'll let everyone know what you did."

"There's nothing to know. Try it and see where it gets you." Peter made a grab for him, to force him to shut up once and for all, but Roger danced away like a boxer among the graves, pointed a warning finger at him from the gate and sauntered away toward the town. Peter stared at his grandmother's name and wondered why he no longer felt so nervous. For a moment, as he'd grabbed for Roger, he'd felt capable of regaining his courage all at once. Suddenly it seemed that everything might have a solution after all.

Chapter XXV

MAGGIE and Steve were sitting by the open patio doors. Apart from a distant waspish sound of motorcycles, the forest was as still as the leafy patterns on the furniture. The only sound in the house was the rustle of the Sunday newspapers that Maggie and Steve were reading. Steve finished his and gazed into the forest, watched trees stirring in a breeze that fell short of the house. He played a lazy Sunday game of willing a breeze to reach the curtains, and at last one did, ruffling his paper too. He made to pass Maggie the paper and found she was staring at him. "Have you called her yet?" she said.

He felt caught out, even though he'd been thinking of nothing but the breeze. "Called who?"

"Now who do you think, Steve? How many candidates are there?"

"If you mean Robin Laurel then no, I haven't called her." The hint of a humorless, justified smile on her face made him say, "But since you seem to want me to, I'll do it right now."

She stood up and stepped onto the patio. "Don't go, you can hear what I say," he said, but she threw him a scornful look and stalked into the forest. He was damned if he was going to trail after her while she was being so bloody unreasonable. As he dialed he realized he wanted to talk to Robin more than he'd admitted, even to himself.

"Oh, Steve." She sounded wary. "How are you feeling now?"

"Could be worse, I suppose." He was surprised how shy and awkward he felt. "Actually, if you had the time sometime, I wouldn't mind a chat if you wanted one."

"Do you think I'm really the best person, Steve?"

"Well, yes, I think so," he said, for who else could he tell about his encounter with Peter? Not Jimmy, not when he must still be worrying about Tanya, even though the last Steve had heard she was improving. "You'll understand when you hear what I have to say."

"My mother's at a friend's this afternoon. Come round now if you like." She still sounded dubious. "I know you need to talk."

Maggie was wandering, head down, between the trees. More than ever he wanted to make her say what she felt and why. He ought to call Robin back and say another time, stay with Maggie until she let everything out, screamed at him if that was what she wanted to do. But as he approached her she looked up and said, "You're going to see her then, are you?"

It was no use trying, or so he felt suddenly. He'd do what she seemed to want. "I'll be back for dinner," he said, and could tell she took that as a sly riposte. He backed the car out of the garage and drove to Robin's.

Robin opened the door almost as soon as he rang the bell. He felt an unexpected surge of pleasure at the sight of her, her long legs, her large brown eyes in her lightly freckled face, her features looking even more delicate than he remembered in their frame of cropped dark hair. "You do look good," he said, and took hold of her shoulders gently and kissed her on the cheek.

He felt abashed at once, both because he hadn't quite known what he was going to do and because he sensed that she was holding back from him. He tried to smooth over the awkwardness by asking quickly, "Has Peter been in touch with you?"

"Peter Priest? No, why should he?"

"That's what I wanted to talk about. You really are looking good," he said, having noticed that the corners of her eyes looked pinched by anxiety. This time she smiled at him, but not for long.

She led the way into the living room. "Tell me whatever you want to tell me, Steve."

He would once he'd tried to put them both at their ease. "Who'd have thought I'd be sitting here in your house after the way we used to argue when we were kids?"

"We did, didn't we. We were just trying to find out who we were."

"Did we ever, do you think?"

"We grew up."

She said that as if she wasn't sure it was an answer. It made him think of what Peter had suggested, but that could wait; he was beginning to relax. "Growing up didn't stop us from getting into fights, as I recall," he said.

She was frowning at him. He wondered if she had a notion of the subject he was avoiding and, if so, why it troubled her so much that he was. "Remind me," she said.

"Well, I was thinking of that party we met at when people in Seaward used to have parties. We'd have been twenty, just about, and we'd come home for Christmas, remember? I kept asking you for a dance and getting more pissed every time I asked until you took pity on me. I never wanted to dance except when I was pissed and then either I got the famous Innes stutter or I was too drunk to talk. What a clown I was back then."

"No, you weren't. Nothing of the kind. I wanted to talk to you, I won't say dance with you. You were just about the only person I was glad to see at that party, and I didn't take pity on you at all."

"My God, that was what we started arguing about, wasn't it? You said that then and I wouldn't believe you. Too busy feeling sorry for myself and how I was only pretending to know where I was going." He snorted at himself, though he was disconcerted by the fierceness of her denial, as if she was trying to reassure him on some deeper level about something more immediate. "Didn't you try to calm me down by saying—I remember, that we'd meet when I wasn't so out of it and have a proper talk? Well, here it is if you like, twenty years later."

"I did say that, you're right. In fact, we made a date and I turned up. I expect you forgot or had something better to do."

"My God, we didn't, did we?" Without warning he felt exactly as he'd felt back then: awkward, nervous, dressed in clothes that he knew fitted him but never quite seemed to, haunted by the threat of stuttering. "Robin, I'm sorry. I don't know what to say."

"Really, Steve," she said smiling, "after twenty years I don't think you need to apologize."

"Yes, but I feel terrible. It's not even as if I forgot at the time, if you want to know the truth. The least I can do is tell you now that I've remembered," he said as she smiled and shook her head. "When I sobered up I was nervous about meeting you again. I know it was five years after that business with Peter and his wishing forms, but it still seemed too soon for me," he said, knowing that hadn't been the reason at all.

She opened her mouth as if to change the subject but seemed not to know what to change it to. "You said when you came in that you wanted to talk about Peter."

"About those forms, actually. They seem to have been on his mind lately, along with all sorts of other problems, my impression was." Now he realized that it mightn't be so easy to tell her what Peter had said about her. "Mind you, I think you always took that business more seriously than I did."

"I didn't think any of us should have got involved with it, if that's what you mean."

"I've begun to wonder about that myself, since I had this talk with Peter. Tell me honestly, do you think it worked?"

"I don't know. I've tried not to think about it. I'm just glad it's all over."

A look in her eyes seemed to add: if it is. "Pete doesn't think it is," he said.

"How can he know?"

"It depends on whether you accept his premise. He thinks that when we signed away something of no value to us that meant of no value to us then, when we were kids."

Her eyes were pinching. "I don't see it."

"Well, you know I used to be a Marxist near as damn it, yet here I am selling houses for a living. And you—" He summoned all his tact. "You didn't care what people thought of you—well, none of us did really, that's kids— and more power to you for not caring."

"But now I do care and my reputation's as bad as they come. That's what you're saying."

"That's what Peter said." He hurried on so that at least she wouldn't feel alone in this. "And we're losing customers at the agency—property, you see. And then there's Jimmy who never had any time for girls, you remember, and his wife almost gets killed. Not that I'm trying to shrug off the responsibility for that, mind you, whatever Pete puts it down to."

Infuriatingly, he'd begun to stutter; the sudden change in her expression had unnerved him. It took him time and effort to pronounce "What's wrong?"

"Steve, did you just say that Tanya had almost been killed?"

"As far as I know, yes," he said without stuttering, his chest feeling hollow and cold.

"Steve, I'm sorry. I thought that was what you'd come to talk about and you were taking your time getting to it. She died yesterday evening."

"Oh, Jesus." He felt as if his being had turned stagnant, his eyes staring at Robin but somehow not seeing. Eventually she knelt by him and took one of his hands. "Do you want a drink or anything?" she said.

"No thanks." He squeezed her hand and stood up quickly, shocked that in the midst of his numbness he felt an urge to pull her to him. "I'd better go," he stammered, and hurried to his car. He was out of the baked streets and on the forest road before he realized that there was no way of simply telling Maggie what he'd learned. He didn't realize fully how difficult it would be until he stepped between the patio doors. "Whatever it is," she said, "I don't want to hear."

Chapter XXVI

FOR A LONG TIME after Steve had gone Robin sat gazing in front of her. The more she thought about Peter's theory the more it seemed to fit, but how did it help? Eventually she took a large gin and tonic with her to the kitchen and went on preparing dinner. She wanted to sort out her thoughts before her mother came home.

Could it possibly not be over even after all these years? She remembered her recurring fear of meeting whoever had carried out her wish. At least that had shown her how irrational she was becoming, and in time she'd almost managed to forget, until recently—until she learned that it had been her mother who had carried out her wish.

It was also her mother who was destroying her reputation. That seemed to imply a solution, if she could only think. Assuming she accepted that she was paying now for what she'd wished—and deep in herself, beyond the reach of skepticism, she did—then wasn't there supposed to be a way of regaining what she was losing? Mightn't that be to

talk everything out with her mother, especially since what
her mother had done all those years ago was preying on
her mind? Robin washed her glass and put it away: she
didn't need that, she felt sure of herself. But when her
mother came home her face made it clear that for whatever
reason, she didn't want to speak to Robin. She went
straight upstairs to her room.

She came down to dinner wearing nothing above the
waist except a stole and a bra that exposed most of her
drooping freckled breasts. She glared at Robin over the
soup, pursed her lips when Robin tried to make conversation while carving the leg of lamb. Abruptly she said,
"You want to talk now, do you? Get on with it, then.
Let's hear what you have to say."

"Mother, I've been thinking about that time at the
museum."

"So have I. I wish to God I were still there. I would be
if I didn't have to stay at home and keep an eye on you
because there's nobody else to." She stared hard at Robin.
"Or so you want me to believe."

"I meant that time with Douglas," Robin said, feeling
the knife scrape bone. "You remember."

"Certainly I remember. My mind's as good as yours, in
fact it's better. I've been around longer than you."

"Just listen while I tell you what I've been thinking."
Robin passed her the loaded plate, which she almost
snatched, and began to carve for herself. "You told me
you didn't know what made you push him under the car. I
think I may know."

"How can you? What are you trying to say now?"

"I don't like to admit this, but when I saw the trouble
you were having with Douglas I got involved in—I suppose you'd call it magic. I only wanted to help you. Four
of us made a wish, only there was more to it than just
wishing. Some power was involved, I'm sure of that now,
something that took advantage of us, God knows why. The

point is, everyone's wish came true in some way. And I'd wished Douglas would stop bothering you."

"Why do you keep reminding me of him when you know how it upsets me? What are you trying to do?"

Robin sighed and looked gently at her, trying to soften her mother's look. "I'm saying that you shouldn't feel responsible for what happened to him. If anyone made you do it, I did."

Her mother stared at her for quite some time before she spoke. "I've never heard such rubbish in my life. Dear God, I know what's wrong with you—you've been taking some of these drugs yourself."

"Mother, for God's sake . . ."

"Don't bring God into it. I wish I'd brought you up to believe in him, then you mightn't have been so ready to get mixed up with drugs. You wouldn't if you'd had a proper father. Douglas would have been." Her eyes brightened. "That reminds me. You nearly made me forget what I heard this afternoon, but you haven't succeeded, even if you did do your best to keep the news from me."

Robin laid the carving knife down. She didn't want to hold it, she was growing so tense. "What news do you mean?"

"Don't you know? Haven't you heard? You won't have things your own way for much longer. There'll be someone besides me to keep an eye on you, someone you'll have to take notice of." She selected food with her fork and chewed it slowly. "Your policeman friend's wife died, as if you didn't know. He'll have more time now to keep an eye on you. You'd better give up this drug business before he has to take you into custody."

"Mother, how can you be so—"

"Don't say it. Robin, listen to me." Her voice had softened, her eyes were almost pleading. "I know he'll need time to recover from his loss, but don't let him get away. He's the man for you, I know he is. I saw how he looked at you. Don't make the mistake I made over Douglas. You'd be doing me a favor as well as yourself, it would be such a weight off my mind to know you'd be looked after when I'm gone.''

Robin took a deep breath. "Mother, I know you mean well, but you mustn't say things like that, really you mustn't.''

"I mustn't care what happens to my only child, mustn't I? My concern for you sickens you, does it? I can see that in your face.'' She pushed back her chair so violently that Robin heard the carpet tear. "Some of the things you're mixed up in make *me* sick, if you want to know. I'm not eating this, you might have drugged it, you probably have. I can't trust you anymore," she said, and hobbled upstairs.

Robin stayed at the table and finished her meal, ate as much of her mother's as she had room for. When she relented and went into the hall to see if her mother was hungry, her mother's bedroom door slammed at once, meaningfully. Robin watched television, though she hardly knew what she was watching, until she began to nod, and then she went to bed. She seemed hardly to have fallen asleep when her mother was shaking her shoulder. "Robin, it's dark and the switch doesn't work. Why is it so dark? I'm frightened.''

Robin dragged herself out of sleep and peered at the bedside clock. "It's five past three in the morning, that's why. Do you want me to give you something to help you sleep?''

"And turn me into an addict? Yes, you'd love to do that, wouldn't you?''

"Barbiturates don't, mother. I could get you some of those.''

"You'll do nothing of the kind. And I tell you the bathroom light won't switch off. It's dangerous.''

Robin stumbled after her and found she was pulling the cord that turned on the electricity for the shower. Eventually Robin persuaded her back to bed and crawled back among her own rumpled muggy sheets. She lay awake for almost an hour, having heard her mother say loudly, "I'd like to know what's making me wake up this way."

In the morning Robin groped her way through washing and dressing and breakfast, scalded her mouth with cups of black coffee: at least the pain went some way toward waking her up. Her patients seemed sluggish with the heat, most of them suffering from hay fever except a man who thought he might have herpes and told her bluntly that his wife mustn't know. He proved to have a minor infection of the urinary tract—"so," she said, gazing levelly at him, "I won't need to tell your wife." That made her feel better, and she was about to buzz for the next patient as this one flounced out of her office when Raquel phoned through. "I think you'd better come out here, miss, I mean doctor."

"What's the problem?"

"Your mum."

Robin heard her mother before she reached the waiting room. "I wouldn't ask you if I knew who else to turn to. The police don't seem able to intervene or they don't want to. I can't do anything with her anymore, she's beyond my control. She'll have to mend her ways if you'll just tell her what you think of her, a doctor doing that when she's sworn to help people."

She was talking to everyone in the crowded waiting room. Some of the older people were frowning sympathetically, most of the patients were avoiding her eyes. "Come along, mother," Robin said. "Don't bother these people, they've problems of their own. Come upstairs and see if you can catch up on your sleep. I'll find you something you like on the radio."

Her mother began to shout. "See what she's doing, she's trying to gag me. She's been giving me drugs because I know the truth, she makes me wake up in the middle of the night not knowing where I am. That's what they do to you to brainwash you. Won't any of you stop her? God help me, are you all just going to sit there and watch?"

By the time Robin coaxed her out of the waiting room two women who'd brought their children for treatment had left, looking shaken. Her mother refused to go upstairs, sat instead in the living room, muttering, "They'll have it on their consciences if anything happens to me." Robin dealt with the morning's patients as swiftly as she could, but afternoon surgery was worse: her mother harangued the patients more hysterically, and Raquel sent in word that one couple had asked regretfully to be taken off Robin's list. "Good riddance," her mother was shouting as Robin went in to her, "if that's all the help they can give me," and Robin knew she had to do something drastic: it was either her mother or her patients. No more nonsense about whatever had happened all those years ago; she oughtn't to have let herself be distracted by that—reality was what she had to deal with. She should have realized at once that Peter's explanation made no sense, for if you were supposed to be able to regain what you'd lost, how could Jimmy when Tanya was dead? Surely he had nothing else to lose.

Chapter XXVII

JIMMY wasn't sure if he was right to take the children to the funeral. Russell fidgeted throughout the stately journey in the limousine, pulled at his tie, and complained that his dark suit was too tight. When the limousine coasted into the graveyard he began to count the stones. "Stop that, Russell, daddy doesn't want you doing that now," Francesca said, and Jimmy wished she would think less of his feelings and give in to her own.

His parents had tried to persuade him the children were too young until Francesca had overheard and run to Jimmy to cling, silent and white-faced, to him. Now his mother came over from the second limousine with a brave smile that said she admired him for concealing his grief, and Francesca shrank against him in case his mother intended to take her away from the funeral. "It's all right," he said, and gave his mother's arm a terse squeeze. She needn't worry that he would break down in front of the children. All he felt was a numb dread that Francesca was secretly close to hysteria.

Sounds of car doors echoed through the graveyard. Soon the small chapel was almost full. Jimmy wouldn't have asked for a mass except for Tanya's parents, who were holding each other's hands tightly and looked aged by their grief. Russell murmured along with the funeral music and stared at the coffin. Abruptly he said, "Is mummy in there?"

"Russell," Francesca said in a shocked voice. Jimmy told him yes, which seemed to satisfy him. When the mass began Francesca concentrated on kneeling and rising in time with everyone else, glaring at Russell to make him respond more quickly. Tanya would have wanted the mass, Jimmy thought, if only so that her parents wouldn't feel she had condemned herself by her unbelief. He felt frustrated and distanced, even from the priest's eulogy: this woman who'd apparently devoted the last years of her life to unselfishly sharing her love of the countryside and wildlife with others didn't seem to have much to do with Tanya. Someone sobbed—her mother, he thought—but Francesca was nodding agreement; Russell was actually smiling as he realized who the priest meant. Jimmy had been right to bring them after all.

The curtains glided around the coffin to hide it until it was taken to the crematorium, and without warning Russell started to cry. "I don't want mummy to go in there. She'll get burned. She wasn't naughty."

"Don't worry, Russ, she isn't in there really," Francesca said, and began to cry too. Jimmy squatted and hugged them and fought back his tears until later. His father led Jimmy's mother away to leave them alone, but Tanya's mother came over. "You know where your mummy is, don't you, Francesca? She's in God's house now."

"Where's that?" Russell said tearfully. Jimmy stared at the worn stone floor as Tanya's mother told them she was sure Tanya was in heaven because at the last she must have remembered what she'd been brought up to know was the truth. He could feel the children relaxing. If they

needed to believe that, he wasn't going to argue. Maybe if
they believed hard enough it would come true, maybe if
you clapped your hands to show you believed in fairies the
fairy wouldn't die. He took a breath that stung his nostrils,
to keep back the tears.

The cars and limousines picked up speed on the way to
the Four Smugglers. Jimmy's parents had closed the pub
for the day. Tanya's mother openly disapproved of the
choice of venue, especially when the children began to beg
sips from people's drinks. "Tanya would have wanted
this," Jimmy told her mother, but she stared through him.
"We'll be in touch," her father said, and Jimmy realized
they were leaving.

His mother made her way to him through the gathering,
which was growing noisier. "Are you still going on holiday? Are you sure you shouldn't stay at home?"

"The children are looking forward to going." They'd
both wanted for years to cruise on the Broads, the Norfolk
waterways, and he couldn't take this away from them as
well; at least the holiday wouldn't bring back memories.
All the same, he'd wondered himself if going might simply delay their having to come to terms with their loss. He
was glad when Francesca said on their way home through
the forest, "Are we still going on the boat?"

"We certainly are." He hitched Russell higher in his
arms. The boy had begged to be carried and had gone
immediately to sleep. Jimmy smiled at her to make up for
not being able to hold her hand, but she frowned at him.
"Daddy?"

"Yes, love?"

"Is mummy really in God's house?"

He couldn't lie; he didn't think Tanya would have wanted
him to. "I don't know," he said, and felt Russell stir.
"What do you think?"

"Granny said she was, and she's older than us. She
ought to know."

"Well, then." He carried Russell home, his back ach-

ing, gave the children a hasty lukewarm bath, and put
them to bed. He sat listening to the silence of the house,
feeling a kind of headachy numbness as he tried to see
Tanya in his mind. Somehow it would have seemed like
cheating to look at a photograph of her. Eventually he
went to bed.

During the night he was awakened, surprised and guilty
that he'd slept so well, by Francesca, who was crying in
her sleep. He stroked her head until she quieted, then he
lay awake, alone with a sudden flood of memories, random and piercing: Tanya sitting on the edge of the cliff a
few weeks after they were married, thinking of names for
the children they wanted to have; Tanya riding a horse on
the common, her hair flowing in the sunlight and the wind,
his heart lurching as the horse stumbled; Tanya calming
him down after he'd discovered the children had been
playing cards for pennies with his father—"Maybe they're
too secure," she'd said, "maybe they need a little risk in
their lives now and then." She'd looked hurt when he'd
snapped that his childhood had been one long risk and not
much fun at all. He shouldn't have spoken to her like that,
it wasn't even as if what he'd said had been entirely true,
and all at once he was sobbing breathlessly into the pillow,
clutching the mattress through the sheet until he felt the
foam tear.

In the morning he felt drained. He loaded the car and
left the keys to the house with Helen, then he drove
through the winding lanes to the boatyard. Russell bounced
up and down and clapped his hands at the sight of the
barge on which they were going to spend the next seven
days. Francesca opened her mouth to hush him until Jimmy
put his finger on her lips. It occurred to him that she was
trying to take her mother's place.

An hour later they were on the Broads, and he felt
calmed by steering the craft, by the prospect of a week
taken at five miles an hour, by knowing Francesca wouldn't
let Russell do anything dangerous. The children watched

the stately parade of the banks, windmills and round-towered churches shimmering in the distance, herons standing on their stalks, bitterns raising their beaks straight up so as to blend with the reeds. He'd forgotten there were so many birds, but either they didn't remind the children of the sanctuary where Tanya had worked or they were coping with the memory. He let them stay up late to see the enormous moon hanging low over the flat land like a mask over a stage. He was in bed almost as soon as the children were, and the moored boat rocked them to sleep.

So the week passed. Now and then his eyes blurred with tears; otherwise the week was proving more restorative than he'd dared to hope, except for the way Francesca was nagging Russell. "Don't say I *seen*," she told him, "say I *saw*. . . . Don't say *fowand*, say *found*. . . . He talks like a baby, doesn't he, daddy?"

Jimmy tried his best to be diplomatic, knowing that he was often more lenient with Russell because he was the younger child. All the same, after a few days she had Russell near to tears. "Don't keep on at him, love, let him be for a while," Jimmy said, and that was how Russell was left unsupervised as Jimmy steered the barge into Hickling Broad.

It was the largest of the Broads. Sails looked small as golfing flags between the expanses of still water and blue sky. "I know it's only five feet deep, but don't lean out as far as that," Jimmy told Russell as the boy scanned the banks for coypu.

"Do what daddy tells you," Francesca said, then caught Jimmy's look and turned sullenly away. Jimmy didn't realize she was no longer keeping an eye on Russell until he heard her almost scream the boy's name.

Jimmy whirled. Russell, wearing only his underpants, was poised on the gunwale to jump into the water. He'd turned when Francesca cried out, and was teetering, grabbing at the air. She was running to him, but it was too far. Jimmy moved without thinking. He spun the wheel as hard as he could, his palms sweating as he wondered if he'd spun it the wrong way.

The lurch of the boat flung Russell onto the deck. For a moment Jimmy thought he was badly hurt, but he was only crying with bruising and shock. "What do you think this is, a swimming pool?" Jimmy shouted, running to him. "What on earth were you thinking of?"

"A baby was drowning," Russell said, gulping. "I was going to save him."

"Where?"

"Over there." Russell pointed shakily at a deserted stretch of water. "I heard him. He said Russell."

Jimmy felt drunk with relief. He stumbled back to the wheel, Russell in his arms. "You must have been mistaken, son. He couldn't have known your name, now could he? It must have been a bird or something. Now listen, don't ever try a trick like that again, all right? I know you're a good swimmer, but this isn't the same as a swimming pool."

"Mummy lets me swim in the sea," Russell said, blinking tearfully. "She letted me. She *did*."

"Francesca," Jimmy said as she started to correct Russell's grammar. "The sea on the beach is one thing, Russ, but we could lose you here. We don't want that, do we? You've got to behave like a big boy now. You are one, after all."

"Francesca keeps saying I'm a baby."

"She doesn't mean it, do you, Francesca?"

Eventually she shook her head. "I don't mean it really. I'm sorry, Russ. You're better than I was when I was five."

Jimmy thanked her silently, not least because it wasn't true. "You've both got to be grown up now and help each other and me. I know you miss your mother, and so do I. We can help each other if we always tell each other what we're feeling if we need to, all right?"

"What are you feeling, daddy?" Russell said at once.

"Sad." He'd no idea how honest he should be, but now he couldn't stop. "Worse than sad. I lived for your mother and you. If I didn't have you two I don't know what I'd do."

Both of them took his hands. "You can cry if you like," Russell said. Jimmy managed a smile instead and let them stay with him at the wheel, let them steer when it was safe. Later they watched mist spread over the fields and swell the moon. He felt almost at peace with the children and himself, so long as he didn't wonder if his relationship with them was developing because they no longer had Tanya. He mustn't feel guilty: it was the last thing he would have wished for.

When the children had been put to bed he gazed out for a while at the sea of mist, bitterns booming and bats flapping through the stillness. Once in bed he slept soundly until Russell's wailing awakened him.

He was forcing his sticky eyes open, trying to see by the befogged glow of the night-light what was wrong, when Francesca padded over to Russell's bunk. "What's wrong, Russ?"

"I want mummy. I want her to come back."

"She can't, Russ. She's in God's house."

"Don't want her to stay there. Want to see her."

"You can. I'll show you how." She sat on his bunk and stroked his hair. "Close your eyes and be very quiet and you will. Can you now?"

"No," he said, crying harder, and Jimmy felt as if he'd brought this on with too much honesty. For the moment it seemed best not to let them know he was listening.

"You can get in with me if you like," Francesca said, and let Russell climb first into her bunk. After a few minutes of restlessness—"Mind your elbow, Russ, put your arm round me, ow, you're taking all the room" —there was silence. Then Russell said, "My mouth still feels sad. I don't want to go back to school."

"What, Russ, not ever?"

"Don't want to go back to *that* school."

"Why not?" She sounded as if she already knew.

" 'Cause it's near where mummy was killed and we'll have to see that place every day."

"I know. I don't want to either. I don't even like going home now that mummy isn't there. It doesn't feel like our house anymore."

Silence for a few minutes, and Jimmy couldn't move. "Will daddy take us to live somewhere else?" Russell said.

"I hope he will. I hope we can go and stay with Granny and Grandpa Waters until we've got a new house. Maybe we'll go and live in London. That'd be great, wouldn't it?"

"Yes," Russell squeaked. Their voices were slowing. Just before they drifted off to sleep he mumbled, "I can see mummy now."

In the morning Jimmy announced casually that he was going to look for a position on another police force—not in London, somewhere not too large. His parents would be happy to look after Francesca and Russell while he went for interviews, he knew. If he'd had any doubts about his decision, the light in the children's eyes made up his mind. Their eyes were just as bright when he left the children at the Four Smugglers. As he drove away, he realized that he felt inexplicably relieved. They would be safe with his parents, he thought, and smiled at himself: surely he had no reason to suppose they were in danger.

Chapter XXVIII

FINDING a house for the handicapped children was an achievement Maggie would have been proud of. She offered the lady who ran the children's home a cup of coffee to sip while they sorted out the details. The children should have been holidaying elsewhere on the coast next week, but they'd been let down without warning. Steve's agency had a large house to let above the promenade, a house divided into holiday apartments that hadn't been booked all summer. "My husband has just the place," she said.

"Oh, does your husband let rooms?"

"His estate agency does."

The lady stopped fanning herself with a Seaward brochure and stared at the name plaque on Maggie's desk. "That wouldn't be the agency that was involved in the dreadful tragedy, would it?"

"I'm afraid so."

"Dear me. I wish I'd known before I came all this way." The lady's earnest look gave way to a brilliant professional smile. "Well, Mrs. Innes, I'm sorry we can't do business. It isn't a matter of my feelings, you understand. I'm very much afraid the governors wouldn't approve."

"I may be able to find you somewhere else." Maggie began to leaf through her accommodation files, her face burning, but the lady was already at the door. "I hope things improve for you," she said, and was gone.

Go to hell then, Maggie thought and almost said. She'd been tempted to offer the children something from the Elsey agency, and now she felt ashamed of being tempted, but why should she feel ashamed? Steve and his parents weren't the only ones to be considered, not when her work was affected too. She reached for the phone, then she pushed it away. She and Steve had more to talk about than what had just happened, and it shouldn't be over the phone. She both wanted to know what was troubling Steve so much and was afraid to know.

Of course Tanya's death must still be troubling him. That could explain his sudden silences, his barely concealed anxiety, and yet she suspected him of using Tanya's death as an excuse, a cover for whatever had really been bothering him when he'd come home from Robin's. She couldn't quite believe that he hadn't already known Tanya was dead.

She prowled her office until it was time to close. She walked out of the town hall without noticing people she knew. She drove home through the forest that looked lacquered with sunlight, and as soon as she was in the house her heart began pounding. You needn't say anything, part of her mind tried to persuade her, you can just let things go on as they are, but that was the worst of her options. She poured herself a drink and wandered out through the patio doors, so as not to seem to be waiting, to Steve or to herself. Shade settled over her; she couldn't see the sky. She was gazing into the distance, between trunks that became stems that became matchsticks, when she heard his car in the garage.

She went into the house, not too fast: mustn't seem to be bearing down on him, the wronged wife, the missus with the rolling pin, a woman scorned. She smiled at him, though automatically, but she couldn't keep it up. "Have a good day?" he said.

"Not particularly. In fact, no, not at all."

He gave her a weary look. "Why, what went wrong?"

"Oh, just that I was getting on quite well with someone until she realized who I was."

"Why, what could anyone have against you?"

"Nothing against me personally. I wish we hadn't got onto this, it doesn't matter." He was staring at her with a sympathetic anger that seemed misplaced to her, and so she said, "I meant she realized who I was married to."

"Is that right. Well, I hope you told her where to go."

He busied himself with pouring a Scotch, but she could tell he was hurt; how couldn't he be? She was about to go to him and hold him, even if that made it harder to say what she had to say, when he said, "You should have been at our office if you think *you've* had a bad day. One of our ex-clients as good as accused us of murder, said it to my mother, the sod. That's how low our reputation's sunk."

"Whose reputation?"

"Haven't you been listening? My parents' and mine, who else's? Well, yes, all right, yours too, if you say so."

She was suddenly so furious she didn't know what she might say. "You think more of just about everyone else than you do of me, don't you?"

"Come on, Maggie, that isn't fair."

"What do you know about what's fair? Taking the side of that girl on the switchboard and humiliating me in front of her, do you think that's fair?"

"Christ, Maggie, you're not still carrying on about that, are you?"

"You bet I am, and I bet she is too. I wonder how many of her friends she's giggled with about it. Let me tell you,

Steve, I care about my reputation even if your lady friend doesn't care about hers.''

"Jesus, what's this now? Which lady friend?''

"Oh, Steve, you can't think I'm that stupid.''

"If you mean Robin Laurel she does care about her reputation, very much so.''

"You're owning up then, are you?'' Maggie felt depressed and fearful. "If she cares about it now, that's news. It isn't the way I remember her.''

That made him think, it was clear from his face. There was something about Robin he wasn't telling. Maggie realized how much she'd hoped she was mistaken to suspect him. "Tell me about it, Steve, for God's sake let's have it out or we might as well split up right now. How often do you see her? When you say you go patrolling? What about that time you said you had to meet Peter for some reason you never did get around to telling me?''

"When I go patrolling I'm checking that nobody has defaced any more of our properties. And when I said I had to meet Peter I met Peter. If you don't believe me I don't know what I can do to make you.''

"You'll be telling me next that Peter was mixed up in what you say you did twenty-five years ago.''

"As a matter of fact,'' Steve said, and struggled to the end of the sentence, "he was.''

Probably she wouldn't have believed him even if he hadn't started stuttering, especially since he'd looked away from her. "Can't we talk anymore, Steve? Is it going to be nothing except secrets that I have to fight to get out of you? Why are you seeing her? At least you'll agree I have a right to know that.''

"Maybe because I can talk to her without every fucking word I say being questioned and disbelieved.''

"Maybe you'd better go back to her, then. You certainly don't talk to me.''

"Don't tempt me or I just might leave. I can do without

coming home to this kind of crap on top of everything else I'm trying to cope with."

"If you want to leave, go ahead. You don't need my permission."

"That's what you want, is it?"

"It's what *you* want, Steve. Don't try and put the blame on me."

"All right, fine. Only if you know so much about what I want I wonder why you've been whining about never being told anything, because you don't need to be told, do you?" He thumped down his glass, spattering the sideboard with whisky, and stalked upstairs.

She thought that was all until the next round, that he would sulk for a while before coming down to reopen the argument or try to be reasonable or apologize. When he stumped downstairs a few minutes later she thought he was going to sulk in the woods. But he was carrying a suitcase, so hastily packed that a shirt cuff was protruding from under the lid. He gazed at her, to make certain she knew what he meant to do or to give her the chance to detain him, but didn't seem to like what he saw. "Fuck it," he said, as the old Steve might have. He marched out to his car and drove away toward Seaward.

Maggie closed the garage door that he hadn't bothered to close and stared along the empty road. She felt helplessly furious, overtaken by events, but one thing she wouldn't do was mope around the house. She went in to the phone and thought of calling Robin Laurel to tell her what she thought of her, but there was time enough for that if she felt it would help. Instead she called a girlfriend she hadn't seen for months and arranged to meet her for drinks. Steve wanted his freedom, did he? So did she, then, at least for a while. Maybe that was what was needed to bring them back together.

Chapter XXIX

IT WASN'T until he heard the footsteps that Peter realized he was alone in the office. He was vaguely aware of having agreed to keep an eye on things until the chief social worker came back, but when he looked up from the case report he realized that everyone else was out on cases or at lunch. The footsteps coming upstairs were too slow, and something else was wrong with the sound of shuffling.

He stood up and saw how far away the world beyond the windows was, the summery crowds, the kites above the common, the sea. He tried to move his awkward legs and wondered if he could reach the door before the footsteps did. But the footsteps quickened as they reached the landing, and it was Hilda Marvle who came in.

Eric was with her, a small wiry man in his early twenties, one of the town hall messengers. Of course, that was what had been wrong with the footsteps: there had been more than two, Eric's rubber-soled steps only just audible. "Still enjoying your work, Hilda?" Peter said.

"I like working here. Specially since I met Eric. This is
Eric," she said, tugging at the young man's hand and
making his face redden. "We have our lunches together
now."

"I'm glad to see you're making new friends." Kissing
had slowed them down on the stairs, Peter realized, embarrassed to have guessed so much. "How about your
brother? He's letting you live your own life, is he?"

"It's all right, Mr. Priest, Eric knows all about him."
She tugged Eric until he nodded, his face even redder. "I
just break the connection now when Roger calls."

"I'm sure that's best. I really meant, does he know
you've made friends with Eric?"

"Not yet. We only meet here at work," she said,
looking suddenly coy, chewing her lip with her prominent
teeth.

"He'll have to know sooner or later, don't you think?"

" 'Fraid so."

Her coyness was meant as a plea to him. If Eric was her
first real boyfriend, it wasn't surprising that she felt and
acted clumsy. She must have brought him to Peter in the
hope that Peter would solve their problem. "I'll see what
can be done," Peter said, "though I do think it ought to
come initially from you."

"If you don't do something about him," Eric said
defiantly, "I will."

Peter could tell by the look in his eyes that would mean
violence, the police, more complications. He might have
brought in the police himself to deter Roger, but what
might Roger try to tell them about him? He went to the
Marvles' house instead after lunch.

Nobody answered the door. Perhaps Roger had already
been following him; perhaps Roger was the reason passersby kept glancing behind Peter, though he could never
see anyone there. He called on Mrs. Alden, the lady who
had almost accepted a home help, but she was out too.

He returned to the town hall as they were closing down

the switchboard. Eric was loitering and looking truculent, more so when he heard that Peter had done nothing. "Don't come out with me," Hilda pleaded. "You go out first and I'll wait until you've gone."

"I'll walk out with you if you like," Peter told her.

They watched from the window while Eric tramped away into the crowds. As soon as they came out onto the wide steps of the town hall, Roger met them. "Where is he?" he demanded.

Hilda stood her ground, and he had to fall back a step. "I don't know who you mean."

"I know there's someone. Is he still in there or did he sneak out first?" He shoved between her and Peter. "I always know what you're up to. Where do you do it, behind a desk? I know—in the lavatories. That's where you should go with him."

Peter stepped up beside him. "You aren't achieving anything, Roger. All you're doing is drawing attention to yourself."

"To you, you mean." He grinned fiercely at anyone who was near enough to hear. "You don't want them to know about you, do you? Stay away from him, Hildy, he's dangerous. I told you about his grandmother."

Peter felt trapped and headachy, but he waved her away surreptitiously while Roger was busy with him. "Go on, slink off," Roger snarled at her. "I'll be after you when I've finished with him."

She hurried away in the direction Eric had taken. "Why are you treating her like this, Roger?" Peter said. "You must see that she's growing up. Soon she'll be a match for you if she isn't already."

"You mean if I don't do what you want you'll take her away from us, but just you try."

"That's exactly what I don't mean. It's what I always try to avoid. I've known too many cases where taking someone into care meant just the opposite." Could this be his chance to reason with Roger? "Listen, Roger, I understand how you must feel about what your father did to your sister, but forming a relationship with a man of her choice is what she needs to help her get over that, don't you see? It shows she's beginning to cope.''

"What do you know about it? Nobody can understand her who hasn't lived with her as long as I have. All you've done is make her worse. She hardly tells me anything now. It used to be just us," he said, and looked furious to have let his wistfulness show.

"Good Lord, Roger, who do you think has made her like that if not you?"

He thought Roger was going to punch him in the face. "What do you know about family feeling?" Roger said through his teeth. "We know what you do to *your* relatives.''

"I won't discuss my affairs with you, Roger, and this is hardly the place to discuss anything. I'd like us to agree on a time and place for a proper talk."

"Didn't think I knew she was your grandmother, did you? I went back and looked. Or maybe she told me.''

"All right, if you won't set a date now I'll contact you when you've had time to think." Peter hurried down the steps, a jagged blur that put an edge on his growing headache, but Roger followed him, demanding, "How did you do it? Poisoned her, did you, or pushed her downstairs? Wouldn't she do what you wanted like you want us to?''

When Peter whirled Roger dodged out of reach, then came close. "Go on, hit me so everyone can see, then they'll see you shouldn't be allowed to pry into other people's lives. Your grandmother won't leave you alone and neither will I. I'll make sure she doesn't unless you stop interfering with my sister.''

He didn't know what he was talking about. Peter strained to grasp that through the pounding of his skull. All Roger knew was that Peter was troubled by guilt, and perhaps that was all that was wrong, surely it was. Peter stumbled home, slitting his eyes against the brightness of the streets.

He turned as he slipped the key into the lock: let Roger try
to follow him into the building and he'd call the police. He
was opening his mouth when he heard the voice upstairs.

He pushed the front door open, hoping to prove his fears
wrong. The voice was at the top of the house, but that
need only mean that he'd left the television switched on
last night, had been in too much of a hurry this morning to
notice. They were broadcasting an old song, a record so
worn he could hear the scratches from where he was
standing, a woman singing "Keep right on to the end of
the road," and what was wrong with that? Only that it
sounded more like "Creep right on," and there was a
vindictiveness about the voice that surely oughtn't to be
present. He tried to make his face blank as he realized that
Roger was staring at him.

Roger glanced up from the sight of Peter's distress to
the sound of the voice. He stared again at Peter, and his
jaw dropped. "My God," he said, shocked and delighted.

Peter slammed the door and ran upstairs. Yes, it was the
television, and the clatter of his footsteps drowned whatever the mouth in the midst of a blur was saying now. He
switched off the set and glared about at the sudden silence.

The flat looked cluttered in a way he couldn't quite
define, though he knew Mrs. Corner had been in to clean
and tidy up; he could smell the pie she'd left in the oven
for him. He shook himself together and went into the
kitchen to turn on the gas.

His headache was fading by the time the meal was
ready. He carried the pie and a can of lager to the table
that had been set for him. He'd cut a wedge of the pie and
was lifting the first forkful to his mouth when suddenly,
revoltingly, he wondered if it had been Mrs. Corner who
had made the pie.

Any other notion was both loathsome and ridiculous. He
stared at the dark gravy oozing onto the plate, he thought
of his grandmother spooning food into her dead mouth,
and then he jerked away from the table, his chair falling,
and fled to the window to see if the view would calm him.

He'd thought the growing darkness was how he felt, but it was out there too. Black clouds were piling up from the horizon, waves were chopping up the sea. He looked down and saw Roger watching him across the road. As soon as their eyes met, Roger grinned savagely and pointed behind Peter.

He was pointing at nothing, Peter told himself. He was just trying to make Peter more nervous. Peter forced himself to turn to the dark room, his whole body shaking. There was nothing but the clutter that was scraping about inside his skull. He groped his way to the bathroom and fumbled in the cupboard for aspirin, took as many as he dared and flopped on the bed.

His headache was beginning to shrink when the doorbell rang. He lifted his head carefully, trying not to jar it, and trudged along the hall, made sure of the keys in his pocket, closed the door behind him and held onto the banisters all the way downstairs. He fumbled in the gathering darkness for the latch and dragged at the front door. "Just wanted to tell you she hasn't come out," Roger said at once. "She's still up there with you."

He stepped back just in time. Peter could feel how satisfying it would have been if his punch hadn't missed, feel Roger's nose crushed like a toadstool. He closed the front door with a gentleness that made him feel powerful and went after Roger.

Roger glanced about as he retreated onto the pavement. Beneath the threatening sky the street was deserted. A streetlamp glared like a floodlight on Roger's face, and Peter saw the nervousness his grin was meant to hide. When Peter stepped toward him he made for the promenade.

The street was darker. Either the lamp had gone out or it had been a flash of lightning, though it had seemed too prolonged for lightning. It didn't matter, what it had illuminated was clear in Peter's mind, so clear that he was no longer aware of his headache. Just let him get his hands on Roger and he'd make sure Roger stayed away from him.

By the time they reached the promenade they were almost running.

The grass on the cliff top was drowning in darkness, the hotels gleamed like slate. A few people were hurrying away from the threat of a downpour, heads down, looking hunted. Roger turned on him while there was someone to hear. "Touch me and see what happens," he shouted. "I'll have the law on you." Nobody seemed to notice, even if they could hear him above the roar of wind and sea. Peter lunged at him, and he backed away and ran.

Peter's lungs were straining, his throat was dry from the chase, but he felt exhilarated and reckless and purposeful. The wind tugged at his toupee, made his head feel lighter. He chased Roger beyond the hotels, along the path that led past the graveyard. Roger hesitated there, thinking perhaps of taking refuge in the church. Peter ran at him, driving him past the gates, down the path that sloped now to a row of cottages where the waves were leaping yards above the seawall.

Between the graveyard and the cottages the rain reached the two men, a downpour sweeping across the torn sea, drenching them at once. By the time they came to the stretch of path that divided the seawall from the cottages, Peter could hardly see where he was going. Roger had halted. Peter rubbed his hand over his streaming face, and saw why.

A hundred yards or so beyond the cottages the path was flooded. Wave after wave rushed further inland, uprooting grass from the mud. There was no way to go except back. Roger glanced toward the cottages as if he was hoping that someone could see him, but all the lit windows were curtained. He backed into the light of the nearest streetlamp. "What do you want?" he cried, his voice thin in the wind. "What are you chasing me for?"

"Just to make sure you stop bothering me. You'll stop now," Peter said calmly and clearly, "won't you?"

"When you leave my sister alone I will and not before."

Either the light was brightening or Peter's senses were, for he was suddenly aware of everything around him: the rain drawn tight as wire through the halo of the streetlamp, Roger's beaded face white as enamel in the light, a wave that leapt up glittering beyond the seawall, the next waves gathering themselves, his body balancing itself in readiness. He'd given Roger a chance, after all. He ran straight at Roger and shoved him off balance, into the dark.

For a moment Roger only looked ready to fight. When the eroded wall struck the back of his knees his expression seemed to cave in. He screamed and flailed his arms as Peter felt him reeling backward. Peter's hands wanted to close on Roger's sodden lapels, drag him to safety; Roger was scared, after all—he knew now what Peter was capable of, he'd leave him alone in future. But Peter thought he would do nothing of the kind. He opened his hands and thumped his palms against Roger's chest, felt the drenched cloth of Roger's jacket squelch as he pushed as hard as he could.

Roger seemed to take so long to fall, grabbing desperately at the air, that Peter felt suffocated by being unable to breathe. As soon as Roger hit the water a wave flung him against the seawall, then the sea dragged him out into the dark. Even if there had been anything for him to grab except weeds on the wall where he'd struck it, the impact had broken his right arm.

As soon as Peter saw the arm forced back over Roger's shoulder, thought how the bone must be tearing through the skin inside the sleeve, he couldn't bear it. He ran for the nearest of the life belts that hung beside each streetlamp. He had to knuckle rain out of his eyes before he was able to make out that the iron brackets were empty. The belt had been stolen or flung into the sea.

He ran back to the wall, almost losing his balance on the drenched path. Roger was screaming for help, but the sea kept cutting off his screams. Another wave rushed in, and Peter heard him smash against the wall. The screams stopped at once.

Peter made himself look down. Roger's limp body was bobbing away alongside the wall, his scalp leaking, a stain that Peter could just make out was red. Peter lurched backward, slithering on the path. It was over, there was nothing he could do. He felt oddly calm and guiltless until he turned toward the lamp and saw the woman watching him.

She was standing under a golf umbrella just inside the garden of one of the cottages. "What are you up to? Chucking the life belts away, were you?" she demanded. "Come into the light so I can see you."

He made himself step forward, thinking frantically: mustn't run away, mustn't seem guilty, she didn't see anything. "Some money of mine blew away," he blurted. "I was trying to catch it. That belt there was already gone."

She lifted the umbrella and peered at him. "True enough, it was. Sorry if I startled you. You're welcome to shelter if you like."

Behind him he thought he heard something thump the seawall. It sounded softer now. "I'd better get home, thanks," he said, his stomach writhing.

"Just as you like." As he turned away she muttered, "Funny sort of evening to go out for a stroll."

He wanted to make sure Roger was gone, but she watched him until he had to make for the promenade. Suppose she was still suspicious? Suppose she described Peter to the police? He needn't worry, he realized, and turned his face up to the rain. They might not find Roger for days or even weeks, and they would have no reason to connect Peter with his death: the way the sea was now, it was impossible that Roger would be found anywhere near the cottages.

Chapter XXX

THE FIRST TIME the police brought Robin's mother home they were kindly and sympathetic. "Here's your daughter, Mrs. Laurel," the large slow policeman said. "See, she was wondering where you'd got to. She isn't such a bad sort after all." Robin's mother glared at him and limped heavily upstairs, and Robin wondered if she was eavesdropping as the policeman said, "She's been telling us tales about you. Don't worry, we can see she's confused."

Presumably most people could, even those who'd asked to be transferred from Robin's list, or were they afraid there might be some truth to her mother's accusations? They couldn't think much of Robin anymore if they preferred to go to Dr. Fenner for a dose of impatience and bad temper. Her mother viewed each transfer as both a personal triumph and a condemnation of the patients. "If that's all the loyalty they can show they weren't worth having anyway."

Now she was plaguing the police as well as Robin's

patients. The second time she was escorted home the large policeman wagged a finger at her. "You mustn't be telling stories like that about your daughter, my dear. Take it from me, we've no reason to suspect her of anything."

When he brought her home from trying to convince visitors to the police station that the police were in league with Robin and peddling drugs, he was much firmer. "We know she's confused, but we'll have to ask you to keep her under control. You're a doctor, you know what to do."

That wasn't the same as being able to do it; didn't he know the law? People couldn't be put away just because they were senile, especially when, in Seaward as everywhere else in the country, their numbers were growing. They couldn't be put away against their will, less and less so, given the changes in the law. There were tranquilizers that could help, properly administered, but that too meant residential care, a course Robin's mother wouldn't .even consider. "I can look after myself," she said fiercely, unaware that meant Robin could look after her.

Robin tried to persuade her at least to visit a rest home to see that it was nothing like a prison or a mental hospital, but it was no use. Once she lured her mother into the car on the pretext of taking her for a drive. They hadn't left Seaward when her mother began to fumble with the door release. "I know where you're taking me. Let me out or I'll jump out, I swear to God I will." Robin drove them back home, feeling caught and desperate—but that evening Mrs. Starr phoned.

Mrs. Starr was in a home in Seaward now. Robin braced herself for another diatribe when her mother put down the phone, then saw that her mother was beaming. "Mrs. Starr's out of hospital, Robin. She's living with Mrs. Fletcher now, who used to play chess with me, remember? They want me to go over on Sunday. Perhaps you could walk there with me. Keep you out of mischief."

On Sunday afternoon a wind from the sea carried music

up from the bandstand on the promenade and set the forest swaying. "What a lovely day," Robin's mother said as they strolled across town to the East Fork. "Listen to the band. We ought to go out for a walk every Sunday when it's like this." They once had, Robin thought, and felt as if she wasn't entitled to the memory when she was planning to delude her mother.

Her face grew hot as they reached the East Fork. At the foot of a street that sloped toward the promenade she could see the Paradise Rest Home—could see not only the large white four-story house, but also the name on the signboard just inside the hedge. Surely her mother couldn't miss seeing that, except that she was busy searching for the numbers on the gates. By the time she was close enough to be sure which house it was the words *rest home* were obscured by the hedge. "What a grand place. I wonder how they can afford it," she said.

A young woman wearing a checked overall answered the door. "The Misses Laurel to see Mrs. Starr and Mrs. Fletcher," Robin's mother said pleasantly but briskly. When the nurse had shown them into a high, bright, spacious lounge to wait, Robin's mother murmured, "A housemaid too. They must be well off."

Robin nodded, swallowing the truth. "It has everything, doesn't it," she said, glancing about at the large television, the nest of tables with inlaid board games, a glass-fronted bookcase full of tasteful bindings. Her mother was surveying the room when the nurse returned to usher them into the garden.

"Emily Laurel, what a surprise. Do you know," Mrs. Starr cried, "we didn't think you'd come." Robin clenched her fists behind her back, sure that Mrs. Starr had told her mother where she was, but her mother was smiling, hurrying forward to take her friends' hands. "It's delightful to see you," Mrs. Fletcher said, levering herself forward with a stick. "I can't remember who won our last tournament, but it'll be jolly to have someone to play with again."

The women were alone in the wide garden with its rustic chairs. That was lucky, Robin thought—lucky there was nobody about who would need explaining. Another nurse brought tea and triangular sandwiches on a tray. "So, Emily," Mrs. Fletcher said as they sipped their second cup. "How do you like our new home?"

"Most impressive. You must be very pleased with yourselves."

"And you see how they look after us," Mrs. Starr said. "Do you want to come and see my lovely room?"

"I'd better, hadn't I?"

"Don't you dare visit hers without visiting mine," Mrs. Fletcher said, and hobbled upstairs with them. Robin gazed up at the house and wondered if everything had been solved, if it could really be so simple. Why not? Even if a problem seemed impossible, there was always luck; life didn't pass you by forever—few people, anyway. She looked down as glass flashed in her eyes.

A gray-haired man was opening the French windows of his office. She went quickly to him, for fear of being overheard. He waited, and kept his voice low. "You're Dr. Laurel, aren't you?"

She hadn't realized how unused she'd grown to being asked that without feeling condemned. "Yes, I am."

"Is your mother thinking of coming to us?"

"She's just visiting her friends today."

"But you hope . . ." He placed a pair of armless glasses on his nose to gaze at her. "I gather you're letting her grow fond of our home before informing her what kind of place it is."

"You don't mind, do you?"

"I'm sure you know best what line to take with her. We do have space at the moment, so long as you let us know before too long. Ah, I think I hear the ladies on the stairs."

He closed the windows and stepped back out of sight as Robin busied herself with clearing the cups and plates onto the tray. The two women helped Mrs. Fletcher into the garden, and Mrs. Starr said, "How are you finding life where you are these days, Emily?"

"Oh, Robin and I have our differences now and then. People do when they're as close as we are, you know."

"I expect you must feel in the way sometimes. We all do at our age. Mrs. F. and I were saying just this morning how nice it would be if you came to live with us."

Robin held her breath. After a pause her mother said, "I'll have to think about that and let you know."

Robin let her breath out slowly, enjoying the sensation of release. Her mother had liked the home and the company, then. Perhaps she even knew what kind of place it was, if Robin dared to hope so much. Robin mustn't say anything, must wait for her mother to speak. But her mother was silent as she toiled up the street to the East Fork. At the corner she turned to Robin. "Well?"

"Well yourself," Robin said, not sure what her mother's tone was.

"Yes, I'm well, despite all your efforts. Yours and the efforts of my so-called friends. You and your cronies in the police force got to them, did you? Told them to pretend that was their house, did you? Don't treat me as though I were as susceptible as you, you'll get nowhere. I knew it was a rest home the moment you started going on about how good it was."

Robin glared at passersby who'd turned to watch. She didn't trust herself to speak to her mother; she walked away fast instead. Her mother limped after her. "Don't you try to lose me. Don't you ever try to get me into one of those places again. I'll kill myself first," she threatened, and before Robin could stop herself she thought: I wish to God you would.

Chapter XXXI

SUNLIGHT through Peter's bedroom curtains wakened him. He drew the curtains and gazed out at the path of light on the sea, and remembered what he'd done to Roger. He thought of Hilda and felt no guilt at all; why, he'd even tried to save Roger—it wasn't as if he could swim. He strode through his flat to the bathroom, feeling refreshed and clearheaded and ready for anything, and realized that he was no longer afraid who he might encounter in the empty rooms.

He'd regained his courage. More, he felt sure that his grandmother would leave him alone now. He'd visit her grave, he promised himself, to keep it tidy and to give thanks for having had the chance to regain what he'd signed away. He could move in with his parents for a while, to make it up to his mother for having upset her by fleeing the house. He ought to meet Steve again, Steve and the others, in case he could learn what they had to do in order to regain what they'd lost. Maybe he could encourage them to do so, without betraying what he'd done, of course. The future seemed primed with possibilities.

He made his way to the town hall through the August streets. He restrained himself from looking in on Hilda: best to wait until she approached him. Some of his colleagues looked surprised he was so jovial today. He sorted through the paperwork on his desk. Nothing was urgent, and he went to see if Mrs. Alden was at home.

Perhaps she'd forgotten their previous meeting, for she seemed almost glad to see him. Her flat was more cluttered than ever, but that didn't bother him. "I need help with putting things in order," she said. "A home help could do that, couldn't she, if I told her what to do? Just remember nobody must know that's what she is."

He was at the door when she said, "Did someone come in with you?"

It felt like a test, and he didn't flinch. "No."

"That's all right then. I just wanted to make sure."

He strolled back to the office, realizing that people were staring at him because he was smiling so broadly. He arranged for a home help to call at Mrs. Alden's, and wondered if he should phone Steve Innes, arrange to meet him for a lunchtime drink. He was dialing when he heard Hilda say "There he is" behind him. He turned and found she'd brought the police to him.

He drew a long surreptitious breath to make his heart stop pounding. Nobody could know what had happened to Roger, there had been no witnesses. He juggled the telephone receiver, which had turned cumbersome and meaningless, and fumbled it onto its rest as he gazed straight into the policeman's close-set eyes. "Mr. Priest," Hilda pleaded, "do you know where my brother is?"

Her anxiety was disconcerting, but he mustn't let it throw him. "I haven't seen him since last Friday."

He hadn't realized how easy it would be to face the police; he hardly even needed to lie. "What time would that have been?" the policeman said.

"Let's see. He was waiting for Hilda when we left here after work. Ten past five or so, that would have been. He followed me home—as a matter of fact, I encouraged him to follow me so as to give Hilda a break. You went after your boyfriend, did you, Hilda?"

"Yes." Her voice wasn't quite steady. "I wish I hadn't now."

"We don't know that anything has happened to your brother," the policeman said. "He may have stayed away from home deliberately to make you anxious. Would you say that's a possibility, Mr. Priest?"

Peter disliked giving her false hope, was disturbed that she needed to be reassured about Roger, but what else could he do? "It might be, yes."

"Just when and where did you leave him?"

"As I say, he followed me home and I left him outside. That must have been half past five, give or take a few minutes."

"And you haven't seen him since?" When Peter shook his head the policeman went on, "Can you think of anything you might have said to make him behave like this? It's apparently the first time in his life he has."

"Well, I did say—" Peter searched for a likely answer. "I did say we might have to consider bringing an injunction against him if he didn't stop harassing his sister."

"Oh, why did you say that?" Hilda was clutching handfuls of her dress, jerking at them. "I'd give Eric up if it meant Roger would come home. I can't bear to think I made him do something stupid."

"I don't think we need to assume anything just yet along those lines," the policeman said, and Peter made a sound of agreement—couldn't bring himself to lie more explicitly while Hilda's eyes were pleading with him. "I'll let you know how our enquiries progress," the policeman told him, and ushered Hilda away, leaving Peter wondering how he could help her now.

He'd have to take it gently, he told himself as he strolled beyond the East Promenade with a wreath in his arms. Children shouted at the subdued waves at the foot of the cliff. Up here on the path to the churchyard it was peaceful, almost cool. He had to guide Hilda toward the possibility that she might not see Roger again, and make sure above all that she didn't feel responsible. However unexpected her longing for Roger was, it would surely be easier to deal with than Roger himself. Peter felt calm as he stepped into the graveyard, and so he didn't start as the old lady grasped his arm.

Perhaps she was one of his cases; her grasp felt urgent enough. The sun was in his eyes, and at first he couldn't see her face clearly, had time to tell himself that he was mistaking what he thought he saw. He lowered his head, his scalp burning under the toupee, and saw how dusty her eyes were now. Perhaps there was nothing but lumps of dust in the sockets.

He was shuddering so violently that he couldn't even pull free of the tattered grasp on his arm when she opened her crawling mouth. "You can't get rid of me that easily," she said in a voice that came and went like the wind. "It's only just begun."

Chapter XXXII

THE LAKELAND TOWN was even quieter than Jimmy had hoped it would be. Climbers surmounted by rucksacks tramped through the narrow cobbled streets toward the mountains. Francesca and Russell could go walking on the heights, he thought, a change from the Norfolk sameness. Or at least they could have, he thought later, leaning on the parapet of one of the bridges over the river that threaded the town, if there had been less competition at the interview for the post on the local police force. He wouldn't need the official letter to tell him he had been passed over for the job.

He should have realized that the police forces away from the major cities would be heavily competed for. He couldn't blame his rivals for feeling as he did; perhaps they had children too and wanted to keep them away from heroin in the schoolyards, violence in the streets. All the same, he hadn't realized how much better qualified his rivals would be at any of the interviews he was going for.

He drove into Norfolk next morning, through fields that brightened as the mist retreated toward distant cut-out pastel trees. His record was unblemished, but that wasn't enough. His career was decent, solid, the rise of a dependable policeman in a small quiet town, and quite undistinguished: no more arrests than average and none that stood out, nothing to show in the way of special aptitude for detection or organization, because Seaward had never given him the chance. Never mind that the officers who succeeded at the interviews would probably be overqualified for the work they would have to do. If only he had just one spectacular arrest, one headline achievement to show!

He let himself into his empty house and went through all the rooms, checking that none of the doors and windows had been tampered with. Of course nobody had got in—if any house in Seaward was burglarproof, Jimmy's was—but patrolling took his mind off the emptiness, a little. All the same, he was glad when the doorbell rang.

It was Henry, Helen's boyfriend. His large, square, ruddy face looked even bushier than the last time Jimmy had seen him, more red hairs than ever poking out of his nose and ears. "We were wondering when you'll be needing a baby-sitter."

"Not for a while, Henry, if at all. The kids are staying with my parents."

Henry looked downcast, so far as the expression beyond the beard and bristling moustache was visible. He and Helen were saving up to get married. "Come in for a minute," Jimmy said, welcoming company, and thought he glimpsed relief in Henry's eyes.

Perhaps Henry wanted a private talk. Jimmy went into the kitchen to pour them both a Scotch, and came back to find him loitering just inside the living room. He perched on the edge of the chair opposite Jimmy's and looked as if he would rather be pacing. "So, Henry," Jimmy said. "How's work?"

"All right, except I get fed up running fares to the

station and back all the time. When she goes to college I want to get the knowledge to drive a cab in London so we can live there.''

''The best of luck to you both.''

Henry raised his glass abruptly and drained it. ''Didn't you like the Broads?''

''Yes, I think they were what we needed. Why do you ask?''

''Helen said you came home a day early.''

''Only to get the kids settled with my parents before I went off looking for jobs.''

Henry bent to tie his shoelace, though it looked secure enough. ''You mean you're moving?''

''I hope to. Seems we all have the same thought.''

''What, soon?''

''As soon as I get promotion or a transfer.''

Henry looked up, leaving the bow of his shoelace more uneven than it had been. ''We thought you might have been ill on holiday, one of you, I thought you might have and that's why you came back early. I've got a bit of a germ myself.''

''Sorry to hear it. Hope the Scotch helps.''

''Yes.'' Henry stood up so quickly that Jimmy's neck twinged. ''You don't mind if I just run upstairs to your bathroom, do you?''

It seemed as trivial a request as it was reasonable, yet Jimmy's instincts told him no. ''I wouldn't mind at all, except something's up with the plumbing. Just nip round to Helen's and then come back if you like.''

''I better had, then.'' He halted, scratching his eyebrows loudly, in the doorway to the hall. ''I used to help my dad when he was a plumber. I'll just have a look and tell you what's wrong.''

''It's all right, Henry, I've already called someone.'' Jimmy saw him out, then he hurried upstairs.

He could see nothing suspect in the bathroom. He lifted the lid of the cistern and unscrewed the panels that boxed

in the bath. Securing the panels again was more difficult,
and left him sweating. He squatted back on his haunches,
then he went to search his bedroom.

That held nothing unexpected either except, at the back
of an empty drawer, a pair of Tanya's panties. Apart from
her jewelry, which he'd kept for Francesca to have when
she was older, he'd asked Helen to dispose of her belong-
ings as she saw fit, anywhere but Seaward. He gazed at
the panties, heard the silence of the house, remembered
how sex had mellowed for Tanya and himself once he'd
had his vasectomy, felt his chest tightening. He closed the
drawer gently and continued searching.

The spare room took longest: suitcases and boxes to
open, furniture to look behind, all to no avail. He was hot
and frustrated as he made for the children's room. He'd
been grateful to Helen for tidying it while they were on the
Broads, but now he was suspicious. He began to take toys
out of the cupboard. What was the package in the corner, a
package wrapped in silver foil?

He lay on the carpet, his shoulder bruising itself against
the edge of a floorboard Russell had jumped on too often,
and fished out the package. It was small and rectangular.
He unwrapped the foil and found the empty carton from a
cake of Tanya's perfumed soap. Francesca had wrapped up
the carton when she was giving her dolls a birthday party.

He lay on his stomach and tried to think. Henry had
been up to something. Jimmy had met too many people
who were trying to deceive him to be taken in now. He
shoved himself to his feet and went down to the garage.

The stepladder had been moved. Nothing suspicious
about that—except that whoever had moved it had tried to
make it appear that the ladder hadn't been touched, had
banked up oily grit against the foot of the ladder. Next
door Henry and Helen were arguing, but Jimmy couldn't
distinguish any words. He hefted the ladder and carried it
to the bathroom, brought a flashlight from the garage and
climbed to the loft.

How would Henry have climbed up if Jimmy had let him reach the bathroom? By standing on the sink, perhaps, however awkward that would have been. Jimmy was sure now that he knew where to look: behind the water tank. He poked the flashlight beam back there, sweeping the bulky shadow away. There was nothing but the roof, sloping to the felted floor.

He almost gave up in disgust then. He swung the beam perfunctorily around the edges of the floor, and then he brought it back to the farthest corner. Why was the felt raised there? He picked his way across the fattened floor, stepping from joist to joist, and peeled back the insulation.

The glare was so fierce he had to blink. The flashlight beam was glaring back at him from a foil-wrapped package that had been hidden under the insulation. He had the impression of a floodlight shining straight into his brain. He was about to unwrap the package when the doorbell rang downstairs.

He let himself down one-handed onto the ladder—the package was too big to fit into any of his pockets—and hurried to the living room, where he hid the package behind the cushion on his chair. He already knew who'd rung the bell. "Could I speak to you, Mr. Waters?" Helen said.

"I don't see why not. Come in." It was years since she'd called him Mr. Waters. He sat on his chair, hearing foil crinkle, and gazed blankly at her. "What can I do for you, Helen?"

Her hands were gripping each other in the lap of her striped cotton dress. "It's really for Henry, Mr. Waters."

"In that case he really should ask me himself, shouldn't he?"

"I told him that. He won't. Only it was my idea to come to you."

"What's it about then, Helen?"

"It's someone he got mixed up with while he was driving. Someone who kept making the same journey until

Henry wondered why. I told him he ought to tell you, but he wouldn't. I swear that's all I knew until just now. I didn't know," she said, her eyes blazing, "that there was someone else involved, someone who said he'd pay Henry real money for driving."

"Sounds ominous to me. So what did Henry say to him?"

"I don't know what he said, but he just told me what he did. He helped them deliver drugs, Mr. Waters, and I never even suspected. I thought I'd made sure he stayed away."

"What kind of drugs, Helen?"

"What they call hash."

"It could be worse," Jimmy said heavily, then wondered if it was. "Do you mean he was making these deliveries while my children were in the car?"

"He says not. I thought of that too. He wouldn't be able to walk now if I thought he had."

"I suppose not. Well, Helen, what are you expecting me to do?"

She pressed her lips together, apparently to keep them under control. "I haven't told you the worst yet. They paid him partly in money and partly in kind, to make sure he kept his mouth shut, of course, only the silly fool didn't realize. And he hid what they gave him—he hid it in your house while you were away. I know where it is. I'll show you."

"Just tell me," Jimmy said, and when she did, "So that's why he didn't like it when we came home early."

"He said he'd check the house for me, save my legs. I ought to kill him."

"That's against the law." He didn't smile. "Is he next door?"

"Yes, that's where he's lurking."

"Then I think you'd better tell him I want to see him."

While waiting he took out the package and peeled back a corner of the foil. The resin was moist and smelled very strong. He left the package on the sideboard for Henry to notice when Helen drove him into the room, his face sheepish and resentful. Eventually Jimmy said, "Well, Henry, what have you to say for yourself?"

Apparently nothing, even when Helen nudged him hard. "Let's forget for the moment that I'm a policeman," Jimmy said. "It's not the way you used my home I find hardest to forgive, or even the way you used Helen. I'm talking about how you took advantage of my wife's death."

He stood up before he knew he meant to, bulking over Henry, but it was Helen who shrank back. She must sense what he felt capable of doing to Henry, who looked as if he would offer no resistance. Jimmy sat down, breathing heavily. "What in God's name got into you, Henry? Aren't you earning enough at an honest job?"

Henry shrugged and glared at Helen when she nudged him harder. "That's exactly what I said to him," she said with a fierceness that was close to tears.

"You know why," Henry tried to take her hand, but she snatched it away. "We won't have much money when you go to college," he said, then seemed to realize how the future had changed. "We wouldn't have."

"I'd rather starve than think you were a criminal."

Jimmy cleared his throat. "I'm afraid you haven't much choice, Helen."

"He won't have to go to prison, Mr. Waters, will he? He didn't actually sell any drugs himself."

"You meant to though, didn't you?" Jimmy waited until Henry had to meet his eyes. "At Helen's college, am I right?"

Helen saw he was, and kicked Henry on the ankle. "That's for even thinking of it."

"Whether or not you go to prison, Henry, may depend on how much information you can give us."

"Mr. Waters means who paid you to drive. Tell him, Henry. He's giving you a chance, more than you deserve."

"I daren't. He said you'd get hurt if I ever told. He did, Mr. Waters, I swear."

"All the more reason for you to help put him away," Jimmy said. "Would it make a difference if I told you I might know who he is?"

"Go on," Helen said furiously to Henry, who mumbled, "I don't know."

"You don't know who he is," Jimmy said, "or you don't know if it would make a difference?"

Henry let his head slump into his hands. "If it'd make the difference."

"Don't you dare play for sympathy here in my house after what you did." Jimmy had to make himself stay seated. "Do you realize how long you can spend in prison just for possession with intent to supply? And how do I know you haven't been supplying it already, just because you say you haven't been? Don't expect me to tell the judge I think you haven't."

"If I tell you who he is—"

"Don't even think of trying to bargain with me. If it weren't for Helen I wouldn't be giving you this chance. Now, answer me a question or get out of my house. Does he often come into town, your generous friend?"

Henry muttered something. "I can't hear you," Jimmy said sharply.

"Yes."

"But you never drive him."

Henry blinked; perhaps he'd thought Jimmy was bluffing. "No, never."

"Maybe you've seen his car, though? A white Volvo, could it be?"

Henry raised his head and stared into Jimmy's eyes with an expression Jimmy couldn't read. "That's right," he said.

"I'm going to say a name. Helen, I want you to forget you ever heard it. Maurice Fox."

Henry was still for a moment, then he nodded. "Can I believe you?" Jimmy said.

"Look, you knew already, didn't you? You didn't need me to tell you. I'll swear it by anything you like in front of you here now if that's what you want, but I won't in court. His friends would come after us, after her."

"Any way you look at it, your marriage is off to a poor start. If it isn't prison it'll be a hefty fine. If Helen weren't associated with you she'd be in no danger, it seems to me."

"I won't leave him, especially not now." Helen's face was white with determination, her lower lip was jerking. "He may be stupid but he isn't evil. If I'd known what was going on it wouldn't have got this far, not nearly. It's partly my fault for not trying to find out. When he's paid I'll make sure he never does anything like it again, I promise you."

Jimmy believed her. "If I agreed to let him go on that understanding," he said carefully, "would you both swear never to tell anyone what he did or what I did for him?"

Her eyes widened. "Oh, Mr. Waters . . ."

"If this ever got out it would be the end of my career. Do you both swear?"

"Oh, yes, I swear," Helen cried, and pinched Henry's arm when at first he didn't echo her vehemently enough.

"You know what will happen to you if you forget, Henry. Get out now before I change my mind." Jimmy saw them out and went back to the living room, which was even brighter than the sunlit hall—at least, the package wrapped in foil appeared to be. He was wondering if he really could carry out what he planned to do.

Chapter XXXIII

THAT WEEK three of the Innes signboards were sprayed with insults. One night, patrolling, Steve discovered that a front door had been crossed out with red paint as well. The owner of the house told him apologetically that she'd decided to conduct her own sale. "It isn't only this vandalism. The neighbors are treating me as if I'm bringing it on myself."

He finished his patrol, his hands aching to get hold of the culprit, then he climbed the steps to the common. Below him in the streets, Elsey boards were multiplying. Weeks of heat had left the parched grass of the common drooping. The sky was clear, yet the heat lingered, an oppressive presence in the evening light. Steve gazed across the bay toward the darkening forest and wondered if it was time to go home.

At first he had enjoyed his freedom, especially once his parents accepted that he didn't want to talk about his marriage. He'd moved into one of the cheaper apartments

the agency had to let, and had felt almost like a student
again when he came home from work, drinking the evenings away with friends, flirting with women in the hotel
bars. With one company executive he'd gone as far as the
door of her hotel room before deciding that it wasn't worth
it. He wasn't that free after all—he hoped not, anyway.

Several times he'd thought of calling Robin. Once he'd
tried, and found he was relieved when there was no reply.
Now that he was on his own he kept remembering the time
he'd stood her up almost twenty years ago, yet when he
thought about it he knew he would only want to talk about
Maggie. He was beginning to think he could see what had
gone wrong with his marriage.

It wasn't just the form he'd signed all those years ago or
what had happened afterward; he was blaming that for too
much. It wasn't Maggie's fault if she didn't understand
why he was troubled, it was his, for letting himself both
drift away from her into himself and take her for granted.
Even if he hadn't cheated with the company executive at
the hotel, perhaps ceasing to be the person Maggie had
chosen to marry was a more insidious form of cheating.

He shouldn't be telling himself all this, he should be
telling her. He stared across the bay, where the fishing
boats from Shipham looked embedded in glass, then he
went down to the woods. Beneath the trees it was cooler,
and he took his time, enjoying the relief. Well before he
reached the house he saw the light upstairs.

She must be reading in bed or watching the portable
television. He felt touched, especially when he saw her car
parked close to one wall of the garage as if leaving space
for him to come back, and oddly shy. Shyness kept him
standing outside the front door while he tried to think what
to say—but he oughtn't to calculate. He found his key and
let himself in.

The hall was dark. He reached for the light switch,
welcoming the familiarity of everything, but the light wasn't
working. He blinked at the dark, which didn't seem about

to go away, then he stepped forward. The burglar alarm began to shrill at once.

He fumbled for the key to turn it off and dropped the key ring. When he made to grab the keys he kicked them along the hall instead, under the stairs. He would never find them now, not when he was giggling so much he couldn't even get the sound out, never mind call to Maggie to tell her he wasn't a burglar. He found the banister and started upstairs, unable to hear his footsteps for the sound of the alarm. The bedroom light was out now, and he tried to get hold of his voice. He had almost reached the landing when someone punched him in the face.

The blow missed his nose and mouth. It scraped along his cheek and bruised his jaw. The hand was too big for Maggie's—he could tell that much even as he flailed on the edge of a stair, carpet fraying under his heels. As the arm swung at him again he grabbed it, as much for balance as to protect himself. The other hand seized his throat and shoved him against the wall. Steve couldn't tell whether the man was trying to keep hold of him or throw him downstairs or heave him onto the landing so as to make an escape. It didn't matter now, for he'd reached out and found the man's testicles.

When Steve closed his fist the man groaned and tightened his grip on Steve's throat. Steve twisted the handful, and the man stumbled violently back onto the landing, dragging Steve with him. They fell in a heap in the dark that was turning red as Steve struggled to breathe. They were still tightening their grip on each other when Maggie flung open the bedroom door, spilling light on them. "Oh, my God. Let go of him," she cried.

She was wearing a dressing gown and nothing else, Steve realized. His hand clenched again before he made himself let go. He shoved the man away and fell back against the banisters, panting for breath. "I thought you were a burglar," the man gasped.

At least he was fully dressed. He had a large head, a

chin like a pair of knuckles, bright blue eyes. "We should hire you as a watchdog," Steve said in a squeezed-out voice, and stared harder at him, realizing, "I know you."

"Jeff. Jeff Boyd." He was sitting on the floor, his hands clasping his crotch as if he feared that Steve might seize it anew. "I met your wife when you and I were at university, remember," he said as if that explained everything or he hoped it would.

Maggie slipped by them, looking at neither, to switch off the alarm. In the sudden ringing silence she said, "Jeff's a reporter with Radio London now. His father isn't well."

"His father's in your bed too, is he?"

"You shouldn't speak to her like that. You're jumping to conclusions."

"Seems there's been a lot of jumping here tonight. Go ahead, tell me I'm wrong. Tell me what you were doing."

"I was at the town hall on my father's behalf and I happened to meet Maggie. I bought her dinner and then we came back here for a drink."

"Do you know, I remember when we kept the drinks downstairs."

"We came up here because I wanted to watch the news," Jeff said. "There was something wrong with the other television."

"You put the light out so you could see the picture better, did you?"

"Well, as a matter of fact—"

"Shut it, Jeff. Just shut your hole." Steve had his voice back now. "You always were a smooth talker ever since we were at school. You used to think my stutter was quite funny, didn't you? I didn't like you then and now I like you even less."

Maggie had come upstairs and was hovering in case she had to intervene. "My God, Maggie," he said, "of all the creatures you could have taken to bed, what made you choose a radio reporter? To get back at me for letting the bad publicity rub off on you, was that what you had in mind?''

"Believe it or not, Steve, I actually wasn't thinking about you."

"Tell me something I didn't know."

"Oh, I'm sure I can, Steve. How about the way you seem incapable of looking at any situation except in terms of how it relates to you?''

"Right, this doesn't have anything to do with me, does it? Forgive me for not realizing. I come home to my house to find another man in my bedroom with my wife, but that doesn't have a thing to do with me."

"It's my house too, you know."

Disconcertingly, what made Steve even angrier was having held back from calling Robin. "Well then, anything goes, doesn't it? You can have someone round for a quickie whenever you like."

"I wish you could hear yourself. Your house, your bedroom, your wife. I'm just one more piece of property to you, and what's worse, you don't even realize."

"Actually, I think she may have something there," Jeff murmured.

"Who gives a shit what you think? Maybe you're right, Maggie, but let me tell you something: property or not, I mightn't want you back secondhand."

"I mightn't want to come back to you, did that occur to you? Every time you open your mouth you take me more for granted."

"Secondhand, did I say? Thirdhand at least for all I know. Shut up, Jeff, don't say a word. In fact, just fuck off out of my house right now."

"You don't tell my guests when to leave. I told you his father's in hospital. Try having a bit of sympathy for someone other than yourself. You make me sick, creeping into the house to try to catch me out when you've probably spent every night in your doctor friend's bed."

"Fine," Steve said, no longer interested in denying it.

"You want it to be your house, just say the word. It'll be yours for as long as the lawyers take."

Maggie opened her mouth and closed it. The mention of lawyers had made them both pause; it seemed too sudden, too close to final. At least it was a boundary from which they could step back. Then Maggie said, "I'd swap the house for the chance to be myself again."

Jeff stared at them and winced, hands back at his crotch. So this was how marriages ended, Steve thought: messily, absurdly, overbalanced by just a few words. "You can have both and welcome until we have to divide everything up," he said, and shoved himself away from the banisters.

Two stairs down he couldn't help turning. He saw Maggie's bare legs beneath the dressing gown, the mole behind her right knee. He must be seeing it for the last time, he realized, and felt like throwing Jeff downstairs. Maggie wouldn't turn to him however hard he stared, even when he said, "At least you could have gone to bed with someone who thinks enough of you to leave the light on."

He closed the front door gently behind him to prevent himself from slamming it with all his force and stalked along the forest road, his skin tingling with anger and unspoken words. A few hundred yards on he glanced back. The bedroom was still lit, the downstairs lights were on now. He was already wondering if he'd been hasty, if she'd meant something much less final, but it was too late now. At least he couldn't imagine what else he had to lose. That felt like freedom—a freedom he suspected he was too settled in his ways to grasp. He thought once more of calling Robin. Perhaps in time he would. Certainly he felt as if he needed someone to show him what to do.

Chapter XXXIV

IT TOOK Mr. Gillespie more than a minute to hobble into the surgery, especially since he wouldn't be helped. He was the last patient of the day, and as usual he wanted to talk. "What can I do for you today?" Robin eventually said.

"I surmise you may find I'm just feeling my age. Seeing my pupils grow up and get married, you know, and now one a widower. . . ." He made the sign of the cross on his forehead and shoulders. "I should have liked to carry on teaching. The profession is crawling with atheists and Communists these days."

Remembering how he'd treated Steve, Robin hadn't much time for his wistfulness. She was about to examine him when her mother wandered into the room.

"Mr. Blackhead, isn't it?" She sat down next to him as if the surgery were a lounge. "Not Mr. Blackhead? You're from the museum, aren't you?" When he told her who he was she gave him a long hard stare. "You're looking well, anyway," she said defiantly.

"I was just saying that news of death reminds one of one's age."

"Who's been telling you that, I wonder? I'd beware of anyone who wants to remind you how old you are. I stay young by keeping up with my research. I'll be back at the museum as soon as they have a vacancy on the staff."

"Let's see what we can do about these pains in your chest, Mr. Gillespie. If you'd like to leave us now, mother—"

"Hay fever, that's what it'll be. Half the town has it this time of year. Don't let anyone tell you different unless you're sure of their motives. Whatever you do, don't let them get you into hospital. They want to pack us all away there where they can do what they like with us." When Robin took her arm to steer her out she struggled free. "Look how she wants to get rid of me, wants to get rid of the truth. You take notice of what I say, Mr. . . . You take notice, that's all."

Mr. Gillespie had a minor chest infection brought on by a summer cold. Robin wrote the prescription and saw him out, then she went upstairs. "Mother, will you please never do that again. *Never* come in during surgery."

"Afraid I'll see what you're up to, are you? Try and stop me. Go on, call your friends in the police. I'll have the law on them and on you too."

Robin tried to reason with her, while the air grew heavier, stifling. When she began to lose her temper she went downstairs, eyes throbbing. Her mother was right, of course: the law couldn't intervene. A few days ago Robin had appalled herself by wishing her mother dead, after so many years of suppressing every wish for fear it might come true, but now she knew that wishes no longer worked for her. She had to *do* something, but what? Before she could think, the phone rang.

It was Steve. "What are you doing tonight?"

Going quietly mad, she thought of saying. "Why do you ask?"

"We never did get together after that party. I promise this time I'll turn up."

Their last meeting had left her with a nagging sense of so much unresolved. Just now the chance to talk freely to someone seemed like the best offer she'd had all year. "I'll meet you after dinner," she said, and told him where.

Her mother refused dinner, wouldn't come out of her room. "I'll cook myself something when I'm hungry, then at least I'll know what's in it," she said.

Suppose she forgot to light the gas or even set the house on fire? "Mother, unless you eat something I won't be able to go out."

"Who do you think you're talking to? You'd think I was the child here, not you. I don't want you to go out, believe me. I want you here where I can see what you're doing."

Robin was shaken by the sudden utter hatred she felt for her mother. Perhaps her mother would starve herself until she was so weak that she couldn't resist being taken into hospital, from where she would be taken into care, except that nothing of the sort would happen. Robin sat down to eat, and had taken two mouthfuls when she stood up. Leaving her mother would make her more anxious than an evening's drinking could deal with.

Steve's wife answered the phone. "Could I speak to Steve?" Robin said.

"He isn't here, as I think you should know."

"Can I leave a message?" Robin said, taken aback.

"He doesn't live here anymore, and don't bother asking where he is, because I don't know. You do, though, don't you? I'm not the fool you take me for, and neither is my lawyer, I'm warning both of you."

The next moment the dialing tone buzzed waspishly in Robin's ear. She replaced the receiver in its cradle and held onto it until she realized it was no further use just now. She felt top-heavy with doubts and thoughts and speculations. She wandered into the dining room and found her mother eating from Robin's plate. "I've wiped your bottom often enough, I'll risk catching your germs. Let's see if you dare eat what you wanted me to eat."

At least Robin could meet Steve now, but Maggie had made her unsure why she wanted to. She ought to meet him, if only to find out what was being said about her now. She gave her mother the phone number of the pub where she would be and walked down to the East Fork.

The sunset lay like honey on the sea, the hot still air felt thick. The pub was in the front room of a terraced house. Steve waved at her through the open window, and she was tempted to walk straight past and away, he looked so delighted to see her. Whatever they had to say, surely they couldn't say it in a crowded pub. "Gin and tonic? I'll bring it out," he said, and she leaned against the lumpy front wall to wait for him.

"Really good to see you," he said when he brought out the drinks. His wide smile was slightly lopsided, which she supposed was a kind of acknowledgment of the circumstances. "I wasn't sure if you were coming. I wouldn't have blamed you if you'd stood me up this time to get your own back."

"I hope I'm not like that, Steve. Besides, I felt there were things that needed saying. I'm sorry I sprung the news about Tanya Waters on you like that. I should have realized you mightn't know."

"I should have kept in touch with Jimmy." He ran his hand through his hair, which was already unruly, and she remembered telling him to let it be itself, all those years ago. "You know what I can't stand about this idea of Peter's? It gives me an alibi, it says I wasn't responsible for what happened at the Grand. I never liked that kind of nonsense, and I'm not going to take advantage of it now."

"Have you seen Peter since you spoke to me?"

"Can't say I have. Haven't tried very hard, to tell you the truth."

"Maybe we ought to go and see him. You know Peter, it must be preying on his mind."

"You don't mean go right now, do you? I'd quite like to relax for a change."

"You seem to be doing that all right." She sipped her gin and felt the alcohol climb into her brain, and then she said, "You're at a loose end tonight, are you?"

"Tonight and every night."

"How's that, Steve?"

"Oh, I'm a gay divorcé now, or soon to be one," he said with an embarrassed laugh. "Well, not *gay*, you understand."

"I'm sorry to hear it. About the divorce, I mean."

"It happens. A lot of it was my fault, not all of it, though. I think it's civilized to know when to split up."

"Go ahead if you want to talk about it," Robin said, feeling unexpectedly nervous.

"We were just drifting apart, that's all. And Maggie hadn't any time for this business with Peter and the rest of us. She thought it was just an excuse."

"For what, Steve?"

He blushed. "Oh, to cover up what she thought I was hiding from her."

"Actually, Steve, I tried to call you at home earlier this evening. I thought I mightn't be able to come."

"You mean you spoke to Maggie?" His blush was growing, and he seemed unsure how to look. "Then you know."

"Well, I've a pretty good idea." She smiled, touched his bare forearm. "Your wife thought we were—"

"Right," he said hastily.

"Why would she have thought that?"

"Maybe she could read my mind. No, I mean, I think she'd already got the idea I was seeing someone before you and I got back in touch, and then of course she found out I was seeing you."

"It's all right, Steve. Don't tie yourself in knots. I think

I understand. If the circumstances had been different perhaps she mightn't have been mistaken.''

He gazed at her smile to make sure she wasn't mocking him. "Christ, I wish I'd kept that date with you after the party."

"Well, we've kept it now." She finished her gin to hide her own confusion; she felt even younger than she'd been when they made the date. The feeling passed. Twenty years had at least given her more confidence, whatever else the passage of time had taken away. She set the glass down with a clink on the stone sill. "Where do we go from here, Steve?"

"Want another drink? Neither do I. I think I've had enough, actually. Let's walk for a bit, shall we?"

He took her arm as they climbed the streets to the common but let go at the top of the steps. A breeze cooled their faces, and he said, "I'm sorry, Robin. I don't know what I could have been thinking of."

"How do you mean?"

"I mean your reputation was already being attacked and now you're being linked with me."

"You think the word's already out about us, do you?"

"I'm afraid it might be."

She thought he sounded hopeful rather than regretful. The breeze lifted her skirt, touched her thighs softly, and she took his hand. "I think my reputation was already just about as low as it could sink. It should be me who apologizes to you for letting your wife think you were involved with such a notorious woman."

"Don't be ridiculous." He was holding her hand as if he didn't quite know what to do with it. "What shall we do now, then? Want to walk?"

"Where to?"

"I thought you said we ought to talk to Peter."

"If that's what you feel like, or we could arrange to meet him. Where are you living now?"

"Just down there. We passed it a few minutes ago."

"You ought to have told me."

"Would you have wanted me to?" He seemed to be trying not to look at her skirt, which was flapping. "Do you want to go there now?"

"I thought you'd never ask. That is," she said, realizing belatedly in the midst of her excitement that was also somehow calming, "unless you think your wife is having you watched."

"Frankly, I don't care if she is or not. If we can't stop the rumors we might as well give people something to talk about, don't you think?"

"I think you've got something there." She'd never felt quite like this before. He took her hand as they went down the steps. She held on tight, and it seemed to her that they managed to say a great deal to each other without speaking. They were in sight of the pub again—Steve must have rooms in the street leading down to it—when she saw her mother.

She let out a cry as she caught sight of Robin, and came hobbling up the slope. "Where on earth have you been? I phoned the number you gave me but you weren't there. Are you trying to worry me to death? I've been looking all over for you."

Robin felt all at once physically sick. "Why did you want me, mother? What's wrong now?"

"What's wrong? What's wrong is that I phoned where you said you'd be to see if you were there and you weren't, that's what's wrong. And then some lout of a barman treated me as if I wasn't quite right in the head. That'll make you happy, won't it? That's what you want them to think."

"Excuse me, Miss Laurel, but we were at the pub for a while. It was my idea to go walking."

She stared at him. "I don't know you. Who are you calling Miss? I've a child, I'll have you know, and God in heaven, don't I know I have. Children are supposed to bring you happiness. I must be one of the unlucky ones.

Sometimes I think they gave me the wrong baby at the hospital.''

"Are you finished, mother?"

"No, I'm not finished, and I won't be until you manage to drive me mad or make me kill myself. Don't think I don't know why you want to get rid of me now. I saw you holding hands. I know what you're up to.''

"That's enough, mother. Come on, we're going home." Robin shook her head when Steve offered to help. "I'll be in touch," she promised, though she felt hollow, robbed. When her mother wouldn't be led Robin walked away, and eventually her mother followed, groaning at her legs.

That night Robin lay awake in bed for hours, thinking of nothing at all but unable to sleep, hearing her mother complaining about her to the crowd in her mother's room. In the morning she got through surgery somehow, though she nearly lost her temper more than once; her nerves felt more present than she did. She watched her last patient out, then she grabbed the phone to call her doctor for a prescription for sleeping pills. Of course a doctor couldn't prescribe for herself, yet she couldn't help resenting it, as if still another thing she'd worked to earn had been taken from her—but then her mind seemed to light up, before she quite knew why. Suddenly it seemed important not to make a secret of the fact that there would be barbiturates in the house.

Chapter XXXV

PETER heard Hilda Marvle's voice as he went into the town hall. She was arguing with someone in the switchboard room. It wasn't for him to intervene, she had to make her own way now, except that as he made for the stairs he heard her say, "But Mr. Priest got it for me."

"Mr. Priest didn't hire you," Maggie Innes said, opening the door, "and he's got nothing to do with whether you keep the job."

Hilda saw him and ran forward, but couldn't squeeze past her through the doorway. "Mr. Priest, they want to take my job away."

Maggie stepped grudgingly aside for him, and he went to her supervisor. "I thought she was doing satisfactorily. I believe that's how you put it to me."

"You must be joking," Maggie cried. "Go on, tell him what you did."

"I only thought someone was Roger. I thought it was him disguising his voice."

"It wasn't the first time either, was it? But this has got to be the end. She kept trying to persuade my caller he was someone else until he got tired of her nonsense and rang off."

"It isn't nonsense. It may be nonsense to *you*."

Hilda was learning to stand up for herself, Peter saw, but it mightn't help her now. "Mrs. Innes, I'd ask you to take into account that Hilda is under quite a lot of stress just now."

"Is she really! You think she's the only one, do you? My God, if I wanted to put *my* life on show . . ." Maggie looked furious with herself for having let that slip. "The difference is that I don't let it affect my job."

"I try not to," Hilda said tearfully. "I just want to know what's happened to my brother. He went away because of me. I only want to know where he is and that he's all right."

He's out there somewhere, Peter thought, holding his face still to make sure he said nothing. He saw Roger floating out of sight of land, his smashed head reddening the water. Getting rid of Roger was supposed to solve everything, but it had made everything far worse. "From what I hear you're well rid of him," Maggie muttered to herself, and the supervisor said, "I think it might be best for all concerned if Hilda could find herself a different job. I'll give her the best reference I can."

"I'll look into it tomorrow. Try not to worry, Hilda," Peter said, and went up the marble stairs, his advice repeating itself hollowly in time with the throbbing of his skull. He sorted files on his desk and attempted to write up the casework he'd carried out today, struggled to remember what he'd done besides try not to look behind him or in mirrors. He managed to write a few facts, and then he thought to call Jimmy. God, he'd almost forgotten, even though Jimmy was the only person who could help.

Jimmy might be at home, the desk sergeant told him, or not even in Seaward. Jimmy's phone rang and rang while

Peter's headache dug deeper. He made himself write in another file and told himself that at least he realized the kind of evil they were dealing with. Only Jimmy had the information that might save him—at least, he prayed that Jimmy had.

He had to get it from him without giving anything away. He mustn't seem too eager, for Jimmy might suspect; after all, that was part of his job. Peter wished desperately that he could tell the others what he'd learned, wished he could find out what they were being tempted to do in order to regain what they'd lost, but he dared not risk betraying what he'd done to Roger. He couldn't let them know that whatever they might do, they would regain nothing—that all the time the assurance had been a lie.

It had taken him in. It must have, for killing Roger to have seemed any kind of a solution, let alone for Peter to have done so. He ought to have known that a power which could kill his grandmother, when all he'd asked for had been for her to be out of the way, could offer nothing except suffering and temptations that led to greater suffering. He could almost sense its feeding on his distress, though he had no idea of its form or where it was. Jimmy knew where, please let him have kept the information, please let it not be out of date, the address he had copied down when Peter had approached him all those years ago.

Next time Peter dialed Jimmy answered at once. "Yes?"

"Peter." Suddenly he was unprepared, and couldn't summon up small talk when Jimmy was so recently bereaved. "I wanted to ask you something. I wanted to ask . . . I know this isn't the best time to ask, but . . ."

"I can't stop now, Pete, I should be up at the Four Smugglers. See me there later if you like."

Peter didn't want to dine at his flat, even if Mrs. Corner had left him a meal, not when he didn't know what hands might have touched it while it was waiting for him, if they were still hands. He couldn't go to his parents, he was too afraid they would see how nervous he was, afraid that he might blurt out some of what was undermining him. He ate in a café overlooking the bay, with his back to the wall and his gaze constantly flickering to the street outside the window, then he walked to the pub.

Two waitresses in pinafores were serving homemade food under the oak beams. People from the sports cars that surrounded the pub were queuing for tables. When he asked for Jimmy, the barmaid sent him upstairs. From the steep uneven staircase he heard Jimmy's father say, "Keep trying, Jimmy. I don't blame you for wanting to make the move."

"It's best for the children," Jimmy's mother said.

"Better than staying here, anyway."

"Don't say that, dad. They love staying with you both, you know that."

"That doesn't mean they know what's best for them."

"There's nobody I'd rather leave them with. You did all right by me when I was their age, didn't you? I didn't exactly turn to a life of crime."

Peter knocked and went into the bright, snug sitting room. "You remember Peter, don't you, my old friend from school? Now I hope there won't be any more of this silliness about my not wanting the children to be with you," Jimmy said. "Come down, Peter, and we'll have a drink."

At the bar he went on, "My dad's so concerned the kids shouldn't end up the way he used to be that he's finally kicked the gambling habit. I won't have him thinking he's a bad influence, it's not right." He took the brimming tankards from the barmaid. "Still, I can see you aren't interested in my problems. What is it that's so urgent, Pete?"

"Did I make it sound that urgent? Maybe you won't think it is. I hope you'll help me anyway. You see, thing is, it's been worrying me."

"Well, are you going to tell me or do I have to guess?"

"I don't know if you remember those forms we once

signed up there on the common. I don't know if you've ever thought about them since."

"I should say so. I sometimes think they're why I'm in the job I'm in."

"Making up for what we wished, you mean? Then you'll understand why it's been preying on my mind."

"If you say so, but what are you asking?"

"I'll tell you." Peter had to raise his voice, which had suddenly dried up. "You remember we lost all the forms, but you copied down the address from that first letter. I was hoping you might be able to turn it up for me."

"I shouldn't think so."

At once the uproar of the pub seemed to be inside Peter's head. "You threw it away?"

"No, I think I may still have it somewhere. I couldn't tell you where, though, and I haven't time to look just now. Anyway, you said it wasn't urgent a few minutes ago."

"It might be, in fact, I really think it is. We had to pay for what we got, remember, and we're doing that now, don't you see? We have to go there and stop it somehow. We'll know how when we see what we're up against. Or I will, I mean," he said hastily, for Jimmy was frowning at him. "You don't have to do anything unless you want to except give me the address."

"How do you mean, we're paying now? Are you talking about what happened to my wife?"

"Well, yes, I mean, I suppose I was."

"Let's change the subject and keep it changed. No offense, Peter, but you aren't helping at all."

"I'm sorry. I won't mention it again." The uproar was forcing Peter's thoughts out of reach. "But couldn't you just look for the address for me? Or listen, if you haven't time yourself, I could look. I'd be careful of your things."

"I can't let you do that. For one thing, the house is upside down now I'm on my own."

Peter had a fleeting impression that Jimmy had something to hide, but what use was that to him? "I'll have to sort out the contents of the house soon, at least I hope so," Jimmy said. "Maybe I'll find it for you then, when we move."

Peter couldn't tell where the uproar in his head stopped and pain began. "Where are you moving to?"

"I'm still going for interviews. Out of Seaward, that's the main thing. The children can't live here anymore. Too many memories."

He'd keep the address locked in his house until he moved, and then it might be further out of Peter's reach if it wasn't thrown away by mistake with whatever he decided wasn't worth taking. Peter began to cry out, though silently. There was nothing he could think of that would force Jimmy to search for the address.

"That's what all the fuss was about with my parents," Jimmy said. "My dad thinks I may want to move to get the kids away from him. I couldn't be happier to have them stay here, except they must be a trial sometimes."

As suddenly as it had overcome Peter, the uproar faded. The light in his mind was forcing it back, clearing his head. "You mean the children are too much for them sometimes?"

Jimmy stared at him. "I thought that's what I said."

"Drink up and I'll buy you another. I'm sorry I was tactless before. I'd like to make it up to you. As long as you're out of town a lot I could take some of the pressure off your parents. I could take the kids out now and then."

"That's kind of you, Pete. They're good kids, they wouldn't be much trouble. Don't feel bound to do it, though. I've already forgotten what you said."

"No, I want to." Peter took a gulp of beer to wash away the nervous dryness from his throat. "I'm spending too much time brooding. Taking the kids will be just what I need."

Chapter XXXVI

"OH, DADDY, isn't it nice to be without Russell for a while," Francesca said with a heartfelt sigh. "The way he babbles on sometimes I can't hear myself think."

"You aren't exactly mum yourself, love," Jimmy said, and told himself to get hold of himself: how could he have chosen that of all words? "Anyway, I think he quite likes going fishing with granddad. Gives him a chance to be himself."

"That's silly. Who else could he be?"

"Who knows who any of us are, love." That earned him a disgusted look. "Well, shall we go and hear what the experts have to say for themselves?"

"I think we'd better," Francesca said solemnly, "before you buy even more books."

He sat down on a leather chair in the foyer of the Royal Hotel to search in his carrier bag for the Star Trek convention program. She was right, there were plenty of books in the bag, several of them by Maurice Fox. They both justified Jimmy's presence there and covered up the package at the bottom of the bag. He found the booklet just as Francesca said, "Look, daddy, there's tribbles."

"Who's that?"

"Daddy," she cried, and several people stared at him. Of course, now he remembered, tribbles were the furry creatures a woman in chains and black leather was pulling along, it wasn't the name of the woman herself. Jimmy had pinned some of Francesca's badges on his jacket so that the Star Trek fans would take him as one of themselves, but perhaps he shouldn't have if he was going to betray his ignorance. So long as he kept his mouth shut, surely he would pass. "Maurice Fox is on next," he said. "Let's go and see him."

"Do we have to, daddy? It sounds boring."

"You can watch the film if you like. The video room's just up those stairs." It was all to the good that she would be out of his way. "Stay there until I come and find you, all right? Or at any rate don't go out of the hotel." He patted her bottom and made for the convention hall.

On the stage several bespectacled people were being quizzed about blasters and ray guns. Jimmy sat on the back row of folding seats, behind a middle-aged couple with pointed rubber ears, and waited for Maurice Fox. Fox had eluded the police for long enough. God only knew how many addicts he'd created since Jimmy had realized what he was doing.

He joined in the applause at the end of the quiz. The audience began to mill about, some converging on the stage. That was bound to happen at the end of Fox's speech, and that might be Jimmy's chance, before Fox recognized him. Otherwise there were the books to be autographed, if Jimmy could think of a way to make use of that. When the time came he would know what to do.

He was watching a girl in a silver tunic rearrange the microphones and keeping his mind as blank as he could when someone sat down beside him. "First convention, James?"

She'd read his name on his convention badge, but still she'd given him an unpleasant shock. At least, taking his cue from some of the badges he'd noticed, he wasn't displaying his surname. "Afraid so," he said as unwelcomingly as he could.

"Mine too. I'm Beer," she said, pointing one fat finger at the badge on her overstuffed T-shirt. "Do you watch anything besides 'Star Trek'?"

"Good God, yes."

"So do I. 'Blake's Seven' and 'Space 1999' and 'Doctor Who' and 'The Prisoner,' of course. Do you know, I was talking to someone this morning who never watches anything except 'Star Trek.' You don't expect people to be narrow-minded here, do you? I mean, sci-fi is about broadening your mind."

"Ah," Jimmy said distractedly, vaguely aware that someone had sat down at his other side now and had placed a bag on the seat between them, where Jimmy's bag was. He reached out and grasped the handles and glanced up as someone leaned over the back of the seat. It was Maurice Fox.

Jimmy's hand jerked, and the bag almost fell. The thought of spilling the contents in front of Fox made him unable to swallow or, for a few moments, even to breathe. But Fox wasn't looking at him—hadn't noticed him. "Sit quietly if you're going to sit there," Fox told the boy who'd just sat down by Jimmy, and strode haughtily toward the stage.

One glance at the boy's badge confirmed that he was Fox's son. The glance showed Jimmy a boy of about Francesca's age, thin, bright-eyed, nervous. He must help Fox look innocent, a family man who visited Seaward purely as a writer and collector. The thought filled Jimmy with hatred, then suddenly with clarity bright as lightning. "Don't you agree?" the girl called Beer said.

"Pardon?" Jimmy said, so sharply that she flinched. "Oh, the stuff on television? I've no time for any of it. I'm just here with my daughter."

"Then you shouldn't be wearing those badges," she said loudly, and moved to another row. At least she hadn't drawn the boy's attention to Jimmy. The boy was watching Fox as he listed his requirements to the girl in the silver tunic. "Got to go," the boy said to himself, and started up the aisle toward his father.

He'd left the bag. Jimmy glanced at its contents without moving his head: beach toys, swimming trunks, a wet beach towel. He turned his head just enough to look over his shoulder. Nobody behind him, nobody watching him, Fox ignoring his son and leaning close to the girl in the tunic. Everything seemed bright and clear as stained glass. Jimmy reached into his own bag as he stood up, found the package wrapped in foil under the books, pinched the foil between the knuckles of his first and second fingers—three seconds since he'd stood up—lifted the wet towel with his other hand and slipped the package deep into the boy's bag. He patted the towel back into place and five seconds later was out of the convention hall.

He sat on a chair opposite the doors that were swinging in his wake and let out his breath, which he hadn't realized he was holding until his chest began to ache. He'd done it at last, then: he'd trapped Fox. There was no other exit from the hall.

He settled back in the lukewarm leather chair to wait for the applause at the end of Fox's speech. He wondered how Fox's face would look when Jimmy caught him at the doors. The man might even challenge Jimmy to search him in public, since he thought he had nothing to hide. But he mightn't be so confident when Jimmy told him to empty his son's bag.

Even Fox might balk at denying all knowledge of the package when that would throw suspicion on the boy. Of course the child was too young to be prosecuted, but Fox would know how the media would handle such a story. In any case, Jimmy would go straight for Fox. He would have ample reason to detain Fox until the hotel room had been searched and he'd obtained a warrant to search Fox's house.

For a moment he felt uneasy, perhaps because what he'd just done had solved so much. Arresting Fox ought to give him an edge at interviews; the children wouldn't have to spend much longer in Seaward. Why did the thought of the children make him uneasier? Of course, he'd forgotten Francesca; he ought to have made sure that she would be out of the way when he made the arrest—she would only complicate matters. Had he time to find her now, tell her to stay away? He wished there were someone to keep her out of the way. Perhaps there was. Peter had offered to take the children, and he might be at home just now.

Jimmy made for the public telephones, which were in sight of the exit from the convention hall. He fumbled in his pocket with his free hand for his address book, next to his warrant card. Yes, better make sure Francesca was out of the way—and then, with a rush of panic so violent that it made him sway, he wondered what would happen if she found out what he'd done.

How could she? He made himself go to the nearest phone and opened his address book on the ledge beside it, dropped his bag between his ankles, turned to Peter's number. Suddenly his fist clenched on the book until he felt the covers bend. Perhaps Francesca wouldn't find out, wouldn't know what he must keep her and Russell from ever knowing, but God in heaven, what *had* he done? He'd taken the first step toward becoming the kind of policeman he detested—the kind his children would have now for a father. He squeezed his eyes shut in the shade of the booth that ended at his hips, then they sprang open. Oh God, she might find out. It mightn't be Fox who was arrested at all.

He'd underestimated Fox. The unnatural clarity of his plan had blinded him to the objections he ought to have raised. Fox would know he had planted the package. Even if neither Fox nor his son had noticed Jimmy, the girl called Beer knew where he had been sitting. "Why should you have thought Mr. Fox was carrying drugs if you didn't already know they were there? Why did you try to disguise your name on your badge?" the lawyer would say, and then Jimmy heard the judge, "This is among the vilest and most wicked crimes it has ever fallen to me to try, a crime that gives ammunition to the enemies of the police and law and order. . . ."

There was still time to take it back, surely there was. Jimmy took a deep breath, though the lingering smell of a cigar in the booth made him dizzy, and heard the applause begin for Fox. He almost ran into the convention hall. He shoved between the doors and saw Fox's son returning down the aisle from the stage. Jimmy hadn't time to reach the bag now, he had to wait until the boy sat down. But when Jimmy glanced at the back row, then stepped forward and stared desperately along it, he saw that the bag was not there.

"Excuse me," the boy said. Jimmy sat down then, his ears throbbing, barely able to hear Fox telling the audience that writing was the easiest job he'd ever had, two books a year, two months to a book. Jimmy stared at him with smarting eyes and swallowed a gasp. The bag was on the stage beside Fox.

He mustn't panic. He still had a chance to reach it, at the end of Fox's question session, when Jimmy could take the books for signing. It didn't matter if Fox recognized him once he'd retrieved the package. He could put his own bag next to the boy's in order to take out the books. He was listening to Fox's boasting in the hope that he could gauge when Fox was about to finish when Francesca ran into the hall and tugged at his arm. "Daddy," she wailed, "some boys took my badge."

"Never mind, love, I'll get you a new one. Don't bother me now though, all right?"

"But it was my best one." She sat down beside him and

held onto him. "They asked for a look and when I gave it to them they ran away."

"I've told you I'll buy you another. Just let me listen to this, do you mind? I thought you wanted to watch the videos."

"I don't want to go out there where those boys are."

"Keep your voice down, will you? All you have to do is tell a grown-up if they come near you."

"I want to stay with you. I'll be quiet. Please, daddy."

"Do what the devil you like so long as you shut up about it," he said wildly, knowing as he did so that he couldn't risk her staying: she might see what he did—even the fear of her doing so would make him clumsy, conspicuous. "Look, here's five pounds. Go and buy yourself a new badge and whatever you like with the change. Just stay out of here until I come to find you," he said low and savagely, but it was too late: Fox was holding up one hand to terminate the questions.

"Stay here now and wait for me. Don't move from this seat," Jimmy said, straining his ears to hear what the girl in the silver tunic was saying into the suddenly uncooperative microphone: "We would like to thank Maurice Fox specially for taking time out from his new novel to come and talk to us. He asks us to forgive him for having to run now. If anyone didn't get their books signed at the autograph session last night Mr. Fox hopes to be here next year."

"Shut up, Francesca," Jimmy snarled as she made to speak to him. What could he do now? Fox had picked up the bag and was stepping down from the stage into the midst of a group of fans. Perhaps Jimmy could sneak among them, except that Fox wasn't letting them detain him but striding down the aisle. A few of them kept pace with him, blocking Jimmy's access to him. Jimmy dodged out of the hall before they reached the exit, to give himself more room, a last chance.

Fox came out alone. Jimmy hid his face in the nearest

phone booth as the man strode through the lobby. Yards of
empty floor surrounded Fox, a girl at Reception called
goodbye to him, and Jimmy could never have got close to
him unobserved. The Volvo was already loaded and waiting outside the front porch of the hotel. Jimmy shoved
himself away from the booth and watched helplessly as
Fox threw the bag onto the back seat, climbed in beside
his son, and drove away.

Jimmy was staring out at the sunlight on the promenade,
feeling guilt cold and hard in the midst of his hollowness,
when Francesca came to find him. "Please may I have a
badge now?"

He watched dully as she chose one, watched himself
hand over the money. "Shall we go now?" she said.
"I've had enough of this." So had he, but he suspected
that what he'd done today hadn't finished with him. He
followed her out of the hotel, wondering how long it
would take Fox to find the package and what Fox would
do then, how much the son would be able to remember if
he put his mind to it, and then Francesca turned to him,
her eyes bright. "You should have made those boys give
me back my badge, daddy. It doesn't matter now, I like
this one, but you should have all the same. They'd have
had to give it back when they found out you were a
policeman," she said.

Chapter XXXVII

"WYMNID, windowshins" Peter sang, dancing and panting, "all fall down," and sat down on the floor of the locked pub. The children jumped up again at once. "What does that mean, Mr. Priest?" Francesca asked, laughing.

"Uncle Peter," he corrected, sitting on the bare boards in the hope of a rest. "I've no idea. I've never heard it before."

"You have. Sing us the rest. Please, Mr. Priest, Uncle Peter. We'll sing ours, then you sing yours. Dance with us again." They grabbed his hands and pulled him to his feet and began to dance him round before he had his balance, Peter wondering if they sensed he felt uncomfortable with them and were deliberately trying to make him feel more so. They fell down and tugged him up. "Again," Russell cried. "You sing now."

"Leave Uncle Peter for a while, children. I think it's very kind of him to play so much with you." Mrs. Waters wiped her floury hands on a towel that she'd taken off the beer pumps. "Would you like a drink, Peter? I'm allowed to serve you after hours since you're a friend of the family."

"Thanks, but I think I'd just like to walk after that lunch."

The children grabbed his hands again. "Can we come with you?"

"Not today." They and the hospitality were making his head throb. "Another time," he said, and let himself out of the pub as quickly as he could.

A breeze ruffled his hair as he stepped onto the deserted sunlit road. For a moment he thought it was his grandmother behind him, being hideously playful. Trees creaked as he hurried away from the pub, in the opposite direction from Seaward. He must have walked for at least a mile before he found a crossroads.

He turned there, along an overgrown road that led toward the cliff. Suddenly he wondered if he was heading for the crossroads he remembered from all those years ago and had never been able to find since, though he wasn't sure why that should help. At least it might clear his mind of the song that was clinging to it, wymnid, wymnid, the chant that had woken him in the night with the impression that a face had been leaning close to his ear, leaning off its own skull. He would do anything to avoid seeing what his grandmother looked like now, though surely what he had to do wouldn't be very bad; he mustn't let himself be hindered by guilt just because the children trusted him. He was nearly at the cliff, well out of sight of the main road. He was about to turn back, since the road ahead was so overgrown, when he saw the van.

It had been driven off the road. That must have been months ago, to judge by the length of the grass all around it, yet none of the windows was broken. Presumably few people came this way. Peter struggled through the grass and wrenched at the rusty handles of the rear doors until they shifted. The space behind the driver's seat and its companion was empty. There was plenty of room.

He came back when it was dark. He had to go slowly even on the unlit main road. Trees stepped out of hiding whenever he took a step, but the stealthy movements didn't bother him; nothing outside his plan seemed to matter. Even on the dark road to the van he didn't look behind him once. Surely he must be right at last if he was no longer afraid.

He didn't switch on the flashlight until he was inside the van. He took the cords and the rest of the things out of the bulging plastic sack and hid them under the seats. He strolled home, watching stars dart from tree to tree, branches swimming through themselves. That night his sleep was uninterrupted for the first time in weeks. The next day was Sunday, and he went out of town to buy a mask.

Chapter XXXVIII

STEVE couldn't remember having seen his mother so angry, even though she was trying to hide it. "Mr. Keaton, my son and his father go out every night to make sure property isn't defaced. I don't see why you feel so strongly about it, since yours hasn't been."

"It hasn't yet." Mr. Keaton sat forward on the chair that was too large for him; his Swiss watch clinked against one monogrammed cuff link. "You can't guarantee it won't be, though, can you? I can't afford to have that on my mind when I'm away on business."

"You're away so much I wonder how you heard about the graffiti campaign," Steve's father said. "From someone by the name of Elsey, would it be?"

"I don't think you're entitled to take that injured tone, you know. If you'd sold my place we wouldn't be having this dispute now."

"Don't you think we've tried?" Steve's mother was losing control, and close to tears of fury at herself. "I've lost count of the number of people we've shown round. When we did find a buyer you turned them down."

"They wouldn't have been happy here, not with nobody else of their color in Seaward. My neighbors were surprised you showed them anything in our part of town." He stood up, dusting his trousers as if the chair weren't clean. "May I have my key, please? I've already given the Elsey agency a spare."

He waited until Steve's father handed it to him before he said, "I may as well tell you this interview hasn't improved my opinion of your professionalism."

"Hasn't it? Just you wait." Steve's mother moved so fast that Mr. Keaton flinched. She went to the display window and snatched the photograph of his house, tore it into as many pieces as she could and stuffed them into his hand. "There, that should confirm your opinion."

"It does, I assure you," he said, his face paling. "You won't be surprised if I advise people not to deal with you."

Steve's father got to his feet. "If I were you I'd be going, my little friend, or *I'll* deal with *you*."

Mr. Keaton threw the scraps of photograph in the wastebin and dropped the key hastily into his jacket pocket. Only the shaft of the key went in. Steve opened the street door for him and watched him stalk away, dodging back onto the pavement as an old lady roared by in a Jaguar. The sunlight made the key flash as it fell.

Mr. Keaton hadn't noticed. He marched across the road and vanished down the nearest slope. Steve heard his mother sobbing angrily, his father murmuring. Perhaps the flash had left an afterimage in Steve's eyes, for the afternoon street seemed unnaturally bright, the point of light that was the key on the edge of the pavement almost blinding. He hurried out and glanced around him as he stooped, to see that nobody was watching. He stood up at once, the key in his fingers that slipped deep into his pocket and stayed there as he sauntered back into the office.

Half an hour later Mr. Keaton phoned. "Have you my key, by any chance?"

"My father gave it to you."

"I know that," he said as though he resented having to speak to Steve at all. "Did I happen to drop it in your office?"

"I'm afraid not."

"Then I must have somewhere nearby." He rang off, and soon they saw him retracing his steps, glaring at the pavement and the agency window. When he reached the doorstep, Steve opened the door. "I shouldn't worry too much, Mr. Keaton. If anyone picked it up they wouldn't know where it belonged to, would they?"

"Then I should think they would hand it to you."

"More likely to the police. If anyone brings it in to us we'll let you have it back."

"I'll be out of town. Please let the Elsey agency have it if you acquire it," Mr. Keaton said in a tone of bitter triumph.

Steve turned away. He'd meant to make a fool of Mr. Keaton, watch the man lose his temper as he hunted for the key; at least, he thought he had. Now he saw how petty that would have been, and turned away so that the man wouldn't see his eyes brightening.

As soon as Mr. Keaton had gone and Steve's parents were out of sight in the office, Steve dropped the key under the window while nobody was watching. Five minutes later a dachshund found it and the dog's owner brought it in. "I'll take it over to the Elseys," Steve called into the office.

Anticipation made the streets dazzling, his throat dry. Ten minutes' detour was all it took to have the key copied. Once the copy was safe in his pocket he began to doubt that he could do what had occurred to him. "You win some, you lose some," Elsey senior remarked with a smirk, his overfed hand that smelled of paper money picking up the key fastidiously between its thumb and one bejeweled finger, and Steve thought he could.

He dined with his parents and helped calm his father down when he launched into a tirade about Mr. Keaton and the Elsey agency that made him look as though he was choking. Later Steve strolled to the pub in the front room of the terraced house. He felt unsure of himself and his motives; he thought he might fling the key over the cliff if he got drunk enough, but did he really want to throw away the chance to even up the competition with the Elsey agency? He wanted to phone Robin, but wasn't sure if he ought to; after all, she'd said that she would get in touch with him. Perhaps she'd taken pity on him the night they'd met but had regretted it since, perhaps the row with her mother had been too much for her. He had another drink and found he couldn't bear not knowing what she felt, wanted to talk to her before he did anything with the key, perhaps was hoping she would sense he was concealing something, find out what it was, persuade him to give it up. He struggled through the pub crowd to the phone.

At first he thought he had a wrong number. "Who's there?" a woman's voice cried.

Just in time he realized it must be Robin's mother. "Could I speak to Robin Laurel?"

"You haven't told me who you are." The next second her panic gave way to hostility. "I know you, I know your voice, you're the one who was trying to lead her astray. She isn't here, she's out with her boyfriend. He's a police-man and he's not long lost his wife, so you'd better stay away if you know what's good for you."

Steve put down the receiver and stared at the wall, then he fought his way to the bar for another drink. "Fuck off," he muttered when he trod on someone's toe. So he wasn't welcome anywhere: a gooseberry at Robin's, a burglar in his own house. He drained his glass and then another before he began his patrol. He glared at the graffiti on an Innes board, he thought of Mr. Keaton and the smirking Elseys; he touched the key in his pocket and smiled grimly to himself, his head clearing at once. He no longer felt unsure of himself. If he was going to be treated like a burglar, he'd be one to some purpose.

Chapter XXXIX

THAT AFTERNOON'S surgery had hardly begun when Robin's mother stormed in. "Tell that woman I want none of her coffee, now or ever. The only drinks I'll touch are ones I make myself."

Robin was in the midst of advising a young husband to support his wife against the sister on the maternity ward, who was trying to persuade her to put her first baby on the bottle. "I'm sure she's taken the point, mother. Now if you'll excuse us, you're interrupting surgery." To her patient she said, "Tell her she can rely on me if she needs to."

Her mother greeted that with a disbelieving snigger. "I don't like that receptionist. Why have you brought her in? Why did you get rid of my friends' daughter?"

"I told you Raquel was only temporary. Jo was always coming back, she just came back sooner because she had a miscarriage. Now, mother, would you *please*—"

"I wonder who gave it to her. I know why you got rid

239

of Raquel, because she was my friend. *She* wouldn't drug my coffee for you.''

Robin sent the young man out and wouldn't see another patient until her mother had left her alone. There were fewer patients today than yesterday, and she wondered if the day would come when there was nobody waiting. Every time the door opened, her nerves jerked in case it was her mother.

The last patient of the afternoon was a little girl with an earache, who began to scream as soon as she saw Robin's instruments. ''Stop being silly or you'll make the doctor hurt you,'' the little girl's father said, and Robin had to reassure the child about that before reaching for her probe. The little girl was gulping down her sobs, since she'd been promised a sweet, when Robin's mother ran in. ''What's wrong with the child? What are you doing to her?''

The child recommenced screaming at once, and Robin closed her eyes. ''Will you get *out*, mother!''

''See, she wants to get rid of me because I know what she's up to. Don't let her get her hands on your child, God knows what experiments she'll perform on her. Look, now she's going to try to have me taken away.''

Robin groped through her blinding fury for the phone and called Jo. ''Will you see my mother out of here while I deal with my patient, please.''

When Jo came in her mother backed into a corner. ''Look, they're in it together, they're trying to drive me mad. They keep drugging me to make me do things. They nearly made me kill someone once so that I'd lose my job,'' she cried after the father, who'd picked up his child. ''I'll take her to the hospital,'' he said and went out shaking his head.

Robin was trembling too badly to speak. ''Look at yourself, that's what taking drugs does to you,'' her mother said and marched upstairs. Jo put her arm around Robin's shoulders, but Robin didn't need sympathy, she didn't know what she needed except to be out of the house, away from her mother. "I've got to go shopping," she said as if that might be banal enough to slow her thoughts down, stop them from piling up inside her head, scraping together, screeching.

She wheeled a supermarket basket through the long cool aisles of the Lux and stared at the garish jumbled patterns of the displays. When she'd thrown a few random items into the basket she almost walked through the checkout without paying for them. She wandered home as slowly as she could, giving her mother time to injure herself, nothing too drastic, just enough for her to be taken into hospital and from hospital into care. But her mother was waiting for her on the front porch, crying, "Where on earth have you been?"

Robin hardly knew. "Shopping," she said as the shopping bag rustled.

"I might have liked to come with you if you'd asked me. What are you trying to do, going out without telling me where you're going, worry me to death?"

"Something like that," Robin admitted to herself.

"You won't get rid of me so easily, don't you delude yourself." A cunning look spread over her mother's face. "Anyway, I'm glad you went out, so what do you think of that, miss? It gave me a chance to deal with your boyfriend once and for all."

"Who are you talking about? Who was here?"

"Nobody was here. Didn't dare show his face, if you ask me. Rang up from a pub somewhere and had the impudence to ask me to bring you to the phone after I'd seen the two of you up to no good the other night. I got rid of him for good this time. I told him you were out with your policeman."

Robin felt her hands clenching into claws. "Go on, attack me, let people see how you treat me," her mother cried. "I know you'd like to strangle me, and that's the only way you'll get rid of me. You'll behave yourself while you're living with me."

Robin thought of trying to find Steve, but he might be anywhere by now. "Just get it into your head that I'll never leave you so long as I'm alive," her mother said as Robin pushed blindly past her into the house.

Robin made dinner and watched her mother switch plates with her, switch them again and again before she ate. Over dinner and later her mother talked at her, but all Robin heard was what she'd said as Robin had entered the house. Soon they ceased to be words and turned into a brightness in her head, a brightness that grew as bedtime approached.

"You go up first," her mother said mistrustfully. Robin stayed upstairs until she heard her mother in the kitchen, filling a saucepan with milk for her bedtime drink. "I'm out of the bathroom," she called down, her heart racing. As soon as her mother bolted the bathroom door Robin tiptoed quickly downstairs and into her office.

She unlocked the desk drawer and took out the bottle. She was shaking the tablets into her hand as she slipped back through the house. She went to the saucepan and opened her hand above the seething milk, then to make sure she dropped in the rest of the tablets. The milk would boil over soon, but she mustn't turn the gas down in case her mother realized she had been to the saucepan. She hid the empty bottle in her pocket until it was time to leave it by her mother's bed, then she hurried to the living room and sat in her chair, her mind blank and brittle, her ears straining.

She heard her mother come flustering downstairs, heard her cry "Oh, the damned milk" and turn off the gas. She heard the clink of china as her mother found herself a mug, the dull ring of metal against china, the wavering resonance of water pouring into the empty saucepan. She must clean the saucepan properly later, she thought, and found herself remembering the summer they'd come to Seaward, her helping her mother to unpack the saucepans and hang them up in the kitchen, her making the bedtime drink that first night while her mother put her feet up, her mother saying, "Now we can just be ourselves, me and my Robin." Her mind turned blank as she listened to the rattle of the spoon as her mother stirred her drink, as she waited for her mother to go up to bed, to sleep, to the peace that was all she could wish now for her mother.

Her mother came into the living room and sat opposite her, stirring the drink while it cooled down. "Do you want a drink, Robin?" she said.

Robin couldn't look at her. "No, thank you."

"Don't, then. Don't have anything I offer if that's how you feel. Good thing I only made enough for one," she said, and took a sip.

Robin forced herself to watch and tried to look as though she weren't watching. Her mother swallowed and made a face, took another sip and grimaced. "What's wrong?" Robin said, her mouth getting in the way. "Too hot?"

"No, a nasty taste. The milk's off, if you ask me. Well, I've made it and I'm going to drink it," she said, and raised the mug to her lips.

A surge of horror shuddered through Robin, jerked her to her feet. "Wait a moment," she stammered. "Why, that's my mug."

Her mother peered suspiciously at her. "They look exactly the same to me."

"Well, of course. That's how you got mine by mistake. I had some medicine in it and I mustn't have washed it properly. You don't want that. Here, let me have it. I'll make you another."

Her mother lifted the mug. She looked stubborn, and Robin was afraid that she meant to gulp down the drink. "Oh, take it, I don't want it. I like to know what I'm drinking," she said, and thrust the mug at Robin.

Robin carried it to the kitchen. Her lungs felt paralyzed, unable to let out a gasp of relief; she wasn't sure that she felt relieved. She went to the sink and held the mug over it, she stared into the depths of the drain and heard her

mother shouting, "Don't bother making me a drink. I
don't want you to, I'll do it myself." Nothing had changed,
and nothing would. Robin lifted the mug and drained it in
two swallows.

Chapter XL

THE STREET where Mr. Keaton lived had the best view in Seaward, but Steve kept his eyes on the house. He advanced down the path between the flagstones that had buried the front garden to the door which divided the bay windows, and rang the bell. The first notes of a symphony Steve had once heard chimed in the depths of the house, then there was only the whisper of a sea breeze.

"I've given the Elseys your key," Steve would say if Mr. Keaton answered the door. He turned and surveyed the deserted street, stared at the real estate agency boards within the garden wall, the Elsey board next to the Innes sign that the contractors hadn't yet taken down. The Elseys couldn't have been quicker, but they'd be sorry they had been so quick. He gazed at the street and listened to the silence beyond the door, then in one swift movement he turned and slipped the key out of his pocket and let himself into the house.

He closed the door at once and stooped to the panel in

the skirting. He found the hidden catch, opened the panel, switched off the alarm with several seconds to spare. The first time he'd shown prospective buyers round the house he hadn't been able to switch off the alarm in time; he'd had to phone the police to head them off. The memory of his embarrassment made him grin savagely. It was something else he would be getting even for.

He drew on his gloves and waited for his eyes to adjust, since he mustn't risk switching on the lights. As his vision sharpened, so did all his senses; he found he could smell the house, the combined odors of expensive leather furniture and antique bindings in the locked bookcases, a smell that made him think of a museum except for its hint of hoarded staleness, a miserly smell. He'd often thought Mr. Keaton hoped to find that someone had been filching so that he could set the law on them—he knew that Mr. Keaton took stock every time he came home. They were both going to get what they wanted now.

He crept past the stairs to the cellar door and switched on the light above the steps. Though that wasn't likely to be visible from outside the house, he dodged in quickly and closed the door behind him. One entire wall of the cellar was occupied by wine racks, while the opposite wall was bare except for a few leaning brushes and a sink. He hurried down the steps to examine the racks.

Leaving gaps among the bottles high up in the racks, where they would be immediately apparent from the steps, was too obvious. Mr. Keaton would still notice gaps here and there whenever he next came home, would be all the more convinced that someone had been stealing his precious wine and trying to conceal the theft—someone who could only be from the Elsey agency. Steve was tempted to drink some of the vintages himself, but he rather thought he'd had enough to drink, even though he felt so clearheaded. He'd empty the bottles down the sink and dump them in the Elseys' trash, which wouldn't be cleared for almost a week.

He bent to the rack that was furthest from the steps and took out one of the lowest bottles, a 1927 port. Mr. Keaton ought to miss that, it sounded vintage enough. He left it by the sink and made for a white bottle in the midst of the racks—a Chateau d'Yquem, he saw it was, the most expensive of the Sauternes. He tugged gently at it when it wouldn't come at once, and it shot out without warning. He had both hands ready to catch it, no need to panic, except that the buckle of his wristwatch caught the neck of the adjacent bottle, jerking it free of the rack. The second bottle slipped out too fast for him to grab it, and smashed on the stone floor.

He gaped at the broken glass and the pool of wine and felt as if whatever bubble had been floating him along, the bubble in his brain, had burst. Christ, what did he think he was doing here? He became aware of clutching the Sauterne and shoved it into the rack, so hastily that he almost dropped it. How did he know that Mr. Keaton had already checked the cellar? Suppose he hadn't had time yet and so blamed Steve or his father for the breakage? Had Steve really expected to be able to smuggle enough bottles to make it look like a serious theft from here to the Elseys' house unnoticed? What in God's name had he been thinking of?

He carried the bottle of port back to its space, holding the bottle tighter as the sweat of his palms made it slip. Could he get in touch with Mr. Keaton, tell him he'd broken a bottle last time he was showing people round the house? He couldn't risk it: the wine would clearly have been spilled since Steve was supposed to have given up the key. But white wine mightn't leave a stain, he thought, and was reaching for a brush and dustpan when he froze. Someone was ringing the doorbell.

He made himself breathe while he waited, though he couldn't swallow. Soon the bell rang again, and again. Perhaps it was someone who wanted to view the house, but what if it was a neighbor who'd heard glass breaking in a house that was supposed to be empty? The bell was silent now, must have been so for some minutes, and he had to assume that whoever had been ringing was gone, not simply going round the outside of the house to look in the windows. Steve mustn't wait any longer, in case they were calling the police. He took a deep breath and ran up the steps to the hall.

He switched off the light in the cellar before he opened the kitchen door. He had to find something in which to take the glass out of the house. He opened the door a crack and peered at the window to make sure nobody was out there, then he made for the kitchen cabinet, staying low, almost on all fours. He found a shopping bag and backed out of the kitchen, closed the door before he straightened up, groaning. He turned on the light in the cellar and hurried down, wishing he could leave the door open above him.

One stroke of the brush and the dustpan was full. He almost emptied it into the shopping bag until he realized that he'd brushed up wine too, enough to soak through the bag. At least now that the pool was shrinking he couldn't distinguish any stain beyond its edge. He picked glass out of the dustpan and then off the floor, and set the heavy bag down in a corner while he mopped up. He'd squeezed the mop into the sink and was turning on the tap to wash the wine away when he thought he heard a sound upstairs.

He screwed the tap shut until it squeaked and bruised his hand. The drain gurgled and chuckled, then there was silence, in which he heard the front door closing. Someone had come into the house.

When Steve remembered to breathe he found he was able to move. He ran on tiptoe up the steps, almost tripping, and switched off the light, wondering too late if that was visible from the hall. He turned in the windowless darkness, one foot groping for the next step down. "Who's in here?" Mr. Keaton said.

Steve lurched away from the sound of the voice, and his

right foot groped into space. For a moment he thought he'd walked off the edge of the steps. He lost his footing and sat down blindly, bruising his hands on the stone. He lowered himself to the cellar floor that way, supporting himself on his feet and hands, and crawled round the side of the steps at once. There was nowhere else to hide.

"Is someone here?" Mr. Keaton shouted. He couldn't have seen the light in the cellar, Steve thought, and then he realized with a gasp he only just suppressed what Mr. Keaton had found. He'd discovered that the burglar alarm was switched off.

He was coming slowly down the hall toward the cellar. Steve made himself breathe, though each breath seemed deafening. If Mr. Keaton switched on the light he would see the bag and the spilled wine, and what would he do then except come down into the cellar? Steve drew a breath just as the cellar door opened, a breath that swelled up behind his eyes as Mr. Keaton stepped in beside the light switch. He couldn't hold his breath much longer, his nose felt as if he was drowning. He clapped his hand over his face so as to breathe, and then the door closed, the dark came back.

The dark stopped jerking as his nerves did. He heard the kitchen door slam, though he hadn't heard it open. "Damned incompetence," Mr. Keaton said loudly, and Steve heard his footsteps creaking overhead. As soon as he was sure that Mr. Keaton had gone upstairs he made himself tiptoe up the steps, one hand brushing the chilly wall, and open the door.

Mr. Keaton was using the toilet, loudly and unself-consciously. Steve ran down on tiptoe and grabbed the bag, holding it in both hands so that the fragments of glass wouldn't rattle, though his bruised hands stung. He ran up and into the hall. He was a few strides away from the front door when the wet paper at the bottom of the bag gave way.

He heard it tear as a corner of one of the heaviest

fragments poked through. He spread one stinging hand beneath it to hold it against his chest while he tweaked the latch of the front door, and almost panicked when he realized there was no sound from upstairs. Was Mr. Keaton listening? Perhaps, for the next moment the toilet flushed.

Praying that the sound would cover his, Steve opened the front door and slipped out, fumbling in his pocket for the key. The street was still deserted and almost dark, but anyone might see him from one of the houses. He slid the key into the lock and eased the door shut, then he dropped the key into his pocket and wondered if he should ring the bell, if he should let Mr. Keaton know the Elseys had the key. Even if that would explain Steve's presence at the house, he'd be crazy to draw attention to himself. Far better to flee before he was seen, and he did.

He left a piece of glass in each wastebin he passed on his way back to the East Fork and the pub. "You're putting them away tonight," the barmaid remarked as he ordered a last pint. She must think he had been there all evening, drinking outside. Oddly, the alibi made him feel less secure than guilty. He thought of calling Robin—he wanted to talk—but he felt too ashamed of himself. Perhaps he'd speak to her when he'd sorted out for himself what he'd done and why, though the way he felt just now, that might be never.

Chapter XLI

ROBIN gazed into the mug she'd just drained, and felt nothing. She supposed that was a kind of peace. That's it, then, she thought, I've done it now. She held the mug under the tap as the water ran hotter and hotter, and observed that the heat felt too distant to reach her. She turned off the distant tap and was inverting the mug on the draining board when her mother came into the kitchen.

Robin would never see her again. The thought made her feel both resigned and vulnerable. "Good night, mother," she said, and was suddenly afraid she would start weeping. "I'm going to bed now."

"Yes, you get a good night's sleep for a change. Perhaps then you'll be easier to live with in the morning." She stepped back suspiciously when Robin went toward her. "Well, what do you want?"

"Don't we kiss each other anymore?"

"I really don't know. Maybe you should think about the way you've been treating me and then ask yourself if we

should.'' She allowed Robin to kiss her cheek and gave
her a dry grudging peck in return, but when Robin made to
hug her she pushed her away and stared hard at her.
''What's wrong with you? Something is.''

''Nothing, mother.'' Now Robin was afraid her mother
would somehow realize what she'd done. If she'd begun
hugging her, she thought, she mightn't have been able to
make herself let go. ''Well, good night,'' she said.

''Good night.'' Her mother's eyes narrowed. ''Have
you been taking drugs while I was upstairs? Is that what's
wrong with you?''

''Mother, I give you my word you'll never have to
worry about that again.''

''I hope I can believe you. All right, kiss me properly if
you want to. I don't like it when we're enemies. We never
used to be.''

Robin gave her a kiss and a quick hug, then she went
upstairs, feeling a little ashamed of her last sly answer,
true though it was. Her head was growing lighter. It must
be because the air was so heavy that she was taking such a
time on the stairs. She reached the bathroom at last,
washed the face on her head that felt like a balloon and
brushed her hair. By now she felt too dizzy to bother with
brushing her teeth. Got to lie down, she thought, and
closed her bedroom door behind her as she stumbled to her
bed.

She lay in the growing dark and listened to her mother's
peevish muttering at the cooker, heard a scrap of a Viennese waltz drifting up from the promenade. She felt as if
she were dreaming the sounds, as if they were dreams she
couldn't quite sustain until she left behind the oppressive
heat, the imprisoning air, the dragging weight of her body.
She played a last game of chess with her mother and won,
she went into the surgery the next day and found nobody
was waiting except the husband her mother had chosen for
her, an overweight middle-aged hotelier who smelled of
gin and old cigars and too much earnestness. She managed

to get rid of him by repeating his usual prescription, then she gazed in resignation at the empty waiting room. Now she knew she could prove she hadn't given out the prescription forms to addicts—could have proved it months ago if only she'd realized that Raquel's boyfriend must have dumped a pad of blanks in the litter basket on the main road along with the forms he'd spoiled, if only she'd realized what the tattered young man had found in the trash that day. It no longer mattered: she was going up to the museum, where she would feel more a part of Seaward than ever, and forever. She could leave her mother, since Robin's father, having learned that her mother was on her own now, had come back. Robin was tempted to linger, to see his face just once. She couldn't linger, only her body would—and then she realized that her mother would find her body.

She imagined her mother trying to wake her, shaking her and calling her name, beginning to sob. Perhaps her mother would refuse to believe Robin was dead, would keep her body there in the bed until it was taken away from her. A wave of appalled pity for her mother overwhelmed Robin, and she staggered to her feet. She had to get out of the house while she could.

She managed to sway as far as the top of the stairs before she began to fall. At once she felt atrociously sick. She flung herself away from the stairs and fumbled along the wall toward the bathroom, and reached the toilet barely ahead of her nausea. She clung to the porcelain lip, at the mercy of her body and her emotions, sobbing or laughing at herself, she wasn't sure which. Her spasms felt as if they were tearing her apart, and seemed unlikely ever to stop. She was still wracked by them when she heard her mother hurrying upstairs.

Robin groped in her pocket for a handkerchief to wipe her chin. As she dragged out the handkerchief it dislodged the empty bottle of sleeping tablets. She heard the bottle thud on the carpet just as her mother reached the bathroom. "Are you all right, Robin?" she demanded, and then, "What's this? More of your drugs?"

Another spasm reached deep into Robin but found nothing as her mother stooped to the bottle. "Oh, God, look what she's done now," her mother cried. "Look what she's done to herself with her drugs after all the care I've taken of her." She let out a shuddering sob, then she came and peered into Robin's eyes. All at once she was startlingly calm. "Stay there, Robin. Don't try to move. I'll be back as soon as I've called an ambulance."

She was. She knelt by Robin and supported her with one arm while she stroked her hair, murmuring, "It's all right, mother's here, we'll get you to the hospital, they're on their way." If only she could always be like this, Robin thought, and began to weep. She would have clung to her mother if she had dared to let go of the pan. "There, there," her mother said as Robin wept. "I know."

When the doorbell rang she gave Robin's shoulders a hug and limped away quickly while Robin slumped against the porcelain. "She took too many sleeping pills. Here's the bottle," her mother said downstairs. Two ambulance attendants carried Robin down on a stretcher, the house lolling around her. All the way to the hospital her mother held her hand.

Someone wheeled Robin through the maze of the hospital. She was unloaded onto a bed, where several disapproving faces converged on her. By the time they'd finished using the stomach pump she was wishing desperately that they'd let her die. Afterward her mother sat by her bed in a long anonymous ward until the doctor murmured, "Your daughter should be fine now once she rests. I should get some sleep if I were you."

"No, I have to go back to the museum. I've left some work unfinished there."

"But it's almost two in the morning," he said, his voice turning away from Robin as her mother strode off. Her footsteps were still dwindling as Robin fell asleep.

Chapter XLII

PERHAPS Coventry might not be so bad, Jimmy thought. Within the ring road that recalled the shape of the city wall it felt quite like a small town. Strolling until it was time for the interview, he came across old buildings and fragments of the wall among the expanses of concrete and paved roadway. He went into the cathedral, which cooled the September sunlight and stained it rainbow, and might have prayed if he ever did. Surely he had a chance at this job.

He had to get away from Seaward. The children would be back at school next week, they'd have to pass the Grand. The theater was being renovated by the council, but it would still remind them of Tanya. If he couldn't bring them up away from city life and all that it threatened, at least Coventry wasn't so big. He took deep breaths to make himself feel optimistic, and was striding to the interview when he caught sight of a display in a bookshop window of books by Maurice Fox.

Fox was another reason for him to leave Seaward, to make sure he didn't encounter the man. Fox must have found the plant by now. Presumably nothing had come of it, or Jimmy would have heard. All the same, he couldn't shake off the fear that the plant would be traced back to him, that perhaps Helen's boyfriend, Henry, would let slip a hint; even if Helen kept him away from Fox, Fox might contact him. He felt absurd and even guiltier for going into the shop to buy Francesca one of Fox's books for children, which she'd asked him to look out for. He rolled up the book in his fist and went on to the interview.

Two of the policemen who were waiting he knew from previous interviews. "Here we are again, then," he said. "May the best man win." He sat down at the end of the line and leafed through *Galactic Chef*, glanced at Fox's dedication—"to my brother, fellow voyager"—before he dropped the book on the floor.

The Londoner next to him glanced at the cover, then at Jimmy. "Bit naughty to be seen reading that here, isn't it?" he said.

Jimmy had to swallow a sudden dryness before he could speak. "How do you mean?"

"After that business with his kid and the drugs."

"I don't know anything about it. What business?"

"All right, I believe you. Bit on edge, aren't you, mate? I should've thought you'd be used to it by now."

He meant interviews, Jimmy realized, and forced his voice to sound neutral. "Tell me what you meant about Fox. I still don't know."

"Just that he was done the other day for drugs. His case comes up next week."

"You said something about his son."

"Yeah, the jury'll love that. He was using his eight-year-old kid to carry drugs. Come to think, you'd know the men who made the arrest, wouldn't you? They were on your patch for a while. Dexter and Deedes."

"Good God." If only to explain his fierceness, Jimmy went on. "They finally got someone, did they?"

"They'd had their eye on him for a bit. You wouldn't believe it except there were witnesses, but the kid spilled his bag while he was getting out of his dad's car, and what do you think fell out of the bag while our boys were watching? Half a pound of cannabis. Of course Fox tried to say he knew sod all about it, but it wasn't our boys who picked it up, it was one of his neighbors."

Jimmy's face was growing hot. "Was that all they had on him?"

"What is he, a friend of yours?" The Londoner stared narrowly at him. "It wasn't all by a long way. They got a warrant to open his safe. Heroin, cocaine, whatever you need to do yourself mischief, it was in there. He'll be put away for years and if you ask me, it's a pity we don't hang his kind of filth."

Jimmy picked up Fox's novel and stared at it without seeing it—anything to save him from having to talk. So Fox had been guilty, and Jimmy might have made the arrest and taken the credit that was Dexter's and Deedes' now. He heard a phone ringing, and then the door opened. He hoped they weren't going to call him yet to be interviewed, not while his mind was so jumbled, not while he was willing the Londoner not to wonder how Jimmy could have known Fox had a son. But the receptionist said, "Is Inspector Waters here?"

He crumpled the book in his hand and made himself look up. "I'm Waters."

"There's a telephone call for you if you'd like to take it. Your mother." Her face was determinedly blank. "Something about your children," she said.

Chapter XLIII

TODAY is the day, Peter thought. It sounded like a march. Today is the day, today is the day, wymnid, wymnid, today is the day. Since he'd taken the day off work, he didn't need to phone and get Raquel, who had taken over from Hilda on the switchboard. He'd found Hilda a job in the office of the Grand, and everything was on its way to coming right. It didn't matter that he'd hardly slept last night. It didn't matter that the police had been to see him.

He'd thought it mattered when he'd turned and seen the uniform approaching across the office. Thinking that they'd pinned Roger's death on him, he had felt profoundly relieved. He shouldn't have expected life to be so simple; they'd found Roger's body, ten miles from Seaward, but all they had wanted with Peter was to tell him so. He still had a chance, he could tell them himself what he'd done, except that when he had opened his mouth he'd found he could say anything but that—couldn't confess in front of all the people he'd worked beside for years. He'd felt as if he'd lost his last chance.

Of course he hadn't. Today was the day. Today is the day, his head sang as he washed and dressed, sang more loudly so as to blot out the memory of the shadow on the wall. How long had he been watching late-night television without realizing his grandmother was in the room with him? He would have blinded himself rather than look behind him, for her shadow had only suggested how little was left of her now. When the television had gone blank and begun to whine he'd switched it off and walked backward to his chair. He'd sat there all night, staring at the dark that had gathered like smoke on his eyeballs.

He'd slept for an hour or so around dawn, and when he'd awakened she'd gone. Perhaps she was somewhere in his rooms, but he mustn't look for her, mustn't let the rooms grow cluttered in his mind. He took the mask from under the tray of knives in the kitchen drawer, folded the mask to fit in his pocket and kept his gaze ahead of him until he was out of the house.

The streets seemed wider and brighter today. Beneath a sun so intense it looked shrunken the sea was a sheet of glass. Peter strolled so as not to be too early, and remembered the idea that had comforted him when he'd been brooding over having been unable to confess: Jimmy and Robin and Steve must have secrets too, things they were compelled to do in the hope of regaining what they'd lost, and Peter might be able to use that knowledge if he needed to protect himself, particularly if he was the only one who realized. The idea made him feel sure of himself, made him stride faster, eager to get going.

He slowed when he came in sight of the Four Smugglers. He was going to do it, then, because he had to. He was going to make Jimmy find him the address. He wouldn't do anything very bad, he didn't want anyone to be harmed, he told himself as he knocked at the door of the pub.

"Oh, Peter, we weren't expecting you yet," Mrs. Waters said.

"I don't mind waiting. Where's Jimmy today?"

"At an interview in Coventry. I've a feeling in my bones he may strike lucky this time." She shooed him in with hands that were plastered with dough. "Are you sure you want to be bothered with them? I mean, on your day off . . ."

"They'll give me an excuse to laze around on the beach. Give me an excuse to get changed." He had a sudden panicky sense of tottering on the very edge of confession. "That's to say I have my swimming trunks on under this. The children will help me relax."

"You know, if you don't mind my saying so, I think you need to." She smiled to take away the sting. "Let me tell you, they're very fond of you. It's more than kind of you to spend so much time with them."

"Think nothing of it," he said, and clenched his teeth so as not to demand that she talk about something else.

"Hurry now, children, Uncle Peter's here," she called up the narrow stairs, and turned to him. "It's a pity you have none of your own when you're so good with them. Have you ever thought of doing something with children?"

"No," he said, not too vehemently, he hoped.

"A job, I mean." She was gazing oddly at him. Here came the children, thank God, the noise of their running enormous in the cramped space behind the bar. "Uncle Peter's going to take you to the beach," she said. "What do you say?"

"Thank you very much, Uncle Peter," Francesca said.

Russell poked the bottom stair with the toe of his sandal. "Don't want to go. My tummy hurts."

"Then I'll just take Francesca," Peter said, feeling deeply grateful to the boy: he only needed one of them, he saw that now, and it would make what he had to do far easier. Leave him, he cried as Francesca said, "Come on, Russ, grandma and granddad want to go to the market and they won't want you getting in the way."

"Are you really feeling ill, Russell?" Peter said. "It'll

be quite windy down there. I wouldn't like you to catch a cold.''

"He just ate too much of what granny was making, that's all. Don't be mean, Russ, I'll have nobody to play with. If you don't come I won't play any of your silly games next time you ask me to.''

"They aren't silly games," Russell said, stamping, and Peter's skull began to throb. "Can I have some sweets if I go?''

"So much for your tummy hurting," Francesca crowed, and grabbed Peter's hand. "Come on, Uncle Peter, let's go and then he'll have to follow us."

"I will not have to," Russell said, but then he followed them out of the pub. Peter turned away at once so that he wouldn't have to keep his face still for Mrs. Waters. "Look after them," she said.

The children waved and waved to her until he thought she would never close the door, thought she was watching because she suspected him. He still hadn't heard the door close when they stopped waving. As he glanced back to make sure she'd gone in, Russell said, "This isn't the way to the beach."

"Yes it is, Russell. It's the way to a different part of the beach."

"No, it goes to where mummy used to work."

Oh, God, Peter thought, the bird sanctuary. It was further along the coast in the direction they were going, and how could he distract them from that? What if they refused to go on?

"Uncle Peter didn't know that," Francesca said. "We won't go that far, Uncle Peter, will we? We don't mind coming this way so long as we don't go too far."

Pray I don't have to, Peter thought, grasping the mask in his pocket and letting go hastily as he heard the rubber crumpling. "Trust me," he said, beginning to loathe himself, all the more so when both of them took his hands.

They were in no real danger. He had to believe that of

himself. It would be an adventure for them, he told himself as he hurried them along the forest road. Birds sang in
foliage patched with blue sky, a squashed tube of insect
repellent gleamed in the undergrowth. Soon the pub was
out of sight, and all too soon he could see the overgrown
road that led to the abandoned van. Russell made to turn
along there until Peter hurried him by. Not down there yet,
he thought as his head throbbed. Soon enough.

Fifty yards further on a trail that started like a path led
into the trees. Russell began to complain that he'd wanted
to go down the road as Peter led them onto the trail.
"Never mind, Russ, this is exciting, isn't it?" Francesca
said.

The trail wound out of sight of the main road. Peter
hurried on until he and the children were almost parallel
with the van. The heat seemed to clamp on him then,
paralyzing him. If he didn't act now he never would. "Just
stay here and don't move, children," he said, his dry
throat rasping. "I won't be long."

"Where are you going?" Russell wanted to know.

"Somewhere by myself."

"Uncle Peter wants to wee, Russ."

"So do I."

"You do it here, then. I'll hold your bucket and spade,"
Peter heard her say as he dodged between the trees. Suddenly he wished he could think of a way to use whatever
Jimmy's secret was to prize the address out of him. It was
too late: he could think of nothing but his plan—everything
on either side of it was blank.

He pulled off his shirt as he ran to the vehicle. He
wrenched at the handles at the back of the van and climbed
in. He dragged his trousers off and threw the clothes onto
the driver's seat, then he squirmed into the old clothes
he'd hidden underneath. The cords and handkerchiefs were
in the pockets of the old trousers but, good God, he'd
thrown the mask onto the front seat with the shirt. Heat

blazed unpleasantly through him as he scrambled out of the van, slipping his clothes out of sight underneath.

He stood still for a moment, dreading to hear someone coming. A bird chirped in its nest, a branch creaked, and faintly through the trees he heard the children arguing. "Just keep a look out that nobody comes," Francesca was saying. "I did for you." The sun beat down on the overgrown road, and Peter felt as if it were burning a hole in his scalp. He unfolded the mask and covered the top of his head with the rubber scalp before pulling the fleshless skull over his face, then he ran back through the trees.

Russell saw him first. The boy gasped and then began to giggle. "It's Uncle Peter," he shouted.

Francesca stood up from squatting and pulled her skirt down quickly. She stared at the advancing figure, stared first at the mask and then at his clothes. "Come here quick, Russ," she whispered. "I don't think it is."

Peter thanked her silently; he didn't dare wonder what he might have done if they'd recognized him. "Stay there. Don't move," he said in the lowest snarl he could manage, and went toward them, pulling out the handkerchiefs.

Russell began to whine. "Who is it? I'm frightened. Uncle Peter! Uncle Peter!" he was shouting as Peter wound the handkerchief deftly round his head, through his open mouth, and tied it at the back.

"You're hurting him. Don't hurt him, he hasn't done anything to you." Francesca's voice was shaking, but she held her ground. "Our daddy's a policeman and our Uncle Peter's coming back in a minute. You'd better leave us alone or you'll have to go to prison."

She was visibly trembling. Peter wanted to turn and run, but he was committed now. "If your Uncle Peter's the man who was with you I knocked him down and left him unconscious," he snarled, tasting rubber. "He won't be rescuing you. Now tell your little brother not to run away or I'll have to hurt you. Open your mouth."

"It's all right, Russ, he wouldn't dare hurt us really,"

she said, her voice wavering. "What are you going to do to us?"

"I'm kidnapping you. What happens then depends on your father." His rasping snarl made him scared he was going to start coughing, he was growing nauseated with the smell of the mask. "That's enough questions. Open your mouth, girl."

He was arranging her gag when without warning, Russell flew at him and punched him in the groin. "Get off her. You leave my big sister alone," the boy cried, just audible through the gag.

Peter doubled over his bruised testicles and forced himself to straighten up. "Tell him if he tries anything like that again I'll break one of your arms," he growled through clenched teeth. He was appalled to realize that, until the pain subsided to a dull ache and he was able to control himself, he might not be exaggerating.

"Do as he says, Russ." Francesca began to weep silently as Peter tied her gag. He pulled the children roughly in front of him and used two pieces of cord to tie their hands behind their backs, then he grabbed each of them by a shoulder and marched them toward the van. His loathing of himself was almost unbearable. Deep in his mind he hoped someone would appear from somewhere, see what he was doing.

The road was still deserted. He struggled to open the rusty doors before the children could think of running: if they tried to get away he was afraid he wouldn't be able to catch them. He prodded them both into the back of the van, onto the blankets he'd spread there. "Lie down," he snarled.

He tied Russell's ankles together, then Francesca's. Both children were sobbing, muffled by the gags. "Stay there and you won't be harmed if your father does as he's told," he snarled, choking on the smell of hot rubber, sweat gluing the mask to his face. "If you try to get away or make a noise I'll know. Someone will always be watching.

If you don't do as you're told you'll never see your father again.''

He was going to cough. If he did, he knew suddenly, they would recognize his cough. He gazed down at their scared faces and wide eyes, then he lurched backward out of the van and tied the handles tight with the last piece of cord. No need to tie the front doors, which were rusted shut. He hid beside the van and retrieved the clothes he'd stowed underneath, and shoved the old clothes under once he'd changed out of them. All the while he could just hear the children sobbing.

He had to look as though he'd struggled with the kidnappers. He tore the skull off his face and stuffed it into his pocket as he began to run. There was a heavy branch at the level of his face, and he ran straight at it, closing his eyes so as not to flinch. He wanted to feel pain, he deserved to suffer as the children were suffering, especially now that he realized he'd threatened them with the loss of their father when they were still recovering from losing their mother. But he didn't notice the stump protruding from the branch until it smashed his mouth.

He fell on the grass and lay writhing, his whole body trying to close around the atrocious pain that seemed to be all that remained of his lips and teeth. He had to heave himself onto his side eventually, because he was choking on blood. When he spat it out, one tooth and a piece of another came with it. He was afraid he'd injured himself too badly to be able to reach the pub, let alone feed the children and look after them if he needed to.

He shoved himself to his feet, staggered toward the main road. His entire head was nothing but grades of pain in which he could no longer distinguish his features. Suppose Jimmy's parents had already gone to market? How long before Jimmy could be contacted? The answer to any question that occurred to him seemed as unbearable as the pain that was blinding him.

He reeled against the door of the pub and pounded on it.

At last, beyond his closed eyes, he heard footsteps. He levered himself away from the door to save himself from falling through the opening. "Oh, good lord, what's happened to you?" Mrs. Waters cried. "Where are the children?"

He tried to blink her into focus, but his eyes were streaming. "Two men took them," he said, or tried to, and found that his plan had gone wrong in a way he could never have predicted: he had injured himself so badly that he could hardly speak at all.

Chapter XLIV

IT WAS Fox, Jimmy thought numbly as he drove back to Norfolk—Fox or someone acting on his behalf. Fox had realized it was Jimmy who'd planted the drugs. Nobody else had a reason to harm the children, but what was the kidnapping meant to achieve? What could Fox expect Jimmy to do? Jimmy ground his heel on the accelerator pedal and tried not to wonder if Fox expected nothing of him, wanted nothing but revenge.

There was no motorway to Norfolk. He drove as fast as he dared on the winding roads, broke the speed limit wherever it seemed safe to do so. At least driving like this gave him less chance to think, to remember the children trooping through the house when they were younger, Russell following Francesca wherever she went and repeating whatever she said, Tanya turning beside him in bed and telling them to go back to sleep, Francesca protesting "But we're awake," Russell shouting "We're awake" in case they hadn't noticed. . . . Once Jimmy almost lost control of the car when he had to brake at an unmarked sharp bend, once he nearly ran over a dog that darted in front of the car. He was beginning to wish he had made straight for London; he could have talked to Peter on the phone before confronting Fox. He was praying that the police would already have found the children unharmed, that they were safe despite the way he'd put them at risk by framing Fox.

By the time he reached the coast road it was evening. A few fishing boats bobbed at Shipham wharf. The shadowy forest swept the bird sanctuary away. Five minutes later he was at the pub, which was already surrounded by cars. He couldn't help feeling unreasonably resentful that his parents hadn't closed it for the evening.

His mother tried to bustle him into the room behind the bar. "At least sit down if you won't have a drink. You must have been driving nearly all day."

"No, I've got to talk to Peter. Where is he?"

"We had to take him to the hospital. He could hardly talk, they'd hurt him terribly. If they did that to him, what might they do to the children?" she said, biting her lip.

"I'm sure they won't do anything yet. They haven't even let me know what they want." He suppressed the thought that it would be far less ominous if they had. "I'll keep you posted on where I am in case they try to contact me here," he said, and phoned the police station, his hand stiffening for fear of what his colleagues might have to tell him.

There was no news. The chief inspector had kept the search low-key. Jimmy fought off disappointment and a dull apprehension and told himself he would have done the same in the circumstances. He struggled through the smoky crowd and drove to the hospital.

Peter was in a ward on the third floor. "Don't take long," the sister warned. "We had to work on his jaw, and he'll still be coming out of the anesthetic. He won't be able to say much."

But Peter seemed almost pitifully relieved to see him.

Jimmy sat down by the bed and made himself look at Peter's smashed face, tried to stop thinking that the thug who had done this to him had the children. "What happened, Pete?"

"Two men." Peter had to keep closing his swollen mouth. "Red station wagon."

"Can you describe the men?"

Peter shook his head stiffly. "Masks."

"Which way did they go, did you see?"

"Told police. Toward Shipham. Going fast. Must be far away by now."

His earnestness was painful. "All right, old chap, I'm not blaming you," Jimmy said. "I can see you put up a fight, God knows. Did they say anything to you?"

Peter shook his head again. "So you can't describe their voices. Anything at all you noticed about them?"

Peter frowned as if he was trying to think, and winced. "No."

"Well, if anything should come back to you, get the hospital to let me know. You did your best, old fellow. Try and rest now."

Jimmy was heaving himself to his feet, feeling weary and driven, when Peter said, "Wait."

"Remembered something? What is it, Pete?"

Peter waited until Jimmy leaned closer. "Told you it wasn't over. Need that address."

At first Jimmy had no idea what he meant, and then he felt close to rage, despite Peter's injuries. "Look, Pete, I haven't time for that now, can't you see?"

Peter seized his hand. "Told you something else would happen. Your wife and now your children. Got to stop it before something worse. You haven't time to find it. Tell me where to look. Please, for all our sakes."

His mouth was bleeding. "Peter, stop blaming yourself, stop brooding about that idiotic business," Jimmy told him, pulling his hand free of Peter's. "It's got nothing to do with this, do you hear? Nothing. Just rest and let them look after you and you'll feel better. I have to go now.''

"For God's sake believe me. You don't know what could happen if we don't find that address," Peter said, choking. Jimmy strode away as the sister came purposefully toward them. "He's bleeding," he said, and hurried out of the ward. At least Peter's urgency had reached him. He was going straight to London to have it out with Maurice Fox.

Chapter XLV

STEVE was listening to the local news in case it mentioned the burglary at Mr. Keaton's when he heard about the kidnapping. Christ, he thought, poor Jimmy, is there anything else he can lose? It took a few seconds for the thought to catch up with him, and then he felt suddenly cold. Coincidence, he told himself, be reasonable, but suddenly he wanted to talk to someone, perhaps Peter. He was hardly hearing the news anymore when the newsreader mentioned that Robin was in hospital suffering from an overdose.

He stared at the radio and felt even colder. Too much was happening all at once, and he felt he knew why if he would let himself realize. It wasn't the kind of thought to be alone with in a flat that hadn't yet had time to seem like home. Besides, he wanted to see Robin, find out how she was. He couldn't help feeling he might have prevented what she had done to herself.

By the time he reached the hospital, visiting time was

half over. He ran into the main building, past a skull mask stuffed into a wastebin. Robin was on the fourth floor. At first he thought she was asleep, propped up by pillows. She looked pale and wasted and, oddly, much younger, so vulnerable that he caught his breath. The sound made her open her eyes. "Oh, Steve," she said with a weak smile. "We choose the strangest ways to meet, don't we."

He couldn't hold back from asking, "Why did you do it, Robin? Why didn't you get in touch with me instead?"

"I should have. I wish I had." She reached out for his hand. She seemed less vulnerable now, almost calm. "As for what I did, it was either me or my mother."

"I ought to have seen how things were. I should have come to see you," he said, writhing inside, remembering how he'd acted like a rebuffed adolescent and drunk himself into housebreaking instead. "I wasn't sure you'd want me to."

She squeezed his hand. "I hope you're sure now."

"I think I must be."

"It takes so long, doesn't it." She sighed and smiled at him. "But it was worth waiting for. Steve, could I ask you to do something for me?"

"Anything I can."

"Could you go to my house on your way home and see how my mother is? I haven't heard, and I'm worried about her. I should be out of here tomorrow, but I don't want to wait that long."

"I'll go now if you like."

"If you wouldn't mind. Here's my key in case you need to let yourself in. You could phone and let them know how things are and they'll pass on the message." She held onto his hand as he stood up, then she drew him down to her and turned her face up to him. Her fingers were cool on the back of his neck. "Thanks, Steve," she said and kissed him. "I'm glad you came back."

He let go of her hand eventually and stepped away from the bed. An old lady grinned encouragingly across the ward at him, but he didn't mind being watched. Robin seemed more like the girl he'd once known, no longer jealous of her reputation. Suddenly she frowned. "Did you hear about Jimmy?"

"The kidnapping, you mean? Why would anyone want to do that to him?"

"I've been wondering." She looked as uneasy as he felt suddenly. "Maybe I'll have a chance to talk to Peter before I leave. One of the nurses was telling me he was with the children when it happened. He got badly beaten up. He's downstairs, in Hope Ward, I think."

Steve wasn't sure if he wanted to talk to Peter, but now seemed the time if he meant to, while the taste of Robin's kiss was on his lips. He reached Hope Ward just as the bell rang for the end of visiting.

Peter was sitting up in bed and staring at nothing. His swollen mouth looked like an enormous purple birthmark. He focused on Steve, and his hand went to his mouth, then flinched away. "Pete, you poor sod," Steve said. "Who were they, do you know? Why should anyone have wanted to take Jimmy's kids?"

Peter looked quickly away from him. When Steve glanced toward the doors to the corridor he thought he saw an old lady looking in through the glass. It was difficult to be sure, since he couldn't make out her face. "You don't want to talk, Pete, I understand," Steve said, feeling unreasonable. "It's all right, you don't have to. I'm not the police."

Perhaps Peter wanted to be left alone to rest, the way he was staring. "I'll leave you to recover, then. We'll talk another time," Steve said with a wink. He went out to his car and drove to Robin's house.

Her street was quiet except for the cry of a sea gull. A notice that said SURGERY CLOSED UNTIL FURTHER NOTICE and directed patients to an alternative address was taped inside the glass of the side door. He could hear Robin's mother

talking inside the house. When he rang the bell on the
front porch, she fell silent at once.

He waited. Though Robin had told him to use the key,
he didn't think he could: one burglary was enough. If
Robin's mother was chatting in there, couldn't he assume
she was coping on her own or being looked after? He rang
the bell again, and she cried, "Go away."

Her shrillness made him uneasy, and so did realizing
he'd been hearing only her voice. Of course she could be
on the phone. He ventured round the side of the house,
toward the surgery. He was almost abreast of the window
of the waiting room when he made out that she was talking
rapidly and animatedly to herself, but what was the crack-
ling sound? He looked in through the net curtains, and
then he ran to the front of the house, pulling out the key.
Red light was flickering beyond the curtains, which were
turning brown. The place was on fire.

He turned the key and the door creaked open. He pushed
the inner door and tiptoed along the hall. She hadn't heard
him, for she was still talking. "That'll teach you to stop
them letting me work at the museum. Let's see how you
like it when you come home and find you've no work,"
she cried as he grabbed a fire extinguisher from the hall
and ran into the waiting room.

She was burning Robin's files, dragging them out of the
filing cabinet and throwing them under the window onto a
pile that was already blazing. The room was full of smoke
and the stench of charred carpet. When he doused the
small blaze with the extinguisher she screamed. "Who's
that? I didn't call the fire department," she cried, then she
saw his face. "She's sending you to interfere now, is she?
Leave my house this instant or I'll call the police."

"I think someone may have to call them, Miss Laurel."

"Oh, I'd forgotten, they're on her side too, aren't they?"
She flew at him, nails slashing at his face. When he
stepped back she burst out laughing mirthlessly and began
to build another fire with Robin's papers. "You call them
and I'll tell them you broke into my house."

He tried to persuade her away from the files, but everything he said inflamed her. Eventually he went into the main part of the house and called the police. They wanted to know where he was calling from, what he was doing in Robin's house, what his relationship with Robin was. He was beginning to stutter and wondering if they simply meant to put him off when he heard a crash of glass in the house. At least that gave his voice an edge, and they promised grudgingly to send someone as soon as they could.

Robin's mother had thrown the fire extinguisher through the windowpane. She was snatching up spilled matches from the carpet to start a new fire. When he went out to retrieve the extinguisher she flung broken glass at him. "Get away from my house, I'll kill you," she screamed, sobbing now because she couldn't find the matchbox to strike a match.

A neighbor tried to calm her, but only the sight of the police did. "There he is, he broke my window," she told them, pointing at Steve. "He tried to break into my house because I wouldn't let him near my daughter."

"She's in hospital, isn't she?" The older of the two policemen stepped forward, glass cracking under his boots. "Dear me, what a mess. You mustn't do that, you know, you could get into trouble. Those are official documents you're destroying."

She flung a shard of glass in his face. "She sent you to guard me until she comes back, did she?" she screamed.

The policeman wadded a reddening handkerchief against his cheek. "How long has she been like this?" he murmured to Steve.

"Months, maybe longer." Someone had to speak for Robin. "Her daughter has been trying to have her taken into residential care, but she won't go. You can see she needs to, can't you?"

"What I can see and what the law can do about it may be two different things." He peered narrowly at Steve as if suspicious of his motives. "Maybe if you make yourself scarce she'll calm down. Now then, Mrs. Laurel, why don't we overlook what you just—"

Her cry interrupted him. She was brandishing a piece of glass a foot long. "Do you think I don't know what you're all plotting? Try and take me out of here and I'll take care of you, I swear I will." She glanced behind her. "Got me surrounded, have you? You won't have me put away, I told her what I'd do if she tried." Before anyone could reach her or even speak, she held up her skinny left wrist and slashed deep into it with the piece of glass.

Steve dashed for the front of the house, for the phone. When the younger policeman grabbed the receiver from him to call the ambulance Steve ran on, to the surgery. He was too late. Robin's mother had slashed her other wrist. She was sitting, eyes closed, against the filing cabinet and waiting to die. She wouldn't speak to anyone, wouldn't move except to kick out when Steve and the police tried to bandage her wrists.

The ambulance attendants had to tranquilize her, nearly snapping a needle in the process. Steve repeated his story to the police, then he drove back to the hospital. Robin's mother was in one of the casualty wards, her wrists bound, her sleeping face pink from a transfusion. He went up to see Robin and held her hands while he told her what had happened.

"So that's what it took. I don't suppose anything less would have got her here. Well, nobody can say now that she's fit to be left unsupervised. They should have the forms here. Tell them I want to sign the forms right now, before I change my mind," she said, and began to weep. "Go on, I'll be all right, I'll have to be."

He went back to the surgery to sort out the mess. A neighbor had boarded up the broken window. Best to leave the charred files for the receptionist to sort out, Steve thought, having made sure the fire was doused for good. At least he could replace the files she hadn't managed to burn. He dumped the pile on top of the cabinet and began to put them back. Good God, he thought, recognizing a name from the past, and then impulsively he opened that file, leafed back as the papers grew yellower. He pulled out one browned page and let his eyes stray down it, peered closer at a date. His mouth dropped open, and all at once he was casting his mind back, trying to be sure. "My God, it wasn't," he said aloud.

Chapter XLVI

WHEN Peter got up he felt worse than he'd feared. He managed to stumble as far as the next bed, which was empty, before he had to seize the metal rail at the foot of the bed to stop himself from falling. His head felt like a balloon full of water that wouldn't keep still. He was clinging to the rail, unable to let go long enough even to lurch back to his own bed, when the night nurse came to him. "What's this now, Mr. Priest? Where do you think you're going?"

"Home."

"None of that, now. Bed's the only place you're going. Don't be afraid to call me if you need me, that's what I'm here for."

As soon as he let go of the rail the ward seemed to heave up. "What's wrong with me?" he moaned.

"Nothing serious. Doctor told you, didn't he? Just a reaction to the anesthetic. It happens sometimes."

She supported him back to bed. "Shall I get you a

bedpan? You're sure you don't want one, now?" she said, and tucked in the sheets. "Get some sleep then and you'll see, you'll feel better in the morning."

That might be too late. He lay with the pillow packed against his cheeks and felt utterly helpless. He didn't dare move his head for fear of making his vertigo worse. At the edge of his vision the nurse sat down in her lit cubicle beside the doors. Even if his dizziness eased, he wouldn't be able to get past her. Besides, he would never be steady enough tonight to find his way back to the woods.

He had to get back to the children. He had to let them go before someone found them—found them not in a red station wagon but in the van. Time enough once he had freed them to discover the address. Jimmy had a secret, he must have been given something to do in order to regain what he'd lost, and surely he would give in to the temptation now, because of the children, if he hadn't already. Peter felt uneasy realizing that he might have forced Jimmy to do it, but there was no point in brooding before he knew what it was.

He closed his eyes so as not to see the ceiling drift, then he opened them as the doors squealed faintly. He strained the muscles of his eyes to see without moving his head who had come in. Nobody had, nobody was coming to arrest him; the nurse had stepped out, that was all. Surely nobody would be searching the forest when he'd told the police the car had sped off beyond Shipham. Surely he would be able to get to the van before the police found out he'd been lying—nobody seemed to go along the overgrown road. When he thought of Jimmy's relief at seeing his children safe, he couldn't help smiling spontaneously.

Then his eyes widened, and his smile. Of course, that would be the ideal time to press Jimmy for the address, while he was so overcome with relief that he would agree to almost anything. Peter felt no longer forced to let the children go but eager to do so. He almost laughed out loud when he remembered that he'd thrown away the mask on

his way into hospital so that it wouldn't be found on him.
Anything would do, an old sock with holes cut in it, a
supermarket basket, just something to cover his face; he no
longer needed to scare the children, after all. He was
grinning up at the dark, and telling himself to go to sleep
so that he'd be ready to leave in the morning, when the
nurse came back into the ward.

There was a man with her, a man whose footsteps
squelched. She and the man were coming down the aisle
between the beds toward Peter. Surely they weren't coming to him, unless the man was a doctor she'd brought to
examine him—surely he didn't want Peter for anything
else. Peter closed his eyes and held his breath and willed
them to stop short of him, or to go on by. He let out his
breath when the squelching footsteps passed him, and then
the bed beyond him creaked. Of course, the beds on either
side of him were empty, and the man was just a patient.
Then he heard the creak of the bed on the other side of
him. The woman had lain down too. She was not a nurse.

He opened his eyes and stared at the ceiling as hard as
he could, as if that might blind him to the shapes on either
side of him. He could hear a slow drip of water from the
bed on which the man, who looked gray and swollen, was
lying. He could make out without moving his eyes that the
woman, or what was left of her, was full of holes. He
hardly needed to hear the thick whisper. "Here we are
again," Roger said.

Peter tried to lie absolutely still, hardly breathing, as if
they might grow tired of his lack of response and go away.
He heard the squeal of the doors as the nurse came back.
He mustn't call her, they were closer than he was, they
would have time to touch him with what had once been
their hands. He could lie there and gaze at the ceiling all
night if he had to, he'd stayed awake like that before.
Never mind that he was trapped from both sides now. He
mustn't mind, he'd feel better once it was daylight—the
nurse had said so—and then he could go straight to the

van. He would be free once the children were—once nobody could realize that he'd lied about the car.

Then he sucked in a breath that felt like a knife in his throat. The children would know that they hadn't been driven anywhere.

He pressed his hands against his ears as soft dreadful laughter began on either side of him. He couldn't let the children tell when it would mean he would be locked up with the horrors, even more trapped than he was now. He might have thought of suicide if he wasn't sure that Roger and his grandmother would be waiting for him beyond. Even supposing that nobody found the children, letting them starve to death would be too cruel. He had to put them out of their misery as soon as he could get to the van.

Chapter XLVII

IT WAS mid-morning before Jimmy was able to see Maurice Fox. The prison wouldn't let him do so until they had consulted the prosecutor. Jimmy would have told them it was more than a routine enquiry, but he was afraid that if Dexter and Deedes learned of the kidnapping they would try to help and simply make the situation worse. He made himself sit still, seeing his parents' bewilderment when he'd told them he had to go to London, fighting off the thought that he would never see Francesca and Russell again, never have the talks he'd meant to have with them, never see them grow up. When the prison warden put down the phone and gave him the nod he was on his feet at once.

Two guards brought Fox from the security wing to the interview room. He looked not so much defiant as arrogant, as if this treatment was the least he could expect. The guards watched him sit down at the side of the table away from the door, then they closed the door behind them.

In the midst of his hatred and anger Jimmy felt a kind of unease at being so close at last to Fox. He hadn't noticed how disproportionately large the man's head and hands were, how smooth his face was except for lines that pinched the corners of his eyes. "We can stare at each other all day if you like," Fox said eventually. "I don't expect to be going anywhere."

Jimmy slapped his hands flat on the table. The vinyl surface squeaked as his fingers struggled not to become fists. "Where are they?"

"Who?" Fox raised his chin to gaze at him more levelly. "Or what? I shouldn't like to misunderstand you."

Jimmy felt his body fighting to rise, his hands yearning to seize Fox by the throat. "You know who I mean."

"Do you think so? Presumably *you* know, since you've come all this way to ask."

That made no sense that Jimmy could see, but his growing fury swept his puzzlement away. Nevertheless he controlled his speech. "I mean my children, Fox, and you know I do."

"Mr. Fox, if you wouldn't mind, or even Maurice is acceptable." Fox sat forward, well within Jimmy's reach now. "I'm sorry to say you have the wrong man. I wasn't even aware you had children. Odd, one never thinks policemen do."

"You're lying."

"I do that professionally, but not in these circumstances. What would be the point? I'd only be inviting you to work me over. I can see how distressed you are. Believe it or not, I feel sorry for you, but whatever has become of your children, there's nothing I can do to help."

Jimmy believed him, and felt hollow and sick. Whoever had taken the children, it couldn't have been for ransom, but he didn't dare think further, not in front of Fox. "Could it have something to do with your marriage?" Fox said. "Could your wife have taken them, perhaps?"

"My wife is dead."

"Whoops. I'm generally more perceptive. It comes with the job."

Jimmy's anger flared. "Why should a man like you get mixed up with trafficking when you can write books?"

"Why not? One shot in the arm can give more pleasure than any book I'm likely to write. I know, I know, the needle kills. At least people choose to die that way and die for pleasure. At least they won't be around when the rest of us are waiting to be burned alive or crawling about with radiation sickness. Maybe my books take people's minds off that, but that doesn't mean they're worth writing. They might be if they stopped me thinking."

"Good God, man, you've a family of your own. How can you talk this way?"

"How would you like me to talk? Am I supposed to break down and say 'Oh, God, I never realized, my son may end up on drugs'? I'll tell you, when the missiles start flying I'd rather he didn't know what's going to happen to him."

"I feel sorry for you. If you care so little for your child it's a pity that—no, I won't say it." It did no good to wish that the men in the station wagon had taken Fox's child instead. "I'm wasting my time here," he said, and stood up.

His instincts as a policeman, dormant since he'd realized Fox had nothing to do with the kidnapping, halted him. He should be leaving for Seaward, to question Peter again and to search the place where the children had been abducted, but something was nagging at him. "Before I go, just tell me: who did you think I wanted to know about?"

"Ah, I thought you'd missed that. You restore my faith in your profession." Fox smiled wryly to himself. "Suppose I were to help you, what would be in it for me?"

"I can't promise anything."

"God, this is becoming predictable. Don't you find it so? Or perhaps you've done it so often you don't notice.

Do you know, I'm tempted to save you from having had a wasted journey. I'd help you before I helped the terrible two. They didn't send you, did they?''

"I've no idea who you mean," Jimmy lied.

"Why, Dee and Dee. They missed their way, those two, they should be doing magic tricks for children's parties. I still don't know how they managed to plant that stuff on my son in front of my eyes. I shouldn't blame you for that though, should I?" he said, gazing at Jimmy, who felt his innards stiffen, felt as if he were trying to hide inside himself. "Maybe I can give you something to take your mind off your troubles. If I were you I'd watch the sea."

"Don't you think we have?" Jimmy was furious. "Don't waste my time, I'm warning you."

"I'm sure the sea was being watched while the terrible two were in your area—in fact, I know it was. But I believe you're less vigilant now."

They were, since watching the sea had achieved nothing. He remembered telling Tanya that Dexter and Deedes were coming to Seaward. Suppose she'd mentioned it to Helen, who'd told Henry? He would never be able to find out from Tanya, and that filled him with a sudden helpless anger that he could only turn on Fox. "Who told you?"

"I won't give you names, I'm sorry. Don't try to make me, helping you isn't that important to me. But since your visit is so opportune, let me suggest that you look out to sea as far as you can tonight. You may learn something to your advantage. Yes," he said, smiling as if he'd turned a neat phrase.

Jimmy left him being impressed with himself and strode out of the prison. "Maybe," he said to the warden's question whether the visit had been worthwhile. Persuading Fox to help, if he had, had taken Jimmy's mind off the children, but not for long. Now he was trying not to feel he'd missed his last chance to find them by coming to see Fox.

Chapter XLVIII

AT TWO O'CLOCK the visitors were let into the wards. When Steve reached the front of the queue for Robin's at last, she wasn't in the ward. "We released her this morning," said the nurse who was checking visitors. "She'll be with her mother, over in Nightingale Ward."

Steve looked in there. Robin was sitting at her mother's bedside, holding her hand. Her mother's face looked slack and bland, but though her eyes were closed he didn't think she was asleep. He stepped back out of sight and waited, mopping his forehead. The heat in here felt as unhealthy as the heat outside, under the blurred sky with its muffled sun.

Robin was the last to leave the ward, ten minutes after the bell. She walked past Steve without seeing him, but turned with a faltering smile when he spoke. "How is she?" he said.

"Completely docile. Of course they've got her on tran-quilizers, but she really seems resigned to going in a home, almost looking forward to it. I think she's given up at last," she said, and let out a sigh that shook her. "She doesn't seem like my mother at all."

"She didn't for a while though, did she?"

"Maybe that would cheer me up if I didn't feel responsible for that too." She took his hand. "Don't mind me. I didn't mean to snap at you."

"I'm responsible too. It was because of me she cut herself."

"She'd have hurt herself anyway sooner or later. Don't worry, I suppose I'll come to accept it was for the best. Let's get out of here and walk for a while, shall we? Or do you have to go back to work?"

"Not just yet. I wouldn't mind talking if you feel like listening."

The sun was a white cocoon in the gathering clouds. On the horizon beyond the dull fields, a windmill lit like a filament as the sunlight caught it, then went out. "I wish the storm would hurry up and get here," Robin said as they crossed the emptied car park toward the shimmering road. "Anyway, if I'm to listen, go ahead and talk."

"I heard from Maggie's solicitor this morning," Steve said, though that wasn't what he'd been planning to say.

"Oh?"

"She's going ahead with the divorce. I gather she's gone to London to work on a radio station, and I've a good idea who she'll be working with. Well, I won't be getting in her way."

"So how do you feel?"

"Pretty good, actually. Free, you know," he said, not looking at her.

"I'm glad."

"Me too." He put his arm around her waist as they made for a stile. "Not only because of that. Something else."

"Not about what we all wished?"

"Exactly. I think so, anyway." He followed her over

the stile onto a faint path. "You know when I went to your place I found your mother trying, well, trying to destroy your files."

"Don't worry, I don't mind if you talk about it. Yes?"

"I went back afterward to sort them out and I found Gillespie's file. I don't know if you remember, but he used to torment me at school."

"Of course I remember. You wished him away, didn't you? I mean, you wanted to."

"I thought I had until I saw his file. I had to call up the school this morning to make sure of the dates. Robin, Pete gave us those forms ten days before the end of the holidays, I worked that out from the newspapers in the library. But Gillespie had his stroke the weekend before that. I didn't make it happen. It already had."

"Oh, Steve, I could have told you that if I'd thought to look. I wish I'd known it was still troubling you."

"Don't blame yourself, Robin, for heaven's sake. It did prey on my mind, I admit, along with everything else. I didn't realize how badly." He felt as if he might begin to stutter as he said, "Do you know what I did? I broke into someone's house after he'd taken it off our list. I was going to make it look as if our rivals had broken in."

"But did you?" She put her hands on his shoulders so that he couldn't turn away. "Well then, you didn't do anything very bad. I almost killed my mother."

"Almost is all that counts. We both stopped in time, at least, you did. Robin, tell me something. Did you feel as if what you almost did would have solved everything?"

"Yes. Did you?"

"As if I could regain everything I'd lost," he said, and gazed at her.

"It wouldn't have, though, would it? Not for me either. Steve, let's promise each other that we'll never let ourselves be trapped into feeling like that again."

"Never let ourselves or each other. Maybe we should seal it in blood."

"I've a better way."

When at last their kiss was finished Steve said, "It won't be over for me until I go and tell this man I broke into his house."

"Do you want me to come with you?"

"That would help. Might stop me stuttering."

He drove them back to Seaward. The car felt stuffed with muggy heat, the road ahead was quivering. He couldn't help feeling that both he and Robin had overlooked something. Perhaps his mind would clear once he'd confessed to Mr. Keaton. But Mr. Keaton wasn't at the house.

Steve went on to the Elsey real estate agency. Now he felt frustrated, less sure of himself. He was damned if he'd tell the Elseys what he'd done, but perhaps he could find out where to contact Mr. Keaton. Robin patted his thigh as he switched off the ignition. At least he might learn whether Mr. Keaton had been to see the agency about the intruder in his house.

Keaton had. That much was clear as Steve and Robin went into the empty showroom, where the video display was playing to nobody, for they could hear Mr. Elsey beyond the closed door of the inner office: "If I thought it was you who took that bottle from his cellar—if I thought you'd been up to more of your tricks . . ."

"I never went near his house, dad," a young voice whined, and a secretary hurried to the counter. "Can I help you?" she asked Steve and Robin, loudly enough to be heard through the door.

"Steve Innes from the Innes agency. I'd like a word with Mr. Elsey."

She had to knock twice on the office door before a shout summoned her. "Mr. Innes from the agency to see you," she said.

Mr. Elsey interlaced his fingers on his desk, jewels clicking. Beside the desk his son, lanky and unemployed, turned away from the door. "What can we do for you?" Elsey said with a smile that looked smug.

"May we come through? I don't want to shout." Steve unbolted the flap in the counter and let Robin through first.

"Sit there," Elsey told his son, pointing at a chair beside his desk, "and see if you can make yourself useful. Well?" he said to Steve.

Steve waited while Robin sat down. He was wondering why Elsey's son, who was facing them now, hadn't looked at him except for one brief glance. He must have been up to some trick, Steve thought, remembering what he'd overheard, and then suddenly he knew. He knew too much all at once—he'd remembered that someone else had avoided his eyes recently, and when—but he had to deal with this first. He swallowed what he'd meant to say and spoke almost without thinking as he gazed at Elsey's son. "Have you been painting any signs lately?"

The father intervened, too readily. "What are you getting at? If you want to talk to us, talk sense."

"I think I am. Looking at his face, I really think so. If I'm wrong, you tell me why he can't even look me in the eye."

"Because he doesn't have to, that's why. You may throw your weight about in your office but don't you try it in mine. Go on, you great fool," he shouted at his son, whose face was bright red now, "tell him you don't know what the devil he means any more than I do."

"Don't you, Mr. Elsey?" Robin said. "Then why are you so angry?"

"People wasting my time makes me angry. Who the hell are you, anyway? I didn't say you could come in here."

"I'm a witness," Robin said sweetly.

"I know who you are, by God. You're the doctor we've been hearing about. You'd better watch yourself. I've a lot of influence in this town."

"I'm sure you have," Steve said, getting up. "But I don't think even you can influence the police, especially not when your son has left samples of his handwriting all over town."

Elsey said nothing, and Steve was sure of himself at last, not merely guessing. He let Robin precede him into the street, where he murmured, "My God, to think I might have let them find out what *I* did."

"I know. Steve, listen, I've been thinking. We both felt forced to do something, but what about Peter and Jimmy?"

"I'm ahead of you. I just remembered, when I asked Peter why anyone should have taken Jimmy's kids, he couldn't look at me. I think we ought to have a word with Peter."

He drove out of Seaward again, to the acres of car park under the lowering sky. He was first into the hospital, and ran up to Peter's ward. Robin was still a doctor; might that help them to see him outside visiting hours? But the sister told them that despite the reluctance of the doctor whose ward it was, Peter had signed himself out two hours ago.

Chapter XLIX

PERHAPS the children were already dead. Perhaps they'd choked on their gags while trying to get loose. The image of their panic, their struggles to free their hands from the cords as their eyes bulged and their small faces turned black, appalled Peter, but at least they would be dead, at least he wouldn't have to do away with them himself. All the same, he'd made sure he would be able to do so if he must. He'd brought something to cover his face.

He almost walked straight past the Four Smugglers. He dodged off the road just in time, into the trees. It wasn't that he feared that Jimmy's parents might suspect him if they saw him: quite the reverse. He didn't think he would be able to bear the sight of their grief or their hope. It would be even worse if they were glad to see him, Jimmy's friend who'd been so kind to the children, who'd been disfigured trying to save them.

He mustn't feel inhuman, that would only make it harder. He had to silence the children or he would be locked

away. Once they were silenced he might be able to stop
what was happening; Jimmy would be beyond caring whether
Peter searched his house for the address. He would be
doing it for Jimmy too, for all of them. It was only right
that he should face the source of all their troubles, since it
was he who'd involved them all those years ago.

He was glad when he was out of sight of the pub and
could make his way back to the road. He didn't like the
way the growing darkness merged the trees so that they
had to pull apart as he moved, a repeated parting that made
him feel he was about to see a face peering through at him,
Roger's drowned face or the remains of his grandmother's.
He was sure the two of them were pacing him, driving him
onward. His bruised face and jaws ached as nervousness
tightened his lips.

The baked road was dimming. A few hundred yards
ahead of him he couldn't focus it at all. Trying to do so
made the ache spread up his face and intensify in his skull.
The road was deserted, that was all that mattered. There
were no cars to be heard, nor anything else. The silence
felt like fog; perhaps that was why he found it hard to
breathe. He took a breath that cut into the gap between his
teeth as he turned onto the overgrown road.

The silence seemed closer. His ears throbbed as he
strained to hear. There was no sound beyond the curve,
where the van was. Perhaps the children had managed to
untie each other, succeeded in sliding open one of the
rusted doors at the front of the van or had even broken a
window, though surely there was nothing in the vehicle
they could have used. They might be untying each other at
that very moment. He reached in his pocket for the stocking, dragged it over his face, and ran around the curve.

The van was as he'd left it, as far as he could tell. He
made himself slow down now that it was in sight, so that
the children wouldn't hear him. Trees flickered and shifted
restlessly under the gloomy sky. He tiptoed to the grubby

windows at the back of the van, above the handles that were still tied shut, and peered in.

The children were either asleep or unconscious. Francesca lay with her knees drawn up and her head tucked into her chest as if she was trying to hide. Russell nestled against her back, his face burrowing into her shoulder, and if Peter didn't look away he would never be able to go on. He ducked out of sight for fear their eyes might open. He pulled off the mask, which dragged at his toupee, as he ran to the end of the road.

The eroded edge fell sheer to the stony beach, which was deserted as far as the eye could see. A dark tide was rushing in, jagged with foam, driven by a wind that made him shiver. Directly beneath the cliff were rocks that the tide would soon reach. He couldn't have asked for better, except perhaps that the children wouldn't wake. If they were unconscious he might be able to carry them one at a time to the edge without their knowing. He turned toward the van and had to lurch away from the cliff as he reeled on the edge, dizzy with a sudden appalled vision of what he was about to do.

He mustn't falter. The quicker he was, the kinder it would be to the children. When he tried to think beyond that, his mind grew cluttered at once. He pulled out the stocking again and rolled it down over his face, though it made him feel suffocated, nostrils clogged with nylon. He ran back to the vehicle and began to pick at the knot that held the handles shut.

He should have brought a knife. He'd tied knot upon knot until there were no more loose ends; he'd pulled each knot so tight that now his fingernails were bending away from the flesh. He found a stout twig and managed to lever the outermost knot loose, still wishing that he'd brought a knife, which he could have used to finish off the children before they knew what was happening. Perhaps he ought to do that anyway, find a rock or a club to make sure they didn't wake as he was carrying them to the edge. His thoughts felt cluttered again in his raw head, and he stopped thinking.

He was poking at the third knot when the twig snapped. Sweat and his panicky breath clung to his face. Not only had the twig sounded like a shot, its snapping had shaken the van. He glanced in nervously, but the children hadn't moved. He found another twig and worried the broken piece out of the knot, then he began to prize the knot loose. Still he'd seen no movement through the windows, and he never knew what made him glance up from the knot. Francesca was gazing wide-eyed at him.

He thought he might never draw another breath. The mask clung to his nose and mouth and seemed to be closing over his eyes. He flung himself backward out of sight, and cursed himself for it; he'd only delayed what he had to do, made it more difficult for himself. He stood there shaking from head to foot, unable to move his limbs as he wanted them to move, then he ripped the mask off his head. It took the toupee with it, but that didn't matter. He would have to finish off the children now, because they would see his face.

At first they didn't see him. Russell had wakened too, and they'd struggled face to face, gazing into each other's eyes and huddling together, unable to hug because their hands were still tied behind their backs. Peter clenched his teeth, and pain burrowed into his skull. He dug the stick deep into the knot, which gave at once, loosening the next. He could untie the rest with his fingers, he realized, and then both children looked at him.

They saw his face, and their eyes lit up. He saw how they were struggling to tell each other it was Uncle Peter, grinning at each other instead. Russell was wriggling for joy; Francesca had started to weep with relief. Peter tugged the last knot free and turned the rusty handles. As soon as they had recognized him, as soon as he'd seen the light come back into their eyes, he'd known that he wouldn't be capable of harming them.

He untied their ankles first and winced at the sight of their chafed skin. He lifted Francesca, avoiding her eyes, and sat her on the edge of the van, then he sat Russell beside her and clambered behind them to untie their wrists. They began to whimper as the circulation flooded back into their legs.

Untying their wrists was even harder than freeing their ankles. He pulled the loops of cord away from the raw skin as gently as he could. He'd left the gags until last in the hope that the children would deal with those while he made his escape. But they pulled off the gags at once, and Francesca turned to him.

He would have pushed past her if he'd been able to move, and fled—anything rather than hear what her eyes were already telling him. "Oh, thank you, Uncle Peter," she said shakily. "I thought nobody would ever save us."

His throat felt as if something sharp had lodged in it. "No," he managed to say, and struggled past her, out of the van.

The children jumped down after him and cried out as their ankles took their weight. Francesca was glancing about nervously. "A horrible man put us in here. He was here just before you came, looking in at us. A horrible man with a mask."

He couldn't bear her trusting him. "That was me."

"No, before you came. We saw you looking in and we knew we were safe."

"Listen to me, both of you." His voice was high as a scrape on a blackboard. "It was me all the time. If you remember, Russell thought it was. He said it was me when I was wearing the skull mask."

She gazed at him and groped for Russell's hand. Of course, she was wondering how Peter could know about that unless he was telling the truth. She looked betrayed and frightened, which made him loathe himself even more. He stooped and grabbed the stocking with the toupee still in it. "Look, this is what I wore just now. Take it and show your father, tell him what I said. Can you walk? Go on then.'' Suddenly he was almost screaming, for they were frozen there, staring fearfully at him. He had to thrust the mask into Francesca's hand before she would take it. ''Run!'' he screamed.

They blinked weepily at him, then they limped away, faster when they looked back and saw him following. He only wanted to make sure they didn't lose their way. He saw them onto the main road and watched them turn toward the Four Smugglers. He kept out of sight then while he paced them. When they reached the pub he turned away and began to run, deeper and deeper into the forest, where there were no paths.

Chapter L

WHEN Jimmy's mother opened the locked door of the pub, she was crying. "What—" he said, and couldn't go on. She seemed unable to speak too, which made him more afraid. The police hadn't even the hint of a lead, and he'd come wearily back to the pub just in case his parents had been contacted, just in case he could rest for five minutes while he tried to think what to do next. She led him through the dark empty bar, up the narrow stairs, and into the spare bedroom. It wasn't until he saw the children that he realized she was sobbing with relief.

Robin had been examining them, but now she stood aside. The children struggled off their beds and ran to him, pressed close to him until he lifted them both, their faces warm against his. He carried them to one of the beds and sat hugging them as if they might never need to speak. At last Francesca said, "Don't ever go away again, will you, daddy?"

"Not for a while, I promise."

"No, not *ever*. Promise," she cried, and Russell added, "Please."

"Not until you feel safe again," Jimmy said, feeling rash.

"Daddy," Francesca said solemnly, tilting her head back to gaze at him. "You only want to move because of us, don't you?"

"Well, mostly, yes."

"We were going to tell you when you came back from Coventry. Don't be angry with us, will you? We'd rather stay at home so we can go and visit mummy sometimes."

How could he be angry with them when they'd come back safely to him? "You mean not even move house?"

"Yes, because that was mummy's house and she wouldn't want us to move."

"Darling, I think she'd want us to do whatever made us happy, don't you?"

"Staying in our and mummy's house would," Russell said at once.

"You know you'd have to go to the same school."

"By the theater, you mean. We don't mind now they've mended it. They're going to have a pantomime there at Christmas."

"Can we go and see it?" Russell said.

Jimmy couldn't be shocked, he was too grateful for their resilience. "I expect you can, since we're staying," he said with a secret wry grin at himself, that faded when he felt her grow tense. "Daddy?" she murmured.

"Darling?"

"They'll have to lock Uncle Peter up, won't they?"

He held her away from him so as to look into her eyes. "Why should anyone want to do that, Francesca?"

"Because it was him who tied us up." She was beginning to tremble, and Jimmy glanced at Robin in case she ought to help. Robin came over. "All right, Francesca, you're both going to be fine but just lie down for a while." She murmured to Jimmy, "Steve's here. He'll tell you everything."

He found Steve in the parlor. "We haven't called the police yet," Steve said apologetically. "Actually, we came here to find out where Peter took your kids that day and then we'd have helped in the search, except that when we got here your kids had come back. He'd let them go."

Jimmy sat down heavily, forcing his eyes not to close. "Who had?"

Steve seemed even more apologetic. "Well, Jimmy, to be honest, apparently it was Peter."

Jimmy closed his eyes and sighed. "Tell me what you know."

Steve told him how Peter had avoided looking at him, told him what the children had babbled as Robin calmed them down, showed him the improvised mask Peter had given Francesca. Jimmy nodded awake, and fury kept him that way. The sight of the toupee in the stocking filled him with a disgust that was almost nauseating. "He wanted that address," he realized. "The address I copied from those forms he made us all fill in. That's why he took my kids, just because of all that bloody nonsense."

"If you think that's all it was."

"I haven't time to argue with you. Sorry, Steve," he added as he heard how he was speaking. "I'm very grateful to you and Robin."

He stumbled to his feet and shook his head awake. He called the police station, told them about Peter, suggested they search the woods. He'd replaced the receiver when it occurred to him that he hadn't mentioned what Fox had told him. Pondering that, he went upstairs.

The children were asleep. "They should be fine now," Robin murmured. "I'll be at home. Don't be afraid to phone if you think you need me, whatever the time."

He gazed at them until he felt convinced they would be safe, then he found his way downstairs to tell his parents there was something he had to take care of. "Don't be too hard on him, perhaps he couldn't help himself," his mother said. He muttered vaguely in agreement rather than tell her it wasn't Peter he would be looking for.

Night and storm clouds were meeting overhead. The air tingled with the imminence of the storm. It seemed to revive him. He took deep breaths of the metallic piny air until he no longer felt weary, then he drove into Seaward, down to the lookout.

A few people were strolling on the promenade, making the most of the suddenly chill wind. Marker flags flapped on the golf course, sand hissed up over the edge of the cliff. Jimmy stood at the railing that enclosed the highest section of the lookout, where the lighthouse used to be. He leaned on the notice that said UNSAFE BEYOND THIS POINT and gazed out to sea.

The fishing boats from Shipham, more than a dozen of them, were lined up on the choppy water halfway to the horizon. The horizon itself looked like a straight line etched in a block of slate. Not only could he see nothing suspicious, it didn't seem possible that anything dubious could be carried on out there, within sight of the hotels and so many boats. Perhaps he hadn't fully understood what Fox had told him. He glanced back at the promenade, then he climbed over the railing.

The land underfoot felt safe enough. It rose at once, so steeply that he had to go on all fours through the spiky grass where a path had once been. He scrambled up fifty yards or so, grass scratching all around him in the wind, until the ground began to feel uneven. Now he was higher than the top floors of the hotels, but he couldn't see beyond the point. He climbed the last few yards carefully, testing each overgrown handhold before he put his weight on it, until his head was above the crumbling edge.

He could see further, but there was nothing to see. The torn black water beyond the line of boats was empty as far as the horizon. Of course he didn't know how long he might have to wait for something to happen, if anything did. Perhaps Fox meant him to wait all night, perhaps Fox

was laughing to himself at that very moment over the trick
he'd played. After all, he cared about nothing.

The lights of passing ships glimmered on the clouds at
the horizon. The hubbub of a crowd and the sounds of a
dance band drifted up from the Hotel Excelsior. He'd been
staring out to sea for half an hour or more when the storm
came rushing at him. He watched lightning leap over the
horizon, watched rain sweep over the boats and set them
rocking, heard the hiss of the sea on the rocks at the foot
of the cliff grow suddenly louder, and then, with a hissing
that made it sound as though the waves had risen to the
parched grass of the lookout, the downpour reached him.

He had to turn his head away to be able to breathe.
Before he'd taken five breaths he was drenched from head
to foot. He clapped one hand over his mouth and nose so
as to fend off the rain, shaded his eyes with the other as he
peered out to sea. Lightning spilled across the shattered
water. Still there was nothing but sea beyond the boats.

Ten minutes later the downpour showed no signs of
abating. They were cheering and applauding in the hotel as
the band struck up again. He felt idiotic and furious. Even
if Fox hadn't tricked him, he would be in no fit state to do
his job if he didn't go home to get changed. The storm
must be undermining the cliff: how much less safe might it
already be beneath him? But he clung to the edge and
raised himself, holding his breath and blinking his eyes
momentarily clear. A flash of lightning had shown him a
shape on the horizon, moving.

It was only a ship. He saw its lights just above the
horizon as the sky went out. What else could it have been?
What did he expect to see out there? Something, for he
was leaning as far over the muddy edge as he dared,
spitting out rain while he protected his eyes with both
hands, waiting for the next flash. It came, and he pushed
himself an inch higher on his elbows. Yes, he'd seen
something else. There was a boat on the horizon, close to
the wake of the ship.

The boat was heading back to Shipham. He held up one hand, edge toward his face, to make sure it was moving. He could think of one reason why a fishing boat might be so much further out than the others, so close to the shipping lanes. It was there to pick up something that had been left in the ship's wake.

Jimmy pushed himself away from the edge, which crumbled muddily in his hands. He slithered down the waterlogged slope and ran to his car. His clothes were glued to him, he could hear and feel how saturated his shoes were, but none of this mattered. The windows began to fog over, and he rolled the passenger window down as he started the car. He had to reach Shipham before the boat did.

Wind swept rain across the promenade and under his wheels. Lightning brought trees dancing forward as he drove into the forest. When he emerged from the forest he had to slow down, for the downpour was intensifying, the windshield ploughing through sheets of rain so solid he could hardly see the headlight beams. He rolled his window down, peered across the bird sanctuary as the lightning flashed. The boat was almost level with him, and much closer.

As soon as the rain showed signs of slackening he drove faster. He could see the lights of Shipham drowning ahead. The road dipped abruptly toward the village, and he almost skidded as he braked. The road twisted several times, blotting out the village, then the first of the cottages swung into view, streaming with lamplit rain. Two minutes' driving through the narrow twisting streets brought him to the wharf, where the boat was coming in.

If it was the same boat. He cursed himself for omitting to take binoculars to the lookout; he would have known the boat's name now. Other boats were coming back to Shipham, and perhaps the boat he'd followed was among them, not ahead of them at all. He could only trust his luck, if he had any left—only hope the chase hadn't been in vain.

A woman wearing a yellow oilskin severa˙ ˌizes too big for her hurried out of a nearby cottage as the first boat bumped against the rubber tires below the edge of the wharf. "Go back inside, mother," the fisherman shouted. "I can manage."

Was there more of an edge to his voice than the circumstances seemed to warrant, or was Jimmy hearing what he hoped to hear? "Don't talk nonsense," the woman cried, "be glad I'm here to help you on a night like this." She planted herself at the edge of the wharf and waited, hands on hips, until her son threw her the rope.

She was right, Jimmy told himself. The fisherman ought to be glad she was here on such a night—unless he had something to hide. He wished suddenly he were in uniform. At least he had his warrant card, and he reached in his sodden pocket for it as he climbed out of the car.

The fisherman peered past the woman, who was wrapping the rope around a bollard, and saw Jimmy. As Jimmy hurried forward across the flooded cobbles, dragging the folder out of his pocket and opening it to display the card, the man must have realized what it was. His hand went to his dripping beard as if he wanted to tear it off, and he lurched toward the wharf as the boat swung against it on the rope. The impact threw him back across the slippery deck. He glared about wildly, arms flailing, as Jimmy reached the point on the wharf he'd made to jump to. "What's wrong?" the woman demanded shrilly, then she noticed Jimmy. "Who are you?"

Jimmy swept rain out of his eyes with one hand and showed her the card. "Police."

"It's the police, do you hear?" she cried. The fisherman was edging toward an object covered with a tarpaulin, but faltered now. "I knew it would come to this," she cried, "I knew you were up to no good. Don't you be throwing what you've got there overboard, you'll only make things worse for yourself."

She followed Jimmy on board and clutched at his arm.

"He's a good boy really, he's always tried to do his best for me. It isn't his fault he's not the man his father was. He never was much of a fisherman even when his father was alive and doing his best to teach him." She pushed her son out of the way and dragged back the tarpaulin, peered at the three black canisters, each about a foot long, that lay tied together on the deck. "What are these?" she demanded. "They look evil, what are they?"

Jimmy unscrewed the top of one canister, pulled out the plastic bag of white powder that took up much of the space within. He tasted the powder and looked up at the fisherman whose eyes were closed as if he was praying, the fisherman's mother shaking her son by the arm, her hands too small to go round it. "I'm afraid they're full of heroin," Jimmy said.

Chapter LI

THE POLICE found Peter's body two days later, at low tide. He had to be identified by the papers in his wallet. Jimmy and Steve and Robin attended the funeral. Peter's parents seemed unable to look at Jimmy after what he'd had to tell them Peter had done, though he'd explained that Peter must have been under a great deal of mental strain, probably incapable of stopping himself. A large young woman called Hilda stood apart from the others, weeping.

Robin's mother went to live in the home readily enough, but Robin could tell she was pining for something, apparently not her. She died before Christmas, in her sleep. Soon after that Steve suggested diffidently to Robin that they should get married, since they were virtually living together now that he was divorced. Perhaps he realized that she didn't want to be alone with her thoughts. "Just for appearance's sake," he said, which at least made her smile. They were married in the New Year.

Patients were returning to her list, and clients to the

Innes agency. Elsey's son had been caught trying to wipe his handiwork off the signboards, not realizing that the sprayed-on writing could never have been identified. Robin had been preparing to confront Raquel about the prescription forms when she learned that the addict she'd seen at the trash, who'd forged some forms and sold the rest, had admitted as much to the police. It seemed he'd heard of Robin's attempted suicide and had felt responsible.

Jimmy was promoted, not least for thinking to check whether Fox had any relatives on shipboard. Fox's brother, the man who regularly dumped the canisters, proved to be the chef on the ship Jimmy had glimpsed in the storm.

Now and then Jimmy and Robin and Steve thought of Peter. They all assumed he'd thrown himself into the sea after letting the children go. They were already forgetting about the forms. Whatever else had happened, it was over now, and no good would come of thinking about it, especially not when it had driven Peter to do what he'd done. Then Jimmy found the address Peter had been looking for.

Or rather, Francesca did. The children were helping him with the spring cleaning when she found the slip of paper in an old wallet of Jimmy's among the clutter in the attic. "Throw it away," Jimmy said as soon as he realized what it was. She was tearing it up methodically when he said, "No, wait a minute."

It was only a box number. He pieced the paper together and kept it in his pocket for days before he decided to trace the address. The post office directed him to an address in central London. The address was false: there never had been any such number in that street. Jimmy felt relieved. There was nothing and nobody to confront. Of course there never had been, he told himself, not knowing what Peter had met on the night of the storm, when he had finally stopped running.

Peter had run for hours through the forest after he'd seen the children to the pub. He was running to hide, but nowhere seemed pathless enough. At last, as the storm exploded overhead, he came to the edge of the cliff. Lightning jerked the waves that shattered on the rocks below him. He turned, almost blinded by the rain, and saw the figures coming toward him through the trees.

Lightning made his grandmother seem to scuttle toward him, made Roger swell like a slug. There was nowhere Peter could hide from them. Finding the address from the forms might have helped, he thought, but now it never would. "You did all this," he screamed at whoever had sent the forms, and could barely hear himself for the thunder. "Where are you? You wouldn't let me find you, would you? Come out, I dare you."

Perhaps the thunder overhead had deafened him, or perhaps it was his sudden terror that made him unable to hear. Yet it wasn't the same kind of terror that had dogged him for months: it was something so different that he couldn't even think of taking back his challenge. As far as he could make out, his grandmother and Roger were smiling, no longer mocking him. They seemed to be gazing beyond him, into the storm.

He turned and saw the storm bearing down on him. For the moment the horizon was clear, and he glimpsed a light there that was either a ship or a star. All at once the onrush of the storm frightened him so deeply that he couldn't breathe, because he thought he understood. He'd never put a name to the originator of the forms and of all that had happened since, perhaps because he was afraid to do so, afraid to think he had signed a pact with something as evil as it had seemed to him. Yet what kind of evil was it that had shown him that giving in to temptation led to greater and greater suffering? Perhaps it was precisely the opposite of what he had assumed.

The light on the horizon was almost clear now. He might be able to make it out if he went forward. He sensed his grandmother and Roger at his back, and wasn't even surprised to find he welcomed them. He wondered if Jimmy and the others would one day experience what he was experiencing. He wasn't conscious of stepping forward, or of falling. He never felt himself hit the rocks, for it seemed to him that the lightning reached for him and lifted him up, toward the light beyond the storm.

Ramsey Campbell

☐ 51652-4	DARK COMPANIONS		$3.50
51653-2		Canada	$3.95
☐ 51654-0	THE DOLL WHO ATE HIS		$3.50
51655-9	MOTHER	Canada	$3.95
☐ 51658-3	THE FACE THAT MUST DIE		$3.95
51659-1		Canada	$4.95
☐ 51650-8	INCARNATE		$3.95
51651-6		Canada	$4.50
☐ 58125-3	THE NAMELESS		$3.50
58126-1		Canada	$3.95
☐ 51656-7	OBSESSION		$3.95
51657-5		Canada	$4.95

Buy them at your local bookstore or use this handy coupon:

Clip and mail this page with your order

TOR BOOKS—Reader Service Dept.
P.O. Box 690, Rockville Centre, N.Y. 11571

Please send me the book(s) I have checked above. I am enclosing
$_____ (please add $1.00 to cover postage and handling).
Send check or money order only—no cash or C.O.D.'s.

Mr./Mrs./Miss _____
Address _____
City _____ State/Zip _____
Please allow six weeks for delivery. Prices subject to change
without notice.